Ghosts of the Unfound

Jennifer Crown

Contents

Dedication   IX

1. Chapter 1   1
    May 27, 1994

2. Chapter 2   5
    November 2019

3. Chapter 3   15
    November 2019

4. Chapter 4   22
    November 2019

5. Chapter 5   31
    1981

6. Chapter 6   36
    November 2019

7. Chapter 7   46
    May 27, 1994

8. Chapter 8   52
    November 2019

9. Chapter 9   57
    4 minutes missing

10. Chapter 10   60
    1 hour: 45 minutes missing

11. Chapter 11   67
    November 2019

12. Chapter 12   71
    5 hours: 14 minutes missing

13. Chapter 13   73
    5 hours: 27 minutes missing

14. Chapter 14   79
    5 hours: 36 minutes missing

15. Chapter 15   81
    November 2019

16. Chapter 16   86
    6 hours: 44 minutes missing

17. Chapter 17   95
    November 2019

18. Chapter 18   100
    16 hours: 27 minutes missing

19. Chapter 19   106
    23 hours: 04 minutes missing

20. Chapter 20   109
    November 2019

21. Chapter 21   114
    23 hours: 14 minutes missing

22. Chapter 22   120
    1 day: 0 hours: 37 minutes missing

23. Chapter 23   125
    1992

24. Chapter 24   130
    November 2019

25. Chapter 25   132
    1 day: 3 hours: 34 minutes missing

26. Chapter 26   136
    2 days: 19 hours: 15 minutes missing

27. Chapter 27   140
    November 2019

28. Chapter 28   144
    5 days: 16 hours: 17 minutes missing

29. Chapter 29   153
    November 2019

30. Chapter 30   156
    6 days: 13 hours: 03 minutes missing

31. Chapter 31   159
    6 days: 17 hours: 5 minutes missing

32. Chapter 32   164
    8 days: 16 hours: 24 minutes missing

33. Chapter 33   183
    November 2019

34. Chapter 34   188
    11 days: 00 hours: 24 minutes missing

35. Chapter 35   191
    11 days: 1 hour: 44 minutes missing

36. Chapter 36   194
    11 days: 4 hours: 57 minutes missing

37. Chapter 37   196
    12 days: 1 hour: 13 minutes missing - Network of the
    Americas Television Report

38. Chapter 38   199
    15 days: 14 hours: 17 minutes missing

39. Chapter 39   203
    17 days: 0 hours: 8 minutes missing

40. Chapter 40   205
    November 2019

41. Chapter 41   210
    22 days: 7 hours: 14 minutes missing

42. Chapter 42   213
    November 2019

43. Chapter 43   217
    25 days: 13 hours: 18 minutes missing

44. Chapter 44   222
    27 days: 00 hours: 23 minutes missing

45. Chapter 45   225
     47 days: 17 hours: 8 minutes missing

46. Chapter 46   231
     6 months: 16 days: 20 hours: 01 minute missing

47. Chapter 47   239
     November 2019

48. Chapter 48   243
     6 months: 18 days: 20 hours: 13 minutes missing

49. Chapter 49   247
     6 months: 18 days: 20 hours: 51 minutes missing

50. Chapter 50   249
     6 months: 18 days: 21 hours: 27 minutes missin

51. Chapter 51   251
     November 2019

52. Chapter 52   254
     6 months: 18 days: 21 hours: 40 minutes missing

53. Chapter 53   261
     November 2019

54. Chapter 54   266
     Late October 2019

55. Chapter 55   272
     November 2019

56. Chapter 56   275
     2015

57. Chapter 57   277
    2019

58. Chapter 58   282
    November 2019

59. Chapter 59   290
    After

60. Chapter 60   296
    Nine Months Later

A Thank You From Jennifer   300

Acknowledgments   301

About the author   305

To my family, who waited patiently as I wrote every tortured word of this book.

To the reader, it's a miracle you are here, and I thank you so much.

Chapter One

Hannah Smoke knew that tragedy had a smell.

Not the smell of the victims, that was something else entirely built of violence and fear. The smell of tragedy that Hannah knew well was on the survivor side. It was thick and acrid, heavy with the desperation that came off someone looking to her for closure about what happened to their loved one. When tragedy was what brought someone in front of her, she could sense before a client even opened their mouth what the nature of the question would be.

She wouldn't get such a warning over the phone, which had been one of many minor worries she fretted about that day.

Up until the phone call, her appearance on *The Judy Show* had been the usual parade of broken hearts and deepest desires. *Will I ever find my soulmate? Should I change careers? Is my – insert preferred deceased loved one here – still with me?* The places changed but the questions never did. Hannah was just as likely to find herself answering these questions in the diaper aisle of her local drugstore as she was in front of a paid audience at a lecture hall, or, as she was at this particular moment, on live television.

Now, trapped in front of a national audience, the sniffling on the phone teetered on the sharp edge of disaster. Hannah steeled herself for the brand of questions she didn't like to answer.

There was a long pause. Hannah held her breath in hope that the line had disconnected.

"Caller? Are you there?" The audience waited in anxious silence as Hannah internally cursed her agent. He probably set this up. It wouldn't be the first time he interfered with his tragedy sells philosophy. Hannah shifted in her seat as she recalled another pearl of wisdom he had a habit of sharing, usually right before he slammed the phone in her ear: "Tragedy has a scent, Hannah, and it smells like fucking money." But Hannah, already feeling like she needed a hot shower without yet knowing the details of what this caller wanted, knew better.

"Live TV," Judy commented, clenching her teeth behind a primetime smile. "Caller?" She tried again with the practiced patience of a seasoned television host. "You're on live with *The Psychic Next Door*."

"Hannah?" a trembling voice cut through the speakers from above.

"Yes, I'm here." Hannah leaned forward, considering whether it was time for a new agent.

"Hannah," the caller sobbed. After a few seconds she choked out, "It's me. Katherine."

Hannah sat up straight as her stomach dropped.

"Go ahead, Katherine. Ask Hannah your question," Judy said, shooting Hannah a tight smile as if to say *and this is where you respond*.

"Oh I…" the voice said. *Katherine.* She was still crying, but her English accent was recognizable now. "Hannah, I'm so sorry."

Hannah's mouth went slack. Precious seconds ticked by before she was able to force it to move again.

"Katherine," she said, elongating every syllable as she fought to keep her voice even. "What's wrong? What happened?" She forgot all about her agent, the audience, Judy, her book—everything save for the one thing that clutched at her now.

"Is Grace okay?" Hannah didn't bother to turn towards Judy as she managed only a clumsy, "It's my nanny."

Judy blanched. "We'll be right back." She turned to the camera with a contained look of panic. A commotion rose in the control booth. The live feed didn't cut off. Judy ran out of frame and started gesturing wildly at a cameraman. If Hannah had noticed, she would have seen a producer throw his hands up in frustration.

"What do you mean we're locked out of our own system?" the man yelled into a headset. "Is that even possible?"

But Hannah didn't notice. "Katherine." Her trembling hands were together in prayer, her eyes closed waiting to hear it was okay, it was all okay, and they would all have a great big laugh about this later while Grace bounced on her lap, her little legs dangling over Hannah's knees with whatever sparkly socks she picked that day, about how silly Hannah panicked over nothing and... "Please, what's happened?"

"Grace, she's... Oh..." Katherine sniffled.

"Where. Is. Grace?" Hannah demanded, punctuating the question with clenched fists. There was a muffled thud, as if the phone had been dropped.

"Katherine!" Hannah screamed. The audience gasped.

The line crackled. "I'm here." She sniffed. "I'm sorry, Hannah, I am."

"Where is she?" Hannah shouted at the sky as the cameras continued to roll and a nation watched.

"I will," Katherine said to someone else. "Just please don't . . ." After a few shuffling sounds, the nanny came back on the line, sobbing. "He says if you are what you claim, Grace will not have to pay for her mother's deception."

"He *who*? What do you mean *he*? Katherine, please..."

Hannah paced the stage in her high-end shoes, pulling at her perfect updo that had a price tag to complement the expensive suit. *Oh please, God, let this be a maniac pretending to be Katherine. Let this be a prank by people who hate me. I can live with a prank but I can't live with...*

An image of Grace's smiling face, baby teeth poking through her cheeky toddler smile and that one curl hanging down that she always was pushing to the side as she waved goodbye to Hannah when she left the house a few days ago was all Hannah could see as she stumbled looking towards the black hole of the studio ceiling, sucking in and devouring every speck of light.

"Katherine," Hannah pleaded with God as much as she did with the voice coming out of the sound system. "Where is Grace?"

Katherine sniffed. "I don't know."

The live audience didn't dare breathe, the common consciousness between them believing any movement might get someone hurt.

A sob, and the final words coming from the other end. "Please find us. Ha—"

The line clicked dead.

Later, Hannah would have no memory that in front of millions of people, her hands covered her mouth as she sank to the floor. She didn't make a sound, like an invisible vise had crushed the air out of her. Across the country, people who didn't know either Hannah or her child would do the same.

Chapter Two

Asha barely slowed down to swipe her security tag as she sprinted to the elevators of the forty-three-story building that housed the offices of *The Metropolitan*.

In a time when newspapers were dropping like flies, *The Metropolitan* was still a respected institution, one of the few papers that had managed to transition from the days of street corner paperboys to a significant online subscription. Every time a former classmate of hers struggled, she knew her position was a bloody miracle—especially after her recent debacle involving a quote that she had not properly sourced, which, Asha was quick to point out, *everyone* did to make deadlines, but was somehow only biting her in the ass because it involved a popular politician. Her stomach churned at the thought, but she resisted the urge to grab for the antacid tablets that rattled in her bag.

She unwrapped her scarf in the elevator and collected herself so that she didn't look like she had just finished a marathon instead of arriving to work, which she would keep doing until someone said she no longer had a job. When the elevator doors opened, she was greeted by Charing's smiling face.

"You're late."

Great. So much for hoping no one would notice.

Charing crossed her arms. "You should be more mindful of making...Hey!" Asha sailed right by as if Charing didn't exist. "I'm only trying to help by pointing out all of your flaws."

Asha scrambled to stow away her scarf, then nodded at the clock. 8:03 AM. "It was probably only 7:59 when I stepped into the elevator, so technically," she made jazz hands, "I'm right on time."

Asha knew she should break down and get an apartment in the city, especially on days like this when the extra hour cushion she allotted to get into New York almost wasn't enough. The trains liked to have technical problems, the ferries liked to have engine trouble, and driving was out of the question, since the bridges and tunnels thrived on snarled traffic. Every morning, Asha played a guessing game of what was the best way to get to work, and even she had to admit it was losing its charm. But there was something about the city that made Asha uncomfortable, even though she couldn't quite understand why the buildings looming over her screamed ominous intentions where everyone else saw endless possibilities. What she did know for sure was that when she stepped off that train in the evening into the countryside of New Jersey, it felt like home—which was the countryside on the outskirts of Cambridge, England. Giving up her peaceful country escape wasn't worth the shorter commute. At least, that was what she told herself when she was sprinting past the unwashed masses because her pre-dawn wake-up turned out to not be early enough—again.

Charing looked her up and down without pretense. Asha knew the senior reporter was judging her and not for the first time under Charing's gaze, she felt inadequate. Charing was the kind of person who managed to pull off the fashion-forward yet work-appropriate look flawlessly.

Asha, on the other hand, had apparently not inherited her mother's high-end fashion sense.

"You're all of what, twenty-something? Time to get a place in Manhattan and have some fun in your youth while you can. I'll let you in on a little secret." Charing looked to see no one was listening. "Jersey is where you go to live in your 40s, when the cool part of you has died to raise children who can't get over how uncool you are." She nodded. "I'm guessing that's something they didn't tell you in the New to New York handbook. It should have come with your resident status paperwork."

Asha sighed and took off her coat. "So, thank you for the cheery welcome, Charing." Asha turned and fired up her desktop. "But I've got much to do and I'm sure there are loads of other youngsters here just waiting for your thoughts on their place of residence and clothing, so I'd rather not keep you." She sat down in dismissal. Asha rolled her chair toward her desk, struggling not to feel self-conscious about her outfit, but Charing stopped her.

"No time. The boss man wants to see you. Now."

Asha hid a flash of panic. An unscheduled meeting around here meant a change of plan. Or, a change of staff. "Do you think it's about...?"

"Made-up quotes?" Charing winked. "Naughty girl."

Asha burned. "It wasn't made up, just not terribly verified." She expected a lecture, but Charing shrugged and turned toward Mike's office, which was somehow worse. Asha just stood there, frozen in place, staring at Charing's glossy black hair whipping down her back as she walked away, and for a moment, the only thought on Asha's mind was how unfair it was that she had to keep her own hair in a sensible bob or risk looking like a schoolgirl. *Get a grip.* Panic came back with full force and she scurried after her mentor to meet her fate.

"Journalism is a dying art, darling, and if you don't want to starve, you're going to have to learn to deal with sources more skillfully." She turned back to look at Asha one more time before opening the conference room door. "Skill, and a better outfit. Oof." Charing cringed and may have kept going after the door was open, but paused when she saw that Mike was accompanied by Stewart Frazer, the CEO of their parent publication company. This couldn't be good.

Mike gestured towards the ample supply of chairs, and Asha was surprised to see it was just the four of them in the room: the two biggest bosses at the paper, Charing as a senior writer, and Asha. There was no logic she could see to how she fit in other than she was getting sacked. She had hoped the reaming in Mike's office and some crappy assignments would be penance enough, but there was no other explanation.

"Have a seat," Mike said, his face unreadable.

Asha smiled to cover up the panic that was building inside. She must be getting fired, and Charing would be taking over her ongoing stories. Asha was about to join the ranks of journalistic roadkill. But she wouldn't go without a fight, pointless as it may be.

"Mike, about that quote..." She blurted.

"Asha, please don't."

"No, hear me out," she pleaded, trying not to vomit. "Look, I know I was hasty."

Mike raised an eyebrow as if to ask, *Ya think?*

Asha put her hands up. "Okay, but aren't we supposed to ask the hard questions? Would you prefer I bury it? We all know he said it, even the readers know he said it."

"But you left open the door of deniability, one of the deadliest of all reporting sins." Charing interjected.

"Enough." Stewart's voice startled the three of them, and they all turned to look at the CEO. "Can we get to the matter at hand?"

Mike pinched between his eyebrows, and Asha held her breath. "Something very big has been brought to us," he began. "An exclusive. What we are about to discuss cannot leave this room."

Stewart nodded. He focused on Asha, his dark eyes staring directly at her, his scrutiny making her uneasy. "About an hour ago, I received a phone call from a lawyer representing Hannah Smoke."

Charing's eyes grew wide. Asha knew this was big, but she couldn't quite place the name. Stewart kept staring at her, and she felt like a student being called to answer a question.

"It seems Ms. Smoke is ready to talk about the events surrounding the kidnapping of her daughter, and she has chosen this publication as her vehicle."

"An exclusive?" Charing asked. Asha could almost see smoke from the wheels spinning in her head. It made sense that Charing was the first choice for this. As her junior, Asha would be on deck to support her whether that be curating old references to the story or fetching coffee. She exhaled at the realization that not only was she not about to be fired, but that this had nothing to do with any of her mistakes.

Mike nodded, glancing at Charing before turning to Asha. "Yes, an exclusive."

Charing took a deep breath as Asha rummaged through her brain trying to remember exactly who Hannah Smoke was. The name tugged at her consciousness, but she couldn't quite bring up the details.

Mike clasped his hands together. "It's a big deal for us, but also comes with some restrictions set by Ms. Smoke. *Non-negotiable* ones," he added, looking straight at Charing. "Since she's spent the last twenty-five years dodging the press, we will go along with them to the letter. We don't want to scare her off and send her running to *The Times* with this."

Charing leaned forward and nodded. "I can work with that. What kind of boundaries are we talking about?"

"Not so much boundaries as demands," Stewart answered. "The first one being that when it comes to putting the story together, the team be as small as possible. And no one on the team is to discuss the story with anyone outside of that select group before it's been published. This won't be one of those stories that has a lot of pre-promotion, it's just going to be dropped out of the clear-blue sky. That was the lawyer's idea. I think he's looking to spare her any harassment before her words even get out."

"I'm assuming this is the team?" Charing cleared her throat and asked with what Asha called her nonchalance voice: the low, relaxed tone she took whenever she wanted to appear in complete control despite having just spotted the journalistic equivalent of prey. Cool and calm were not Charing's default. And even had Asha not known that, the pen Charing was about to snap under the table was a dead giveaway to how big this was.

Stewart nodded.

"My apologies, but who is Hannah Smoke again?" When Mike rolled his eyes at her, Asha tried to backpedal. "I know I've heard the name, I just can't remember exactly where."

"*The Psychic Next Door*?" Charing pounced, unable to hold in her frustration. "Only the biggest tabloid story of the nineties. Outside of OJ, of course."

"It's all right, Asha," Stewart said. His voice carried a balance of kindness and warning. "This goes back a bit and you're not American.

I wouldn't expect you to know every detail." He sat back and folded his hands. "It would have been helpful but here we are," he added under his breath giving Mike a side glance. He turned back towards Asha. "Hannah Smoke was a psychic and reality television star who was making an appearance on a live show when she found out her child and nanny had been kidnapped."

"Oh, yes, I have heard about that," Asha started, but Mike held up his hand.

"There's no time to review. We asked for a day." He shook his head. "One lousy day to do exactly that, but it was declined."

He tossed a file across the table at them. "This is what we were able to throw together for you on short notice. Much of it is our work from that time." He jutted his chin towards the file. "Apparently, we were among the first to do a story on how the slew of attacks on Hannah as a mother were unjustified. That's part of the reason she's coming to us. Charing, since you're familiar with this case, you can explain the details to Asha on the way to the interview. Ms. Smoke is insisting on doing this today."

Charing looked up from flipping through the file contents. "Today?" She shook her head. "Way to give us no time, Hannah." She slapped the folder shut and passed it to Asha. "Everyone has finally left her alone and now, out of the blue, she wants to talk? Decades later? There's something there. And I am just the person to find out what it is."

"Charing," Mike said. "You have never let me down and I don't expect you to now."

"Of course. I'll…"

Stewart cleared his throat. "As was stated before, there are restrictions. Ms. Smoke's lawyer made it clear that any attempt to circumvent her requests means she will take her story elsewhere."

Mike leaned forward. "The interview will be one-on-one." He looked between the two women. "Asha, you are to do the interview."

"What?" Asha and Charing gasped at the same time.

"Charing, we have called you in for prep before and to help craft the story after. She allowed us that concession."

Charing jumped out of her chair, her face turning red. "Are you kidding me? I am the best goddamn reporter you've got here."

Asha swallowed. "She's right." She meant it. Charing was the best reporter they had, it was another reason Asha didn't object to her abrasiveness—there was a lot to be learned in her seasoned if harsh shadow.

"With all due respect, I'm not even familiar enough to know what to ask." Charing shot her a nod in agreement. "I'm not trying to sound like I don't appreciate the opportunity, but Charing being at the front end of this makes the most sense."

Asha was ambitious, not stupid. She knew that when the story was this big, even a small credit would be huge for her career. There was no reason to risk screwing it up by jumping in head first having no idea how deep the water was.

Stewart rubbed the back of his neck with his hands, his face otherwise impassive. "She stipulated that we send the least experienced on staff reporter. One of her restrictions. No veteran journalists."

"If we send anyone but the most recent full-time writer hire, she will go to another paper," Mike added.

"She doesn't even know who Asha is!" Charing gestured with the tortured pen at her. "Just send me and tell her I'm 25. I look fresh out of college for God's sake." That was true. Charing could have passed for a graduate student, because besides being a gifted reporter, she had the gift of Asian genes.

The editor shook his head. "Too risky. We have to assume she's done her research. It's in the reporter bios on our website." His fingers drummed the table. "I should take that down. Charing, we'll make sure you get credit." Charing responded by rolling her eyes so far back Asha wondered if it hurt. He looked at Asha, "Not to mention if you pull this off your career goes into the stratosphere."

Charing gripped the back of her chair so hard it appeared the stuffing might burst out, Asha hoped her armpits weren't developing sweat stains.

Today. This is going to happen today. Asha went through a mental checklist in her mind of all the things she would normally do to prepare, but there was zero time. She suspected that wasn't accidental. "When are we expected?"

Mike ignored her question. "She has agreed to being recorded, so bring your equipment. Her home is about one hour from here."

"We're going in her *house*?" Charing waved in Asha's direction. "She hides away for years and now is suddenly inviting reporters into her home? I don't like it. She's up to something and she's counting on an inexperienced reporter not to know it."

Asha burned at the thought of being considered a chump and wondered if her bosses agreed with Hannah on that point.

"The lawyer was vague," Stewart interrupted Asha's indignation, "something about some new information coming to light and Hannah wanting to bring attention to the case again. If she's up to something, I guess Asha will have to find out what that something is."

"Yes," Mike said. "Asha, this is your big chance to do that hard-hitting journalism you came to the States for." He held up his hands in a gesture that could be for emphasis, but if they had reached her neck would be choking her. "But in the *smart* way. If you ruin this..."

"I won't." Asha sat up straight. She looked up at Charing who was still fuming. "I can do this, but we both know I'm going to need your help." Asha stood. "It doesn't matter who deserves what if both of us are on the line."

Charing's mouth dropped open and she considered Asha for a moment, a darkness flashing through her eyes as she exhaled. "You're right." She put a hand on Asha's shoulder and squeezed. It hurt but Asha refused to wince. "Let's go get our story."

"There's no time for this, you need to go," Stewart interrupted. "Now. Before she changes her mind. And ladies?" They both turned back towards him, Charing looking pissed and Asha feeling ill. "This is not just your futures, but probably the whole future of this publication. Do your best not to screw it up."

Chapter Three

The car ride to Hannah Smoke's home morphed from interstate highways, to winding, narrow country roads, to barely maintained dirt paths.

Charing drove as if she were daring the road not to cooperate, still smarting from the sting of not taking the lead on this.

Asha couldn't blame her as barely an hour ago the question of whether or not Asha had a job was still up in the air, and now here she was getting the top assignment. Asha felt a burst of anger for this Hannah Smoke, who was probably trying to look good at the expense of a young reporter. If she messed this up, her career would be over. If she nailed it, she'd still not be respected by her fellow reporters, who wouldn't feel she'd earned it. Maybe she should title the story "Between a Rock and a Hard Place" when it was finished.

She thought about her parents back in England.

Just yesterday, her father had called, trying to intervene in yet another feud that had taken root between Asha and her mother. "Love, it's been two years. You haven't moved up from that junior reporter position, you haven't done any big stories. Don't you think it's time you moved back home? What you're doing there can be done in London, you know that. And then things would be right smooth with your mum..."

She'd cut him off, saying she was on the verge of something big. She'd stuck out her neck and upset too many people to tuck her tail between her legs and go home. It would be humiliating. Her mother would suffocate her.

And Lily, absolutely not. Asha couldn't bear the thought of running into Lily, jobless and tossed out of America, to see Lily's look of pity that she so often bestowed on others, being directed at her. The only thing worse than running into an ex is running into an ex fresh off of spectacular failure.

"... and that interview was insane..." Charing's dialogue broke into her thoughts. Rubbing her eyes, Asha tried to clear her mind's chatter and focus while Charing summarized the events of 1994. Google filled in when it could, but the internet was cluttered with opinion pieces about whether or not Hannah was a fraud who tried to pull off the ultimate swindle and paid with her child's life. Charing scoffed at those.

"First of all, the child's death, while likely, has never been confirmed." She snorted. "There's those who say Grace Smoke is living somewhere under an assumed identity so she can spend mom's millions and live in peace while her Hannah avoids prison. I'd say that's crazy but it doesn't even get an invite to the crazy dance when compared to some of the theories floating around." Despite her anger, she was invested in this story and to her credit didn't want Asha's perspective clouded by writers who were likely funking up the basement they lived in with the smell of stale chips and body odor.

"So, you don't think she was involved then?" Asha pressed one hand against the roof of the car, trying to keep herself steady while she reached into her bag with the other hand to grab some antacids.

"I wouldn't go that far." They hit a pothole, and Charing cursed Hannah for potentially damaging her car while being so obtuse as to pick a newbie for the interview. "Asha," she frowned when she saw the pastel tablets spilling into Asha's hand. "You've got to stop with that."

"I'm nervous," Asha answered through a mouthful of flavored chalk.

"What else is new?"

"I'm not fond of this situation, and" Asha paused for a moment to swallow, "I don't like ghosts."

Charing huffed. "Please tell me you're joking."

"I didn't say I believe in them, but ghosts and," Asha checked her teeth in the sideview mirror, "people who claim to talk to them give me the willies."

"Yeah I'm sure there's a story there..."

"There's not." Asha lied.

"... but there's no time for it. As I was saying, people like Hannah Smoke mean well, but manage to fuck things up anyway. It's like a gift for her kind—and when I say her kind, I mean the frauds. Do I think she ever intended for her child to be hurt?" She took her eyes off the road for a moment to look directly at Asha. "No. Do I think she was completely honest about everything she did know? *Hell no*."

She looked back towards the road to try to minimize any more damage to her car. Asha could have suggested she slow down, but decided against it.

"Let your guard down only enough to make her let her own down. She's a professional manipulator, so I don't care how many times you need to remind yourself there's no such thing as ghosts today, just don't forget it for a second."

"I just said it was creepy, I didn't..."

"As much as we see ourselves as being good at getting what we want out of people, remember she's likely even better. This woman padded her bank account to the tune of millions using her manipulation skills. You can't let that slip your mind for a second today. Shit!"

"What?"

"I can't believe I didn't see it before." She slammed her hand against the steering wheel. "The newest hire thing is bullshit, Asha. You had better be ready."

Asha smirked. "You made that clear and for the record, I agreed."

"Think about it. Making that request means she knows exactly who's walking through her door today." Charing stabbed the dashboard with her finger.

"Right, but she said she'd back out otherwise."

"It's not just trying to take advantage of a less experienced reporter though. I'm saying she made the request because it gives her the opportunity to research you, surprise you with things she knows about you to try to get under your skin. Bitch!" Charing slapped the steering wheel again. "That's an old trick and I almost missed it."

"Bloody hell." Asha grabbed at the door as some rocks kicked up beneath the tires. "Are we sure this is the right way?" She'd wanted to ask a few miles back but didn't dare question Charing, seeing as she was already pissed. It seemed strange that a former psychic to the stars, who was reported to have made millions in her time, couldn't afford a neighborhood with paved roads.

Charing chuckled. "Oh, we are definitely headed in the right direction. The worse the roads, the richer the people that live on them." She nodded towards the gate at the end of a gravel driveway as they passed. "This isn't McMansion Boulevard where people want you to drive by and admire their behemoth to satisfy their ego. Real rich people do everything they can to avoid the eyes of beggars such as ourselves. That driveway entrance may look like it leads to the Texas Chainsaw Massacre house, but trust me, you get beyond the trees and it probably opens up to friggin' Versailles."

"*In a quarter mile, destination is on your left*," the GPS said in a smooth tone, as if it too wanted Charing to slow down.

"I don't feel ready," said Asha, looking over the substantial pile of articles she had not had a chance to look over.

"Yeah?" Charing slowed the car, and Asha couldn't help but feel they were stranded in a forest. "If it makes you feel any better, you're not." She squinted through the windshield. "But relax anyway. Play along with her bullshit a bit if you have to. Being nervous or upset will not help put Hannah at ease."

"Relax with my guard up." *Brilliant.*

Like a mirage in the middle of the woods, a man in an expensive suit stood at the side of the road by an unmarked gate. A Jaguar idled behind him. Charing pulled over and rolled down her window.

"Asha Bennett?" the man asked.

Charing put on a dazzling smile and pointed back at Asha. "That's Asha. I'm Charing Tan from *The Metropolitan*. I don't believe I've had the pleasure." She held her hand out the window.

The man frowned. "From here on, it will have to be just Ms. Bennett."

Charing had a way of keeping the charm going when she was boiling but had to get something done. A coworker referred to it as her third-degree smile. "I'm sorry," she said, stepping out of the car, once again offering her hand. "I didn't catch your name."

"Randall Newman, attorney for Hannah Smoke." He gave her a tepid shake. "I'm afraid, Ms. Tan, that Hannah was quite specific. Ms. Bennett is the only one permitted to pass through that gate."

"Mr. Newman." Asha exited the car and stood at Charing's side. "While I realize Ms. Smoke had requested me, my colleague here is more familiar with Hannah's tragedy, so she accompanied me to make sure I do the best job for..."

"I'm going to cut this short because nothing you are about to say matters. My client's wishes are her wishes, and I suspect you won't be doing much of the talking anyway." He looked pointedly at Asha. "I'm going to assume you're not so inexperienced that you don't know how to listen and write things down?"

Asha bristled and straightened her blazer. "Of course not."

"Good." He looked at Asha's empty hands. "You—you did bring a tape recorder or whatever you kids are using these days to record interviews, right?"

Asha looked stupidly down at her empty hands, and Charing huffed as she stalked back towards the car, adding being shut out for the second time today and Asha's incompetence to the list of things that made her want to choke someone.

"Ms. Tan can assist you in crafting the article after the interview. That's fine." He turned to Charing. "But this place is rigged with cameras and an alarm at the next gate, and I'm telling you, if you try to so much as peek around a tree, it will be game over."

"The next gate? One isn't enough?" Charing said, and Asha knew she had been considering peeking.

"For a long time, it was nonstop around here." Randall Newman shook his head, as if seeing the whole media circus again. He turned towards Asha. "Shall we?" He opened the passenger side door of his car.

Asha looked back at Charing and swallowed. "I'll call you when it's done."

"Yes, you will." She inched closer and lowered her voice. "Make her comfortable. Let her talk. Go along with her nonsense when you sense it will help. Only interrupt if absolutely necessary."

"I can do that." Asha nodded. "It's how I survived having you as a mentor."

"Good. And whatever you do, make sure every second is recorded. Don't fuck that up or, so help me God, your family will need a psychic to find your body parts. And don't forget these." Charing pulled Asha's antacids out of her pocket. When Asha went to take them, Charing didn't let go and said, "Don't let her intimidate you, you've got this."

Randall gave Charing the side eye and tilted his chin towards his car. "Get in. I'll drive you to the door." Asha pulled the door shut and looked straight ahead as they rode towards the next gate. She didn't dare look back because she knew that over Charing's look of disapproval she would see her mother's scowl, standing there with her arms crossed in stern judgement of the only child who left her family behind to pursue her career. A career that now hinges on Asha doing the impossible, and doing it right.

Chapter Four

The driveway to Hannah Smoke's house was a quarter mile long. The second gate, which appeared around a bend in the road, provided passageway through a stone wall topped with wrought iron fencing, and beyond it, Asha had her first glimpse of the main house. Manor might have been a more appropriate word.

"Wow." Asha allowed herself that one word out loud. Apparently, there were two jobs in America that paid well with no proof of legitimacy required—TV psychic and TV preacher. The car came to a stop as she gazed at the ivy-covered entrance. "I guess this is a good paying gig if you can get it."

Randall chuffed and turned off the ignition. "If you're trying to trick me into answering questions about her, you're wasting your time."

"I'm not." Asha took in the house, feeling like having the interview here might be part of the intimidation. "But can you tell me what new development prompted all this?"

Her feet crunched on the white stone driveway as she pulled herself out of the car. Weeds peeked out here and there, and there were areas where stones were missing. At the center of the driveway loop, the still fountain seemed more likely to welcome mosquitos than houseguests.

In better days, the house might have had a casual elegance that managed not to scream *everyone look at me and be impressed,* despite having all the qualities of a luxury home. But right now, at least from the outside, it looked habitable but with about as much cheer as a sepulcher. She stopped when she heard Randall speak from behind her.

"Hannah likes to make sure I earn my retainer, so I'll be finding out when you do."

Asha turned back towards him in surprise. "You don't know?"

He let out a frustrated sigh and slammed his car door. "It's been a long time since Hannah has spoken with the press, so I'm going to say something to you now that I haven't needed to say in years." He rested his hands on the roof of the car. "There's been a lot of ugly speculation. Stories about Hannah and what happened have been thrown around for decades. People, especially reporters, when they see these things on TV or in the paper, forget that there are actual people living it. As Hannah's lawyer, I don't want anyone doing a hit piece. But it's more than that." Randall stepped away from the car and started towards the house. "As a human, I ask you to remember that even if the worst lies ever told about her are true, she still didn't deserve what happened." He gave Asha a pointed look and added, "neither did Grace or Katherine."

Asha didn't bother crafting a response. She had too much to worry about already without some lawyer getting in her head, seeing as her angry boss and disappointed mother already lived there rent-free. The stones shifted under their feet as they approached the house, the sound reminding Asha she wasn't on solid ground and making her anxious again.

The door cracked open before they had a chance to knock. A woman with a lined face and a long braid of thick silver-accented hair resting on her shoulder looked both of them over. For a moment, Asha thought this couldn't be Hannah Smoke. But then she saw those same pale brown eyes she'd seen in those old pictures, the color of weak tea. And, more importantly, she saw the determination in those eyes, a woman resolute and ready for battle.

"Ms. Smoke?" Asha hesitated, suddenly self-conscious at the idea that *Smoke* might be a stage name and she didn't even know because she knew *nothing.*

The woman gave her a tight smile as she opened the door wider. "Glad you could make it on such short notice, Ms. Bennett." As they both moved to enter, Hannah held her hand up. "That will be all for today, Randall."

The lawyer, pausing mid-stride a few steps behind Asha, huffed. "You can't be serious. Hannah. You should not do this on your own."

Hannah moved so that she stood between him and the doorway. "I keep you on payroll precisely because of all the things I do that I shouldn't."

Asha had to bite back a startled laugh. The wit in her response and the certainty in her posture were definitely not what Asha had been expecting from a reclusive grieving mother. *Interesting.*

"Scratch that," Randall said. "You really shouldn't do this at all."

When the man still didn't move, Hannah sighed. "I've got it, Randall." She waved Asha inside and started to close the door. "I'm not going to say anything that will land me in jail."

"That's what all the jailbirds say," he yelled as Hannah snorted and the door clicked shut. She shrugged. "He's not wrong. I said that to him right before I went to jail, but I'm jumping ahead."

Hannah turned around, and Asha felt uncomfortable under the weight of her silent stare once the banter was gone. She waited for Hannah to direct her somewhere, but she stared at Asha like she forgot why she was there. The older woman stood a good five inches above her and looked down at her in an uncomfortable way Asha had experienced many times when she first met people—it was as if Hannah were wondering where the rest of the girl was.

"So, where should we set up?" Asha finally asked, eager to brush off the goosebumps Hannah's scrutiny gave her, along with the thought that maybe they weren't entirely alone. *Which is stupid.* She admonished herself and straightened her posture.

The question snapped Hannah out of her trance and she let out a nervous laugh. "Oh, I'm sorry. It's been so long since I've talked to a reporter, much less talked about," she waved a hand in the air, "all of it." She clapped her hands together, and her voice was pitched higher when she said, "I figured we could talk in the kitchen?" She gestured towards Asha's bag. "It's comfortable in there, and you'll have the table to set your things on."

"Ms. Smoke…"

"Call me Hannah," she answered as they walked through the entry hall. The place, while beautiful, didn't feel like a house someone lived in. Asha wasn't sure what to expect, but noted that despite Hannah having lived there for decades, it lacked anything personal: no pictures on the walls, no art, or tchotchkes that made a place feel like any home, much less Hannah's home. There was a disquieting quality to it, as if ghosts had gathered to watch them.

"Hannah is my real name," she called out over her shoulder, oblivious to Asha's discomfort. "Smoke was a name I took for work. Even then it felt silly." She shrugged. "My mother came up with it one night when she couldn't find her cigarettes." Hannah laughed. "She was fluttering around the house getting frustrated and talking to herself, at one point she blurted out Hannah, Smoke! Everyone said it sounded so mysterious. I use it now because..." Hannah paused, looking at something in the distance Asha couldn't see.

"Because?" Asha leaned to try to get a peek of her face.

Hannah turned back around and wrung her hands. "Because it's Grace's name. At least, that's how everyone knows her. Grace Smoke." She turned back around and they entered the kitchen. "You have an accent," Hannah said with her finger in the air. "Are you from the UK?"

"Yes, Cambridge to be exact," Asha said. She was relieved to see that the French-inspired country kitchen had a homier feel to it. The room was functional and, with a bit of polish, it would be the kind you'd find in *Architectural Digest*. Hannah gestured to Asha to have a seat in one of the cushy chairs at the table, right next to the large stone fireplace where a fire danced, relieving Asha of the chill from the damp November mist.

"I was in Cambridge once, briefly," Hannah said. "It looked like a lovely place. I regret not getting the chance to go punting." Noticing the recorder Asha had pulled out of her bag, Hannah waved her consent. "Feel free to start recording. It's all on the record, I guess." She turned back to the stove. "Coffee? Tea?"

"I'm fine, thank you."

Hannah turned her back as she reached into a warming drawer and retrieved a tray of pastries. "You should know that my history with reporters isn't a good one," she said. "But I'd been thinking about coming forward again for a while, and once I decided to do it, that was it. I needed to do it right away."

She pulled a platter of cut fruit and cheese out of the refrigerator and added it to the growing collection of treats on the table. "And, in my nervousness about doing so, I'm afraid I may have rushed things a bit, and thrown your own plans for the day a bit topsy-turvy."

Asha placed her notepad on the table with the pen laid precisely across the top as she liked it and folded her hands. "Not at all. Of course, we would make any accommodations necessary to help you tell your story." Asha adjusted her glasses and hoped Hannah couldn't hear her stomach rumble. She had, in fact, not eaten.

Hannah placed two steaming mugs on the table between them. "It's going to be a long day, I suppose. And worrying about starving you is only going to make me nervous. So please, don't go thinking it's not appropriate to accept food. We should eat." She sat down across from Asha. "Anyway, needing to run out to the store gave me something to do instead of just pacing until you got here."

Asha gave a polite smile and took a croissant. "When was the last time you were interviewed? Formally?"

"Well, it depends about what and where. In the U.S., it's been over twenty years since I've willingly spoken in public about Grace or Katherine."

"That long?" Asha paused in setting up her recorder.

"I would release statements and such when appropriate, but no interviews like we're about to do." She held up a finger. "But, I do a lot of missing children work overseas these days—that includes anything and everything from rescuing exploited children to reuniting adoptees and birth parents. That's just regular work, not psychic work," she said, predicting Asha's next question. "I have participated in stories about that, but those interviews are never about what happened to my family."

Her fingers tightened around her coffee mug. "They'll mention it in a tagline or something, but I find the foreign press a bit more willing to respect my wishes." She shrugged. "Maybe it's cultural, or maybe it's because I wasn't as famous there so all they see is the loss and not the scandal. I can't be sure."

Asha smiled. "That may be the first time I've heard the word press and respectful used together in a sentence."

Hannah's face lightened a bit as she realized something. "I'm guessing all you've seen are old pictures, right? My bottle job blonde was the first to go, and after that it wasn't long before I learned my hair was not only a mousy brown, I was going gray." She paused with her coffee spoon in the air. "In my prime celebrity days I was always dressed up. I'll admit that sort of thing was important to me before. Hell," she used the spoon to gesture around her, "even my house isn't as dressed up anymore."

"Well, you look great now, only different."

"I guess I am." A cloud of sadness passed over Hannah's face. "Different, I mean."

Sensing the chitchat had relaxed Hannah enough, Asha nodded and put her mug down to double check that all her supplies were in order. "So, tell me. Why this interview now? What changed?"

Hannah's posture deflated and all of her nervous fidgeting went still. She took in a shaky breath and tried to recover but all that came out was "Um…" Asha internally cursed herself for bungling the most important assignment of her career in record time. She watched Hannah's hands tremble as she lifted her mug, then give up when the contents threatened to slosh over. She secured her coffee on the table but kept her white-knuckle grip on it. "There's not an easy explanation for that," Hannah murmured.

Calculating what Charing would say next, Asha's heart pounded at the idea that there was *something* to tell. "It's alright. Whatever it is," she reached out to brush Hannah's hand with her fingertips, "not before you're rea..." She was cut off when Hannah's hand flew up in response to her touch, spilling hot coffee over both of them.

"Shit!" Hannah's eyes, which had glazed over, came back to the present.

"Oh, I'm so sorry!" Asha sprang up to grab a dishtowel from the counter. She could hear Charing's scolding in her head. *Rule number one: don't spill hot beverages on grieving mothers.*

Hannah stood up, shaking the coffee off her hands. "No, it's completely my fault. I guess I'm a little on edge." She gave a nervous chuckle and gestured with her chin towards the sink. "I'll get the mess, you cool your hands off first."

After multiple assurances to Hannah that she was fine, Asha wiped the table while Hannah cleaned what made its way to the floor. Once they were settled, Asha couldn't help herself from offering another apology.

"I'm sorry." She winced and rubbed at her forehead. "I wasn't trying to rush you or make you uncomfortable."

"Are you sure your hand is okay?" Hannah ignored the apology. "I don't like that redness. And it's my fault. I invited you here today, and yes..." she swallowed and her eyes turned glassy as they drifted to gaze out the French doors to the backyard.

Asha followed Hannah's eyes to a crumbling slab of concrete and the hairs on the back of her neck stood up. "Hannah?"

Hannah turned back and regained her composure. "There is something new, and, uh," she squirmed, then shook her head to clear it, "but it's difficult to explain. I don't know that I completely understand it myself." She took a deep breath and looked at Asha with steady eyes. "But the only way my story and my desire to tell it now will make any sense is if I start at the beginning." She winced. "Only just now I realize I'm not sure where to begin."

Asha smiled because she knew exactly how to respond, a first for today. A softball question would get Hannah talking, and this one would have the benefit of a lengthy explanation that gave her time to settle in and get comfortable. The story would be familiar like the back of her hand because she would have told it a million times before and Asha needed to learn more. Not just about the kidnapping but about Hannah herself.

"I know where, because the first question I have goes back before the tragedy. I want to know, how exactly does one become a famous psychic?"

Chapter Five

Hannah pitched forward with her arms wrapped around her stomach, looking younger than her eleven years. She bent her knees and folded herself in half in the passenger seat of her mother's canary-yellow Camaro, looking tiny for her age, her tennis shorts and a t-shirt revealing the skinny limbs of a spider.

"What's the matter baby, you cold?" her mother asked.

The pre-teen did her best not to be annoyed by the question. She was smart enough to know you couldn't expect enough light to clear a path from a dim bulb, no matter how badly it wanted to show you the way. "My stomach hurts."

"Well," Joanne paused to pull the wad of gum out of her mouth and chuck it out the window, "this won't take long." She flashed her daughter a bright smile. "If you want, when we're done, I can take you for ice cream."

She's trying, Hannah reminded herself. "No, thanks, mom. I just don't feel well is all. And this..." Hannah paused for a moment. She was surprised by the tears welling up in her eyes. Hannah was just old enough to know there was more to this than what the adults were telling her, but not old enough to sort it all out.

"It's all right, baby." Her mother reached down and patted her leg as if Hannah were nervous about jumping off a diving board. "Don't treat it any differently."

Hannah uncoiled herself and fell into the back of the seat. Her stomach somersaulted as they turned into a residential neighborhood. They were getting close. "But it is different, Mom. This isn't the same as telling Mr. Winfred that his neighbor is letting his dog loose so it might run away, or telling Mrs. Barlow that her great-aunt is with her." She looked out the window. "It's not even telling Fannie that her husband is cheating." Hannah had sort of enjoyed that one. She hated Fannie with a capital H.

Joanne sighed and rolled her eyes.

"It's *Aunt* Fannie—who—I shouldn't need to remind you—is responsible for a good chunk of the people that come walking through our door, paying good money so you can have some nice things like the rich kids have, those tennis lessons." She smiled and gave Hannah a playful shove. "You know you feel fancy with those lessons, and you deserve them. But I can't do it on my salary." She fluffed her hair in the rearview mirror. "Not unless there's some big demand for drop-out stock girls on the horizon." She turned serious again. "So, no, baby, it's not any different. And don't you go treating it like it is, okay? You just," her mother waved her hand in the air like it was a magic wand, "do your thing. You do your thing and we can keep this car that doesn't break down every thirty feet."

"Ok," Hannah agreed with the volume of a church mouse. "I'll do my thing." But she wouldn't agree that this was just like any other time. Mom and *Aunt* (ugh) Fannie could pretend it was all they wanted, but deep down, Hannah knew they were liars, and that they were aware of their lie. They may have thought they were protecting Hannah with the lie, but she knew they knew better, making the protection worthless.

The police car that prevented them from parking in the driveway of the home of six year- old Kylie Keegan was all the proof Hannah needed that this was not the same. Not by a longshot. Her stomach lurched again.

"Mom?" she said through the nausea.

Her mother was already out, tapping her foot. "What?"

Hannah lowered her head. "Never mind."

Hannah didn't have to look up to know neighbors were peeking out their windows at her long walk to the front door.

The disappearance of Kylie Keegan had sent everyone into a panic. Rumors of white vans and strangers with a missing puppy flew around. Since the news broke that a little girl one town over had disappeared, Hannah had had to shrug off uncomfortable questions and pretend not to notice people giving her the side-eye. Her *teacher* had even suggested she should help if she could.

The rumors about Hannah were already local lore. She knew at that moment, a web of gossip shot out from the epicenter that was the Keegan residence, as neighbors hiding behind curtains picked up the phone to say *you will not believe who is in that poor missing little girl's house.*

Hannah was relieved when the officer answered the door. No one had said anything to her about a policeman in this meeting, and she had a glimmer of hope that this reasonable adult, one whose eyes were laced with the weight of responsibility, would put a stop to this. She knew the eyes of the other adult, the one who waited inside, would look different. Hannah didn't want to look at those eyes, the ones that had the pain.

"Thank you for coming." He nodded his head at Joanne. "Hannah, I know this is scary, but we just want to see if..."

Confusion came over Hannah like a wave as he spoke. He didn't believe in her. She didn't need him to say so, she just knew it. Then why was she here? His face, with just a touch of lines forming, flinched when he looked back towards her, like she somehow had communicated back to him that he didn't believe in her and he was embarrassed.

"Come on in," he removed his hat and used it to point down the hall of the upper-middle class colonial, much nicer than where Hannah currently lived despite the extra income she provided. "Mrs. Keegan would like to see you."

Kylie Keegan had been missing four days when Hannah walked into the kitchen and was greeted with pain that required everything she had not to lose her lunch. *Oh God, I want to help her*, she thought. She tried to forget about the officer, both the one that was there and the others that must be working on finding Kylie. The pain. She had never felt that kind of pain before and it was too much. She wanted to help make it stop.

"Hello," Mrs. Keegan managed to croak out. "Thank you for coming here, Hannah. I've heard about your..." She shook her head to clear it, while Hannah wiped the slick sweat that had gathered on her brow. "I... I am desperate." Her voice broke. "And I guess I'm in that place where I'll try anything."

Hannah nodded, certain that if she tried to speak she would vomit. She turned her head towards a door she suspected was a powder room—these big houses always had one of those—but the adults probably believed she was tuning into Kylie.

"Anyway, if there's anything, no matter how small..." Mrs. Keegan was interrupted by the sound of a lanky teenage boy stumbling through the back door.

He looked about as well as Hannah did.

The room came to a standstill. The boy regarded Hannah with open curiosity, his eye twitching as he tried to figure out how the young stranger fit with his mother and the sheriff. He didn't know exactly what she was doing there, but Hannah sensed he knew it would be related to *her*.

Hannah didn't move. She didn't blink. She didn't breathe. She just held his gaze and tried to fight what was happening inside of her.

Tears spilled from Mrs. Keegan's eyes, and the officer locked his stare on the wordless exchange happening between Hannah and Kylie's brother.

"Hannah?" he started. "Do you have any...feelings about..."

He didn't get to finish because the girl who would become Hannah Smoke vomited all over the kitchen floor once inhabited by six-year-old Kylie Keegan.

Chapter Six

Hannah lifted her cup and paused. "He ran. It was useless, but he ran anyway. I heard everything moved rather quickly after the girl's remains were found, but I avoided the details." She looked out to the patio again where the wind dragged dead leaves like bad memories across the pavers. "Looking back, it was the turning point that took me from local curiosity to national celebrity. I wasn't an overnight sensation. I didn't get a TV show that day, but I was put on the path that led there." She frowned. "I wasn't wrong for feeling sick."

"I didn't realize your career started when you were so young," Asha said.

Hannah smiled. "I can barely recall a time before it. That case brought a new sense of legitimacy due to my work with *law enforcement*." She made quotation marks with her fingers and rolled her eyes. "Can you believe it? People referred to the vomiting incident as 'work with law enforcement.' Even then I knew that was a stretch."

Asha shook her head. "Not exactly a typical American childhood I imagine. What about school? Did you have friends? How did any of that work?"

Hannah shrugged. "Who is going to let their kid be friends with some creepy little girl solving murders?"

"That sounds lonely," Asha sighed, pushing down her own feelings about being the neighborhood outcast. Not that she hadn't tried to fit in, but it finally dawned on her at fifteen that pretending to be into boy bands and skimpy clothes had become more unbearable than solitude. Complicating matters, around the same time she threw away her last pushup bra, her mother started to wear a permanent mask of disappointment.

"You know how every town has a local place that's haunted?" Hannah asked. "A big, old, abandoned building with some weird history that kids dare each other to go in?"

Asha grinned. "England is an old country. We had loads of those places."

"Well, in my town *I* was the haunted house after what happened with Kylie's case. Kids kept their distance, but occasionally they threw a rock at me to see if a ghost would come flying out or something."

Asha picked up her pen and scribbled *bullying* in her notebook. "But I imagine the media had a very different reaction. How did that play out?"

Hannah twisted her napkin. "It started with some minor local coverage and then someone—I hate to say I suspect my mother—gave a tip to a regional news station about my involvement in the Kylie Keegan case. Looking back on it with adult eyes, that poor girl, it was like she didn't matter anymore. What mattered to everyone was that a child psychic had cracked the case."

"Did you ask her if she did it?" Despite her flaws, Asha couldn't imagine her own mother putting her in the line of fire of an unforgiving media for financial gain.

Hannah went to bite a nail, then looked at her hand in disgust and forced it back into her lap. "I couldn't. I still couldn't later as an adult. Isn't that crazy?"

Asha smirked. "Nope. It's always complicated with your mum."

"I learned early that when it came to my mother, certain questions were useless, since the answer would always suit what she wanted reality to be. And once Barbara Silver showed up at my house to tape a segment that was going to be broadcast in all 50 states, it didn't matter. Even if Mom hadn't alerted the press, she was sure ready to thank whoever did."

"Oh." Asha looked up, alerted by the name. "I didn't realize you were interviewed by Barbara Silver back then too. How did that go?"

At that, Hannah laughed. "Better than it would a decade later. I didn't know how these things worked, so I thought the interview would be the end of it."

She shook her head. "I thought everyone would see that I was just some kid and this was no big deal. It turned out the opposite was true. A kid who is nervous on camera can also be the most charming. Once that interview aired..." Hannah pursed her lips "Well, that was when people who were willing to pay more than ten dollars, a lot more, started showing up. It wasn't just Fannie's dim-witted friends anymore, and my mom no longer had to stock the shelves at the local supersaver."

Asha whistled. "That's a lot of pressure, Hannah."

"No," she replied. "Pressure is when you find out there are more missing people out there, and all of their families want your help too. And you want to help, even when you can't. Do you know what I mean?" Hannah shook her head. "No, of course you don't. People think they do but they don't. It's not like wanting to help a sick relative or something. It's desperate in an immediate kind of way, and people are looking to you for an answer or a miracle and they want it right now."

Hannah stared out into space, seemingly lost in thought. Asha realized she would have to take a leap of faith to make her feel understood. "I think I do, in fact, know what that's like to some extent," she said in a whisper.

That caught Hannah's attention. She looked at Asha, one eyebrow raised.

Asha squirmed in her seat. "There was a pond not far from our home. We would go there as kids, play in the muck, get filthy... Brilliant childhood fun." Asha gave a small smile, which Hannah returned. "We were all good swimmers and it wasn't deep—you could see the bottom even standing in the middle—so our parents didn't worry too much about it. I was there with Rory, a boy from the neighborhood."

"How old were you?"

"We were both eleven. There were some plants growing in the muck towards a far end, and he decided to try to pull one out. Once he got close enough to reach for one, he took a step and plunged in the water up to his shoulders. It was a bit like when someone goes down a step they weren't expecting. We both laughed."

Asha swallowed, realizing that she shouldn't have started this but couldn't stop now.

"It was funny until we realized he was slowly sinking in the mud and when he tried to get out, he was stuck. I grabbed his hand and pulled, but he wouldn't budge. The mud was sucking him down and the water kept getting higher, first covering his shoulders, then his neck, then his ears. I desperately wanted to help, but nothing was working." She looked up at Hannah. "I was trying everything I could think of and it was getting worse and we were alone. I don't think I've ever been that scared in my life." *Except maybe that one other time*, Asha pushed the thought aside.

Hannah's fingers pressed into the table, her eyes wide. "And?"

Asha paused as a ripple of fear from that day silently worked its way through her. "I remember saying *I've got you Rory*. But I didn't. I knew it and I could see in his eyes he knew it too. I'd rather not see a look like that ever again."

Hannah nodded, intimately familiar with such looks. "I'm sorry, Asha."

Asha recovered. "Thank God an adult who was jogging nearby heard me screaming and came to help. He could have easily assumed it was just children playing. By the time they got the rope that pulled him out, the water had just started to cover his face. He was okay."

Asha admonished herself to not lose sight of why she'd told this story, even though she knew every time she told it she had difficulty sleeping. Tonight, she would close her eyes and see the water creeping up his chin, reaching for his mouth, until it finally spilled in to fill that void and take away her friend.

For Asha, something very important died that day, but some part of it came back for her more than a decade later. *I will not hand that over to Hannah.*

"My point is I imagine that's how you felt much of the time, with so many people begging you to help."

"When I can't," Hannah replied.

"Even when you want to," Asha picked up her pen, eager to move on.

Hannah licked her lips. "Color me corrected." She sat up, looking genuinely concerned for younger Asha.

Asha shrugged. "I had the experience once and it was quite traumatic. I can't imagine having it happen again and again."

"Trauma again and again has been the one constant in my life." She held Asha's gaze, sadness in her eyes. Then she looked away.

"I understand this is difficult. But you're going to have to trust me a little, or at least trust my ability to see your perspective." Asha lowered her head to meet Hannah's eyes. "Even though you don't like reporters. Sometimes we deserve it."

Hannah smiled and her shoulders relaxed. "I like reporters just fine when I'm not the focus of their story." She stood up to throw another log on the fading fire, watching the flames get excited by the new fuel. "There was a method to my madness when I requested the newest reporter your paper had. I know they all think it was because I wanted to catch someone off guard, make them give a sympathetic account of what happened."

Asha had not anticipated such candor, but of course Hannah would have known what people thought of her. "That did come up," she acknowledged. To do otherwise would have felt like the kind of lie Hannah could see through.

"I don't think I could have taken that hungry look a journalist gets when they know you're getting to the good part." Her eyes narrowed as she said the word *good*. "Telling someone about the time your heart was ripped out of your body," she closed her eyes and drew a shaky breath, "and seeing their eyes start glittering with the promise of what this will do for their career. Some actually start salivating." She shook her head. "No, I didn't think I could get through today in that case."

Asha hesitated. "They've already said this will help my career," she admitted without mentioning in this case help meant save. Hannah just nodded.

"I hope it does." She hesitated. "I promise I didn't call you here today to hurt you, Asha. I guess I'm just hoping not to see the celebration in your eyes as I tell you the worst of it."

Asha pressed her lips together. "No cause for celebration as far as I can see."

Hannah nodded, and Asha reminded herself that she didn't believe in psychics as she took on the full weight of Hannah's stare.

Hannah shook her head, snapping out of her trance. "So. Where was I? The national segment, right?"

"The one with Barbara Silver, yes."

"Soon after that, there was enough money coming in that we were able to move to the right side of town. I thought maybe things would be different for me, but the only thing that changed were the names I was taunted with. The kids at my new school called me 'ghost girl.' They suggested I should just kill myself so I could be with my own kind."

Asha felt a wave of familiar disgust. "Makes you wonder what kind of parents they had."

Hannah scoffed. "I didn't have to wonder, because the second their parents ran into difficulty—financial problems, a sick loved one, a cheating spouse—whose house do you think they came running to? Many wanted to come late at night. They were embarrassed, like someone buying lottery tickets when they're having financial problems, but they did come. I guess it didn't matter, but it was the first time I really felt *used*." Hannah reached for a roll.

"It wasn't long before my mother pulled me out of school, and while I'd like to say I was home-schooled, that wasn't really a thing back then, and I probably wasn't anyway unless you count adding up cash as math class." Asha noticed she didn't actually eat the pastry, she just tore it into bite-size pieces that never made it into her mouth.

"But bullying wasn't what kept me up at night. I had bigger fish to fry than other kids not liking me and once I was pulled out of school, what they thought ceased to matter."

"What did keep you up at night?" Asha asked.

"The more successful I became, the more missing people there were. A lot more."

"How did you handle that?"

Hannah pushed her food away as if she had suddenly lost all appetite. "Have you ever seen it? What happened that day, on *The Judy Show*?"

Asha startled at the sudden change in topic and cleared her throat. "I found a brief clip, but this all happened so fast I didn't have a chance to give it the kind of attention I normally would."

Hannah nodded. "The full segment is not that easy to find, even though so many watched it happen live. My understanding is that clips pop up on YouTube from time to time, but the administrators are quick to pull them down. Technically, *The Judy Show* owns it, and I'm pretty sure they consider that segment a valuable property to sell the rights for. Maybe before we continue, you should see it. Then everything else will make sense. The events before and after will be in better context."

She stood up. "I'd put it off all day if I could, but you should see. You should understand. I considered just sending you home with a copy to watch later without me, but you will have questions. Also, I'm not in love with the thought of another copy of this circulating out there."

Asha hesitated, a pit forming in her stomach. It sounded like watching one of those awful terrorist beheading videos with the person that was beheaded. "Are you certain? It's quite understandable if you don't want to see it." Still, she followed Hannah through glass doors into a small office. She would have to get her hands on it somehow, since now she would be mostly paying attention to Hannah's reaction as opposed to the video itself.

"My whole life has been an experiment in *I'm not sure*." Hannah chuckled and pulled out a VHS tape. "Have you ever seen one of these?"

"I'm at least old enough to remember those, yes."

Hannah gave her reserved smile again, but Asha noticed her mouth twitch as her eyes fell back to the toxic tape in her hand and she sat down on one of the sparse chairs.

For such a grand house, the room was decidedly utilitarian. Bankers boxes loaded with files lined the walls, and Asha wondered if they were all about Grace's disappearance. A TV/VCR combo sat on a folding card table, and they each sat in a folding chair.

"I use this room for research. It's the black hole of my house, where I keep any shred of information about what happened. If I keep it all in one spot, I won't be having an okay day and suddenly come across something that drops me into the abyss. I have another room like it, but that's for other missing kids."

Asha studied her. "Does it help? Keeping all of this in one room?"

"No," she said without humor.

"I can watch by myself," Asha offered.

"No. You will not do this alone."

There was an attentive quality to Hannah that Asha made note to bring forward in her article. Despite losing her only child, she had not lost the protective traits of motherhood and that would be important for readers to see.

Hannah pressed play.

Chapter Seven

Hannah stared out the window as the limo provided by *The Judy Show* crawled through the congested streets of Chicago. The cool glass soothed her skin as the symphony of voices in her head demanded to be heard, so she granted them a few minutes of her time now because she would need to actively shut them out later. The movement of Rick's body as he studied her caught her attention, which she would have otherwise ignored if not for that mischievous grin that always got her.

"Nervous?" he asked.

She flexed her fingers against the leather seats, working out the tension building inside of her.

"A bit."

Her impending appearance on *The Judy Show* was adrenaline pumping on its own, but the potential for what it could do to sales numbers of her upcoming memoir, *The Curse of My Gift: The Story of Hannah Smoke,* was enough to make her already frayed nerves tap dance.

Hannah's agent was only half-joking when he said that if Judy liked the advanced copy she had been sent and said so on live TV, Hannah could be knocking out the current number one, a horror novel from a hit series, when it hit stores. "One set of ghosts replaces another," he'd joked. To be fair, that book would be cooling off by then regardless, but the thought was still inconceivable to Hannah.

An unconvincing smile plastered across her face as Rick slid across the seat so that he was right beside her. "Here is what I would suggest," he said, reaching into his bag and pulling out an overstuffed file.

She turned her head and gave a pointed look at the papers in his hand like he was offering a used tissue, but didn't say a word.

"Do it, Hannah," he encouraged, gently placing the file in her lap because he didn't want to upset her and understood her distaste for the situation. "Do it because it's the biggest appearance of your life, and there's no point in feeling bad about ensuring you give people what they came for. That's all it does. Helps you focus and turn off the noise." He kissed her forehead and sat back.

Hannah bit the inside of her cheek and looked back at the scenes that flashed by as they whizzed down the street and spotted a messenger boy, zipping on his bike between cars. She wondered if she should yell out to him if he wasn't more careful that he was going to get himself killed, and that she didn't just know that because she was the cautious type and worried about these things but that she knew because she *knew*.

She didn't tell him. Just like the countless people she didn't tell before. Because with some people, it won't make a difference. And with other people, like that messenger boy, it will only make it worse.

Peeling her eyes away from the window and all she couldn't do, she turned her attention to the file and began leafing through it because Rick was right, as usual. At seventeen years her senior, almost to the exact day, it was a joke between them that he was Hannah's responsible adult. "How much time do we have when we get there?"

She could see Rick stifle a laugh. Hannah knew exactly how much time they had, she had the entire schedule memorized by now. Her preferred method of preparation had always been over-preparation. "There will be two hours from when you arrive to when you hit the stage," he replied anyway.

Hannah's assistant, Rebecca, was already at the television studio, making sure things were properly arranged. This was not Hannah's first time appearing before a large audience, so she already had her routine down: quiet meditation in a private area, the only interruption being getting camera ready and then straight to the set.

"And while you're in makeup," Rick trailed a finger up her leg, which made her giggle and slap him away in annoyance, "I will blend in with the audience, doing a security check. If there's anything you should know, I'll make sure you do."

Studio audiences always presented challenges, but they had certain advantages too. One was that people tended to come to these events in groups, openly discussing what they were looking for.

Hannah looked him in the eyes. "You always do."

The quiet moment between them was broken when the volume on the television in the corner increased for a commercial.

Tonight, on the Knowledge Network!

"Oh no," Hannah groaned and rolled her eyes.

"Oh yes." Rick grinned and reached across the empty space to turn the volume up.

America's Favorite Psychic Next Door, loses something? "Rebecca!" Hannah laughs. "I can't, ugh... I can't find my keys!" Rebecca then shakes her head and says to the camera, "Apparently the spirits don't give a rat's butt about your keys."

"Oh my God, Rick." She used the file to slap the back of his head while he sat up at attention watching her on TV, grinning like a buffoon. "Turn that off. You know I hate watching myself."

"Shhh." He didn't turn around. "I want to watch. This chick is super-hot."

And finds something else. On screen Hannah stops and bites her lip, studying a stranger in the market. *"Hello. Um, I'm sorry. I know this is rather strange. But did you lose a close friend recently?"*

"I can't." Hannah reached past Rick to turn the television off. When he pouted, she pointed back at her file. "I have to study." And with that, Hannah was back in the moment. "Hopefully the phone calls go smoothly," she murmured.

"There it is." Rick sank back and looked at her from the side of his eyes, while hers never left the paper she was absorbing zero information from. "It's a live show, Hannah. You will be interacting with the audience first, so that's going to eat up a lot of time. The phone calls, yeah, that's a new wrinkle, but you'll be fine."

She wasn't hearing him, shaking her head in frustration and leafing through the papers in the file haphazardly. "These are all missing people."

"Four of them. Their families have tickets to be in the studio audience today."

Hannah crossed her arms, letting the file slide down her leg. The lightheartedness that filled the car a moment ago had vanished.

"Yeah, I know." He crouched in front of her with his hands on her knees. "But they will be there."

Hannah nodded and, fighting a wave of nausea, picked the file up.

What felt like only five minutes but was, in reality, a few hours later, Hannah stood at attention as an assistant attached a microphone to her blouse. What she hadn't told anyone was that if today went well and the book went on to be a hit, *The Psychic Next Door* would be going on an extended break. No big announcement. She planned to just slowly disappear from public life and not make a whole thing out of it.

Grace would be old enough to start asking questions soon, and she did not want her daughter raised in the spotlight. Hannah was financially secure, and if this book did well Grace would be too. No reason to keep it going.

Rick gave her a supportive but unaffectionate nod as she walked by. The true nature of Hannah's relationship with her security guard was kept secret, since a psychic sharing a bed with a private investigator didn't exactly elicit trust.

A production assistant led Hannah to an opening behind the stands where the audience was patiently waiting to have all their questions answered from the beyond. Judy was already on stage because the first segment of the show had already been taped, and the excitement mounted with the murmurs and applause that rose through the crowd as Hannah made her way to the empty chair beside Judy.

"Thank you for being here today." Judy smiled and looked Hannah over. "Oh, I love your suit!" She looked away and made some hand gesture Hannah didn't recognize to someone in the wings. "Sorry for the rush, but we're back in less than a minute."

"Thank you. It's great to be here and to meet you." Hannah smoothed her hands over the fine fabric Judy had just complimented. "Very exciting."

The host smiled back. "Well, from what I've heard about you, I suspect things haven't even started to be exciting yet."

In the background, someone in a headset shouted, "Get ready to go live in 30!"

Hannah realized that if today went well—if today went *exciting*—then that was her chance to get to ordinary. She looked at Judy, put on a dazzling smile and thought, *cheers to ordinary.*

Chapter Eight

The length of videotape was just enough to hold the infamous television segment. Neither of them moved as the screen went from a younger version of the woman sitting next to Asha sinking to her knees, to snow.

Asha didn't dare breathe, as if it were disrespectful to the dead.

The whir and click of the tape automatically ejecting from the VCR was a welcome, if obscene, intrusion to the silence. It meant one of them had to do something, even if it wasn't right or comfortable.

Since Hannah was still frozen in place and the only sign of life was the rise and fall of her chest, Asha gave in. "Do you need a minute alone? It would be perfectly understandable, Hannah."

Hannah's throat clicked with a difficult swallow. "Perhaps you're right. Feel free to make yourself comfortable." Her voice pitched a few hoarse octaves higher. "There's a restroom down the hall if you need it."

Her chair scraped against the floor as she abruptly got up, and Asha was grateful that she had left the room. She was certain Hannah was crying, and Asha had not yet figured out how to deal with that and still maintain professionalism at the same time. Striking a balance between Hannah's potentially questionable version of events and her unquestionable heartbreak was harder than she had anticipated.

Using the bathroom gave her the welcome excuse to leave the office and the sad echoes of that videotape behind. After Asha splashed some cold water on her face and turned to find a towel, she found herself face-to-face with a small black and white photo on the wall. A photo of a baby covered in bubbles, holding a rubber duck in the same bubble-covered condition.

Her brain tried to escape it, tried to say that maybe it was one of those kitschy baby photos that came with the frame. *Don't be daft.* Hannah was about as likely to have random baby photos in her home as Asha was to still be employed if she mucked this interview up. She forced herself to really look at the picture and felt her heart get heavier as the weight of it sank in—Grace was the little girl everyone knew and the woman no one would ever know.

She felt her phone vibrate and pulled it out, thankful for the distraction. There was a text from Charing.

Just had a call with Phillip from Endzone Publishing on the 18th floor. The same company from Hannah's book! Mentioned that I was working on a review of the biggest scandals of the past 50 years - he spotted Hannah in the café downstairs a month ago! His boss had some secret do not disturb type meeting that same day. Don't let her manipulate you. No coincidences!

Asha didn't respond, but nodded to herself and put the phone away.

Looking at the house, it made sense. Not much was being spent on maintenance, so it wouldn't be a stretch to assume Hannah might need the money a new book deal would bring. Asha would have to find a way to bring up money later.

But as she rubbed at the redness lingering on her hand she had to admit that didn't feel right. Whatever new information Hannah had to reveal today Asha felt in her gut it was one of 2 types: incriminating or devastating. *Explanation first means you know your ass is in trouble and you're trying to get ahead of it,* Asha thought as she gave the baby picture another glance. *What has Hannah done that she needs to explain?*

When Hannah reemerged in the kitchen, she threw a pack of cigarettes on the table. "And now," she announced, "well, I guess now is when we get down to it. Because everything that was in the before I've been through a million times. I help solve a murder, it makes me famous, reality TV comes along and I have a show. Everything that comes after..." She pulled out her chair. "I guess everything that will come after is why talking to you is a big deal."

Asha tried hard not to "salivate," as Hannah had put it, but she sat up straighter and discretely checked her recorder to make sure it was still on not to miss a single detail, because she knew in her gut that when it came to Hannah, the devil would be in some small detail.

Hannah paused halfway to her seat. "Oh." She frowned slightly. "You saw the picture."

"What?" Asha startled at the change of direction.

"I can see it on you. It was the picture in the bathroom, wasn't it? Grace was 6 months old when it was taken."

Asha dropped her pen, astonished. "Are you...you know."

"What?" Hannah sat.

"How shall I put this?" She bit her lip and leaned forward, her voice dropping to an almost whisper. "I mean I'm not saying I believe in this or anything, but are you reading me?"

There was a tense pause. Then Hannah threw her head back and laughed. "No," she said when she finally caught her breath. "But thank you, because with all this sadness, the occasional laugh helps." She shook her head, still laughing. Asha felt her face burn with embarrassment.

"No," Hannah repeated. "You're just that obvious. And it's a look I've seen before so don't feel bad because it's not exactly a fair fight." She lit a cigarette. "I've thought about moving it, but I just can't. It's a happy memory."

"Of course." Asha willed the blood pooling in her cheeks to dissipate.

Hannah waved her hand through the tendril of smoke that danced in front of her. "I promise I won't chain smoke through this thing we're doing here. My hands having something to do helps manage my nerves." She offered a nervous smile. "Cheaper than therapy. Anyway," she shook her head, "We should probably start from the time immediately after the phone call disconnected."

"Were they able to trace it?"

"Yes." Hannah nodded. "But that took time. It wasn't like in those crime dramas where you see them keeping someone on the line and then the police are kicking down the monster's door before he even hangs up. In reality, it was like untangling a ball of knotted up fishing line and would take a few days to sort out. The call had come from a stolen cell phone—remember we're talking about one of those old flip phones. When a phone was just a phone, texting wasn't even a thing yet, and you didn't have it in your hand every second of the day. The owner thought he'd just misplaced it and wasn't even sure where he'd lost it."

She gripped the arms of her chair, and Asha could sense her trying not to get lost in the horror of that day.

"From the second I heard Katherine on the phone, I needed to get home. The first FBI agents were mobilized from the Chicago office and met us on the plane so we could start answering questions. They will get involved in any case where a child is considered in imminent danger, and the planning involved in hijacking a live television broadcast just cemented the deal. Some people said it was my celebrity, but I can promise you that's bullshit." Her frown deepened, indignation showing between her eyebrows. "I've met with plenty of regular people who had the help of the FBI when the worst happened, but the fun of slinging mud my way at any perceived advantage doesn't stop."

"I imagine being on live TV didn't eliminate you as a suspect," Asha commented, jotting down a note to herself—*research celebrity vs. private treatment.* "Parents are always first on the list of suspects, right?"

"Yes. Especially when that parent is famous and trying to sell a book in the age of *there's no such thing as negative publicity.*"

Chapter Nine

4 MINUTES MISSING

Hannah's first memory of after would be sitting in a chair just to the side of the stage, not aware of how she got there, but vaguely understanding that her legs weren't working properly and that the only thing that could make them function would be the precise location of her daughter.

A murky rumble permeated the room as the stunned studio audience was ushered back into the waiting area. The same waiting area where Rick had gone earlier to overhear the misfortune of others on Hannah's behalf.

Now, their own misfortune was taking all of the air out of the room.

Hannah didn't realize she had begun to slump forward until Rick leaned in and caught her with his free hand, the other hand holding a phone, his baritone words cutting through the ringing in her ears. He was in full law enforcement mode now—for him, it kept the insanity at bay. Hannah's alternative mode, which was an invasion of the voices that lived in her head, would not be nearly as helpful.

"Hannah? The police are racing towards the house. Along with EMS, fire, anyone with a transponder in a ten-mile radius."

His steady brown eyes focused on hers, and the small wrinkles at the corners elicited trust from Hannah. Rick was an adult, hers and Gracie's.

He knew about these things. He would know what to do, how to fix it. "It will be a hoax, Hannah. It won't be the first or the last. We just have to hear it from them."

Hannah could have reminded him that was definitely Katherine on the phone, but she wouldn't because she needed it to be a hoax too. "But did anyone call the house?" Hannah gripped at his arm. *Please please please let it be a hoax. An English accent is not hard to imitate, that's all. A stupid hoax. Or a mistake. Just not...*

Rebecca whipped around from a few feet away, where she was tethered to a wall-mounted phone. "I'm on it, Hannah."

"And?"

Rebecca's face was ashen. "No answer. Not yet."

Hannah's hands dug into the top of her head, trying to claw for answers. "The pool house! They would be in the pool house!"

Rebecca's face lit up at that reminder and she whipped around again to dial the pool house number and Hannah's heart flooded with hope. *Yes, of course. Rebecca always calls me on the main house phone, but Katherine stays in the pool house. When I'm away, Grace stays there with her. And that will be why they didn't answer the phone. That has to be it. Come on...answer.* Hannah's eyes were glued to Rebecca's back as she prayed silently.

"Yes!" Rick's voice boomed as someone came back on the line. "Yes, I'm here! Are they in the house?" Hannah's heart skipped a beat. Rick's face went slack and Hannah's heart stopped. She could read him easily—not that you would need to be an expert to identify shock.

It wasn't a hoax.

Grace was gone. So was Katherine.

Rick sank to the floor next to Hannah. "Yes, I'm still listening." He said into the phone. Hannah could hear chatter and shouting from the other end, but couldn't make out anything specific. She tried to imagine her house, a place so peaceful, currently being overrun by chaos.

"No. No no no," she croaked. Hannah gripped Rick's arm. "Maybe they went out?" It was all she had left.

"There are some things..." Rick hesitated and reached down to grab Hannah's hand. "The door to the pool house was left wide open and one of the planters next to it was knocked over."

A rush of adrenaline shot through Hannah's body and, with no place to go, it made her tremble. Rick positioned the phone under one ear while he grabbed Hannah's face with his hands and forced her to look at him. *Yes. It would be okay. Rick would know what to do.*

"There's no sign of injury," he said. "That's important. There may have been a scuffle—God bless Katherine, but there's no," he paused to swallow, "massive pool of blood, or anything obvious that makes it look like someone was injured. What we need to do, for Grace and for Katherine, is to get on a plane and get home, get the girls back safe. Someone wanted a public spectacle, and they've got it. Now we get them back. Then we find who did this, and hang them for the world to see by their insides."

Hannah nodded. Yes, it sounded like a plan to her.

Chapter Ten

The first time Hannah was asked if she had a "feeling" about where Grace and Katherine were was courtesy of an FBI agent as they flew back to New Jersey.

They were somewhere over Ohio, and Hannah was trying not to be suffocated by the opulence of Judy's private jet. A few hours prior, she would have coveted such a luxury. The Knowledge Network had sprung for her to fly private exactly twice, but she wasn't in the same orbit as those considering private jet ownership.

It was an appreciated gesture to be sure, Judy's offer to get Hannah home without the added confusion of flying commercial, but it also served as a reminder to Hannah of the consequences of her greed. As she cast her eyes downward, it slapped her in the face again with her suit, the Dolce and Gabbana she had finally settled on after hours of agonizing deliberation, when she'd thought that the worst thing that could go wrong today was a bad live reading. She knew better now and had the overwhelming urge to burn it, the only debate being whether she should take it off first.

"Uh, Ms. Smoke?" The FBI agent who met them on the tarmac hung up a phone mounted in the service area and ducked as he turned around and made his way back to where she was sitting. Another was deep in conversation with Rick towards the front end of the plane.

It was a circus but Hannah had the sense that the FBI was in charge of the situation, which granted her the fleeting illusion that the people in charge knew what they were doing. They handled this sort of thing daily, after all—minus the celebrity part.

The agent sat down in the seat across from her and Hannah could see he was young, probably relatively new to the FBI, and decided she would have preferred the old "has seen it all" type. A responsible adult. A Rick.

"Ms. Smoke?" he repeated when she didn't answer.

"Hannah is fine." She flinched at her own reflexive response and smile. *My God. Even in this I can't drop my on-air habits.*

"Hannah, I am Agent Jeffrey Watts. There will be a lot of questions coming. Some of them will be intrusive, but you need to answer them directly and honestly. We don't ask them to embarrass you or your family—it's all to find Grace and Katherine."

Hannah nodded. "Of course. Ask anything you want."

"When it comes to details, give them all. You can leave it to us to decide if something is insignificant. At the same time, if there is something you think we might overlook as insignificant but may not be, we encourage you to speak up. That's not just the FBI, ma'am, that's all law enforcement. Although considering the circumstances, the FBI will take the lead in your situation—my understanding is that your local police department is welcoming the assistance, that this isn't the type of thing they normally handle."

Hannah chewed at her lip. "Privileged teenagers racing their parents' expensive cars is the big crime where I live." She flexed her hands and said a silent prayer that she would see Grace become a privileged teenager, wearing some outfit Hannah didn't like and stomping off to her room because she's pissed at Hannah for saying she wasn't to leave the house dressed like a tramp. "Before today..."

He gave a sympathetic nod. "You will be asked, probably within the next 24 hours, to submit to a polygraph."

"Yes, of course," Hannah agreed. "I understand. You will need to test Rick as well."

She let her eyes pass over Rick, knowing the suspicion they would both be under. She watched him in his subdued suit, looking polished yet unremarkable as they planned. To a casual observer he didn't look tortured, but to Hannah the hands on his hips and shifting of his feet revealed it took everything for him to not break down the cockpit door and insist they fly faster.

Hannah had worked on cases in the past where a parent turned out to be a monster and had congratulated herself on despite being unplanned, she had a stellar father for Grace. *Look at that*, she thought. *Turns out it's me. I'm the monster.*

"We will be looking to do this with anyone that has a regular presence in your home. My understanding is he is Grace's father?"

"Yes. It was a thing we kept quiet." When he didn't respond, Hannah felt the need to explain. "A psychic in a relationship with a private investigator raises eyebrows."

"I see," he nodded and jotted something down on a notepad. "If you could, it might be helpful if we had a list of anyone who was aware of the relationship, particularly in regards to Rick being Grace's father."

She shrugged. "It's a short list."

"I mean everyone—that could even include people like your pediatrician."

"Right." Hannah's mind raced, realizing that maybe her relationship status wasn't the secret she thought it was. She wondered how many people knew but turned a blind eye and kept a shut mouth to keep the money flowing.

"And I have to ask this..." He paused and dropped his pen on the table between them as if he was afraid of either the question or the answer. "Do you have, any, um, *feelings* about where they are?"

Hannah bristled, even while recognizing that this was to be expected. "You wouldn't have to ask. I would have volunteered that already, no matter how silly the source."

The agent lifted his hands. "I meant no offense. Is there anyone who you think would want to do this to you, Katherine, or either of your families?" he continued. "Anyone at all? Even if it's just a weird feeling about someone. Maybe someone who's been giving you what we'd normally call 'the creeps'?"

"No one that stands out." Hannah shook her head in frustration. "I am in a line of work where even when the people I meet aren't creepy, their requests often are. Creepy is part of the job."

He nodded. "Does anyone come to mind that may have been angry?"

Hannah rubbed her forehead, surprised that there wasn't anything that stood out, nobody that she had been particularly wary of recently.

"Shit, I don't know. The idea in my job is to make everyone feel better, but that doesn't mean I make everyone happy. My existence alone is often enough to piss people off." She rubbed her eyes, smearing makeup across her face in the process. "God, the list of people I don't even know that wish me ill is probably a mile long but I'm not aware of any specific threats. Rick might have some better insight on that though. He handles my security." Hannah's eyes welled up. "Which before today was a joke between us. Or..."

"Or, what?"

"I mean, I treated it like a joke." As she said it Rick caught her eyes. "He would get frustrated with me."

The agent sat back and gestured she should go on.

"He said I should mix up my routine. And that I should ask more questions about security at appearance venues. He said when they tape my reality show I shouldn't go to locations I actually visit privately."

"It's good advice." He jotted something down. "Did you follow it?"

"Um..." Hannah's voice wavered and she looked up to see Rick was still looking at her. He gave her a nod that indicated he thought everything would be okay, or that he needed Hannah to believe that, which only made her feel worse since if she had followed his advice...

"Hannah?" The agent interrupted her spiral.

"Not always." She clucked her tongue and dropped her hands. "Maybe not ever. I mean some of these businesses were local and I like the people who own them and you know how appearing on a show helps them out..."

"Here." The agent dug in his briefcase but instead of a tissue offered her a blank notepad and a pen. "Things will occur to you at unpredictable times. In all of the chaos, I don't want you to assume you'll remember to say something later. Get into the habit of keeping this with you. Anything that occurs to you—remembering a weird fan following you, a service person at the house, or maybe something strange that Katherine said—I want you to write it down so you won't forget to tell us. Everything counts, Ms. Sm... Hannah."

"Habit?" Hannah swallowed. "I mean," she fought but failed to maintain her composure, "how long can I expect them to be..."

The agent folded his hands on the table and leaned forward. "Kidnapping is not unusual, but the circumstances surrounding this one are, at least as far as motive goes. We always want parents thinking ahead but the goal is to get them back as quickly as possible."

Hannah's eyes spilled over at the thought that maybe even the FBI felt out of sorts.

"Hey." The agent looked around and located a napkin to hand her before he leaned in further. "This person, whoever has them, the fact that they needed it to be broadcast on television tells us a lot."

Hannah nodded and blew her nose. "The need to embarrass me."

"Yes. That can be very good news, Ms. Smoke. Non-custodial kidnappings often occur with darker motives."

Hannah started to turn away.

"No, please." He reached for her hand. "Hear me out. Those kidnappers don't go through the trouble of broadcasting it on live TV. In fact, in this case, if whoever took Grace and Katherine hadn't done so, they would have given themselves several hours of a head start. That's something when you're trying not to get caught."

Hannah felt a glimmer of hope and sat up, understanding what he meant.

Encouraged by her posture, he went on. "I'm not trying to fill you up with false hope, but you should have hope. Hang on to it, as it will make you a stronger participant in getting them back. The kidnapper wants all eyes on *you* and went out of their way to get that. It is logical to think the motive might have nothing to do with actually harming Grace or Katherine."

"Yes." Hannah wiped her eyes again. "That does make sense. And I tried to keep her—actually, both of them—out of my celebrity as much as I could. That one piece of advice I did follow." It was why they hadn't fought about Hannah's casual attitude even more. Flaunting Grace in the public eye would have been a deal breaker for Rick, and Hannah saw eye-to-eye with him on that.

"That's even better news. Because if Grace and Katherine weren't constantly on TV for the world to see, it's less likely we're looking at someone who had an unhealthy interest in either of them specifically. They appear to be a means to an end, the end being you. The unhealthy obsession is likely with *you*."

Hannah sat back and considered this, her mind rolodexing through all the people with missing loved ones she couldn't help, or, to be more accurate, *avoided* helping. "Right," she said, centering the pad on the table. "I think I know where we should start."

Chapter Eleven

"I made it through that flight. I made all sorts of promises to God about how things would change when I got them back. How I wouldn't take them for granted anymore, how I would be grateful for everything I had been given and stop obsessing over material shit." Hannah looked up at Asha. "God wasn't impressed."

Asha nodded but was well-aware that the blanket of regret Hannah wrapped herself in was, at least so far, superficial and could be used to cover more than just maternal guilt. It was something she could spot, having had ample practice when Asha's own mother would wrap herself in all of her maternal sacrifices to manipulate Asha when they had different wants. With Hannah, Asha could sense there was something there, something more than the what-ifs surrounding Grace's disappearance. *Because just like mum,* she thought, *it's not sacrifice if you only did it to get something in return, and it's not guilt if you're only feeling it after getting your hand caught in the biscuit tin.*

She bit her lip and looked around them, for a moment seeing the ghosts of chaos from that day: the flashing lights, the people rifling through every corner of the house frantic for clues, trying to imagine what Hannah knew that she wasn't saying, both then and now.

Asha decided to return to the events and let Hannah lead. "I'd like to backtrack just a second, to the gauntlet of press when you arrived home."

"Oh yes, *that*." Hannah fidgeted with the pack of cigarettes again. "The insanity started once we pulled onto the street. I knew we'd be overrun with emergency vehicles and such, but if you were to count everyone, there was, without a doubt, more people here to cover the story of Grace and Katherine being taken than there were people working on locating them. This is a big property, and it was wall-to-wall people working on finding them, so you could imagine what it was like where the press were being held back at the gate. Not to mention this location. It might feel like you're out in the middle of nowhere but we're actually a short drive from New York and Philadelphia."

"Two major markets within a short distance."

Hannah nodded, looking mildly annoyed. "And countless smaller ones. Even Boston is only a few hours' drive. So, they all came."

Hannah put the cigarettes down and picked up the lighter. "The damn news trucks." She flicked the lighter on and frowned at the flame. "I'm not exaggerating when I say they were parked on the side of the road going back a half mile. To get to the driveway, we ended up scraping the sides of the car because once they realized who was inside, no one wanted to move without getting a picture." She let the flame go out and looked at Asha. "This was back when news vans had those huge satellite dishes on the top." Hannah held her hand above her head. "Do you remember those? They haven't been a thing for a while, I guess."

"Vaguely."

"That agent from the plane, the young one, he rode to the house with us. As soon as he spotted the activity, he made me duck. He threw his jacket over me and said news coverage would be important."

Hannah put down the lighter and gestured with her hands. "All the shouting and pounding. The car was this giant SUV and was still rocked from all the pounding. I think someone's foot got run over. 'We have to use them, Hannah,' he'd said. 'But because of the celebrity angle, we have to take extra care to control the narrative.'"

Asha's brow furrowed. "The FBI was worried about a missing child narrative going wrong?"

"It makes perfect sense. Think about when a local child goes missing. All eyes turn to the parents. 'They *should* have done this, they *shouldn't* have done that.' Add a dash of celebrity and people skip the pretense of benefit of the doubt since, to them, you're not even human."

Hannah looked at Asha's recorder. "I wasn't aware yet of the commentary in the hours that followed. It was massive. Stations cut into their regular programming to cover this story, and that was a good thing. I am grateful for any effort that had everyone thinking about Grace and Katherine. But there's nothing more dangerous than a television reporter with all that damn time to fill and no new information to share. Because no matter how careful they think they are, the opinions start leaking out." Hannah stopped to again look out at the slab that once was the foundation of the pool house. "And if the bullshit they're slinging is getting eyeballs and ratings, the bullshit is repeated, eventually reborn as fact...

"but when their opinions meant people would be led to think my child wasn't actually in danger, those opinions weren't so harmless."

Asha was surprised to feel a stab of guilt. She remembered the commentary she had come across in her mad dash to learn about the case, the accusations that were lobbed, but those had been written after the fact. She'd not had a chance to watch any old news footage to see what it was like on the day they were taken, the stuff that was reported by real journalists like herself. "What were they saying?"

Hannah's fingers touched her lips, and she broke eye contact with Asha and spoke through clenched teeth. "Before I even pulled into my driveway to see that my baby was really gone, before I dodged news vans and helicopters to come back to the house where they were last seen, it was already being theorized that *I* had done this. That I'd staged the fake kidnapping of my own child on live TV to sell books."

Chapter Twelve

5 HOURS: 14 MINUTES MISSING

Judy sat in the familiar plush chair on her familiar soundstage and smiled her familiar smile into the camera. Every news outlet had been notified that she would be making a statement, and every one of them was carrying her beloved image live. Hannah watched in a slack-jawed daze surrounded by agents and officers, trying to comprehend that all of this was about *her* Grace and *her* Katherine. Time had become the most precious commodity, and what had passed since she had been in that room with Judy felt like months instead of hours.

"Earlier today, during a live broadcast of our show, we were all rocked by tragedy — the kidnapping of Grace Smoke, daughter of our guest Hannah Smoke, and her nanny Katherine Willard," Judy said with gravitas. "You will be seeing a picture of both of them on your screen, and I am begging all of you to take a long, close look at it."

Judy balled her hands into fists and shook them in front of her. "In cases of kidnapping, time is critically important, so you should not hesitate to call if you have either seen them, or think you might know something of their whereabouts. Law enforcement has made it clear: it is better to say something and be mistaken, than to say nothing and miss something important.

"We have shared what limited knowledge we have about the situation with both local police and the FBI. We will continue to cooperate in any manner necessary to get these girls home. My understanding is Hannah arrived home about an hour ago and is fully cooperating with law enforcement."

She paused and gave the camera a stern look. "It has been suggested, by some unscrupulous news sources, that someone associated with this show may have staged this event to boost ratings. This is a disgusting accusation, and as a child abuse survivor, I find it especially repulsive. While I cannot speak for Hannah's team, there was nothing I witnessed to suggest this was planned. While I may have the same questions many of us share about psychic powers, I would never knowingly have someone on this show capable of such dark deception as faking a kidnapping."

Judy looked down for a moment, deflated, before she looked at the camera again. "Even sadder is that, if it were fake, it would mean Grace and Katherine would be safe. That's the horror of this, ladies and gentlemen: the nasty rumor being spread by some unethical reporters is the theory to hope for. But we cannot assume this to be true. We have to assume it's real and do everything in our power to get them back. God knows that's what I'm doing. I pray all of you do the same."

Chapter Thirteen

The pool house. That was Hannah's destination. She ignored the curious glances at the distraught celebrity striding through the kitchen and made a beeline for the French doors in the back.

"Ms. Smoke..." A hand shot out over hers, stopping her from turning the handle. She looked up at a man whose slicked-back salt-and-pepper hair, imposing height, and dark suit screamed *law enforcement,* like a caricature come to life. "I'm sorry, but that area is off limits. We must ensure that every bit of evidence is collected before we let anyone in."

"So that is where they were when..." She gripped the handle tighter. "You're certain about that part?" They all craned their necks upward as the blades of a helicopter whomped overhead and cut Hannah off, dragging a spotlight along the backyard. "Is that your people?"

"No." The caricature sucked his teeth.

The first time Hannah comprehended that nothing was off-limits to the press was when she realized the helicopters flying over her home were *news* copters, hoping to grab a glimpse of her for their hungry viewers. She pressed her face against the glass to get a better look. "They can do that? It's legal?"

"Even when it's not, in a time like this we have to make sure every resource we've got is put to best use. Right now, Katherine and Grace are the priority."

She followed his gaze to the backyard where people swarmed like ants, ignoring the roar from above. He put his hands on his hips. "Our people won't be distracted. They're focused right now on collecting every shred of evidence they can find to help get them back. Once we can spare someone we'll find some excuse to get the choppers out of here, even if it's some obscure noise ordinance."

He looked back at Hannah. "I am special agent Thomas Wolinsky. I am the FBI coordinator for this investigation. Your local police department is doing everything they can to help, but..."

"I know." Hannah interrupted. "They don't have the experience or resources for something like this." She didn't take her hand off the handle or her eyes off the commotion outside. *Something like this,* she thought. *How does one have resources for something like this, the total destruction of everything you care about?* But instead, she said the one useless thing she could manage. "Call me Hannah."

"Call me Tom." He seemed about to say something else, but paused as she loosened her grip on the handle, and her hands came away an obscene neon pink. "Fingerprint powder," he explained. "We dusted all of the access doors to the main house just in case."

The color struck Hannah as odd, grotesque in light of everything. "Why is it pink?"

Tom gestured towards the door handle. "The handle's dark in color and we need to make sure we can see any prints that develop, so the technician picks a color that will contrast. Makes it easier to find what they're looking for."

"Oh." Hannah's hackles went down. "Of course."

"It's not my intention to be pushy, but time is of extreme importance."

"It's okay." Hannah turned to him. "I'll do whatever you need whenever you need it."

Tom referred to a notepad. "We've got our people putting together a statement for you to make at a press conference later. That will be the next time you publicly reach out, to try to get whoever has Grace and Katherine to contact you. It seems he wants everything done in public, so I would say it's more likely he'll communicate with you through the press than through private channels. Still," he pointed to her kitchen phone, "we've got all of your lines, private and business, bugged with a tracer, ready to go just in case."

"He?" Hannah perked up.

"Just a turn of phrase, ma'am. Not based on information other than Katherine using the phrase 'he says'."

Her face fell with disappointment as Rick came over and put a protective hand on Hannah's shoulder.

"I know that you both have already answered what feels like endless questions. That list you provided on the plane, we've already got people at headquarters following up."

"Headquarters? Isn't this headquarters?" Hannah's head spun at how quickly things had been organized.

"In cases like this, where there are a lot of moving parts and time is a factor, it's standard practice to have a location that all people involved in the investigation report to. Local stepped up, and before the first agents were even on the scene they had secured use of an old office building a few miles from here." He put his hands on his hips. "The press doesn't seem to have caught on to that yet. They will, but for now they're all either at the end of your driveway, camped outside the police station or…" he made a pained face and pointed to the sky that was now black, but still filled with the sound of whirring blades.

"Would you like to sit?" He gestured towards the kitchen table.

"Yes," Rick said and gently pushed Hannah into a chair. It wasn't chivalry, it was because Hannah looked like she would collapse at any moment. As she sat, Hannah smoothed her white pants, smearing pink powder all over them, getting an odd satisfaction from further ruining her perfect façade.

Tom pulled out a notepad. "There will be, if you are both agreeable, a polygraph. We're aiming for sometime tomorrow."

Rick nodded and exchanged a look with Hannah. "We both already agreed to that on the plane."

"Rick—that's correct?" Rick nodded the affirmative. "You have a history in law enforcement?"

Rick stiffened. It was slight but Hannah sensed it. "Yes."

Tom gave him a polite smile. "There may be times I gloss over something then, assuming it makes sense. I'll try not to but some of this is second nature."

Hannah sensed Rick relaxing, and decided she didn't have the energy to sort it out.

"If at any time something isn't making sense, slow me down and ask questions." He looked at Hannah. "I had a case where the victim's surviving family member was in law enforcement, and it took him days to tell me he didn't know what the hell I was talking about when I referred to signature. That was my fault. Those of us that work in kidnapping and…" He stopped short and Hannah knew what he had glossed over.

She didn't let herself go there though, not yet. He went on. "...other crimes, have a different focus."

"What *is* signature?" Hannah asked.

Tom clasped his hands in front of him. "You've worked with law enforcement as a psychic?"

Now it was Hannah's turn to stiffen. "Yes. On occasion."

"Then you're familiar with the concept, just not the term. 'Signature' is the thing a suspect, in this case whomever has Grace and Katherine, needs to have happen to be fulfilled by his crime. It often gets confused with modus operandi, the way the crime is committed. Modus operandi can change. If our suspect has captured people before, he may have evolved his method of subduing a victim over time. Generally, as a suspect figures out how to make it easier or less risky to commit the crime, modus operandi may change. Signature doesn't."

"So, the phone call during the show," Hannah started.

"Is signature. Or part of it. The person needed you, needed some sort of public interaction with you, to be satisfied. It doesn't make the kidnapping part easier, that's for sure."

"Um, sir?" Another agent in a black suit, Hannah was beginning to wonder if there was a special FBI store somewhere, leaned over and whispered something in Tom's ear.

Tom's face registered the tiniest bit of surprise, just enough for Hannah to catch it.

"What?" She reached across the table and grabbed his arm.

"A woman claiming to be your mother is at the gate."

Everyone stopped to look at Hannah. Rick grunted and rubbed a hand over his exasperated face before he turned to Hannah and nodded. "You should let her in, Hannah."

"I just can't with…" Hannah rubbed her forehead.

"I know," Rick squeezed her shoulder and held her gaze in a way that conveyed it was for her own good.

"Fine," Hannah relented. "No need to check I.D. if she's made a scene because in that case it's definitely her." Rick rubbed her back as her voice went up a few octaves. "So now I've got a fucking signature but no name, and this monster has my kid. That's great. I'm an episode of *Law and Order*."

"Actually, Hannah." Tom sat down to catch her eyes. "We may have something more. Something—or *someone,* to be precise—we need to talk about."

"Well if it's my mother that storm is incoming."

He grabbed his pen. "I need you to start from the beginning and tell me everything you know about your nanny Katherine Willard."

Chapter Fourteen

The storm that was Joanne White introduced herself to the press amassed outside Hannah's driveway by attempting to run them over. It wasn't entirely her fault, not when the threat of bodily harm was the only way to get them to move.

"Ma'am!" A local officer ran towards where she was using her Mercedes as a slow-motion battering ram. "Ma'am this area is off-limits."

"Don't you tell me what's off limits, that's my grandchild in there!" Joanne pointed towards the house. "Or at least she should be," her angry face softened. "Is she there? Did they find them?"

She stumbled out of the car, her usual dazzling sparkly top and skinny jeans identifying a woman ready for a night out, but not her face. It was her tortured face and long blonde hair that was a ringer for Hannah's that told the officer she might actually be who she claimed she was. She ran up on him and clung to him like a lifeboat.

"All I could get on the drive here was the news and they don't know anything and when it happened I tried calling but of course I couldn't get anyone..."

The officer wanted to interrupt her so he could see about getting her access to the house but she held on to him and kept babbling.

"...and then I'm in the car and I can't get in touch with anyone but I figured I needed to be here and I just came right I haven't even spoken to her yet but I have to come right?"

He pointed behind him, "Let me just..."

"Hey!" A bright light zeroed in on Joanne and a microphone was thrust into her face, almost knocking her off her feet. "Are you really Hannah's mother? What can you tell us?"

It was a matter of seconds before others noticed what was happening. "It's Joanne! It's Joanne White! Joanne, is it true you and Hannah were estranged after you did that *A Current Affair* interview?"

"Joanne, when was the last time you saw your grandchild?"

"Does Grace even know you?"

"Does she call you Grandma?"

Joanne whipped around at the frenzy that was keeping her from getting inside. "You sons of bitches!" she howled, and swung her purse at the nearest reporter. He lost his balance dodging it, and fell into the cameraman behind him, clearing the beginnings of a path to Hannah's gate. Two officers grabbed Joanne by the elbows and lifted her through the crowd. At home, people watched shaky camera footage of Joanne White, in a perverse version of crowd surfing, screaming "You Bastards! That's my granddaughter! That's my Hannah!"

Chapter Fifteen

"That may be the only time I'd say there was a scene my mother was in that wasn't her fault," Hannah chuckled. "We were estranged at the time but, you know, family is family." She looked at Asha and paused for a moment, considering what to say next. "My mother may have prioritized money and the spotlight over feelings, but even she had her limits."

Asha nodded. If there was anything she understood it was mother issues. "When push comes to shove..."

"I look back fondly on the good old days when we were fighting because she used my name to get VIP treatment, or spoke to the press while in the same breath assuring me she valued my privacy." Hannah shrugged. "I understood why she needed to be here, and at that point I had bigger fish to fry."

"Like Katherine," Asha said.

"It didn't take an expert to figure out why they were seriously looking at Katherine."

Hannah's hand glided across the table. "These types of crimes often involve a family member or someone close to the family. And the logic was sound that Katherine may have pursued the job with the intent to get access to Grace. We found her while I was still pregnant." Hannah shivered. "The idea that someone was planning this before she was even born made the whole thing feel even darker, if that was possible. And the scene they left. A few random items knocked over but no sign of serious injury. I overheard two detectives discussing that it must have been quick and with little resistance, that the whole thing looked staged."

Hannah pulled a cigarette out of the pack and tapped it on the table but didn't light it. "It turned out there was something else, but I wouldn't know until they let me see the pool house. We'd found Katherine through an international agency that had experience placing live-in help with celebrity households. Did you know Katherine was also from England? She was from Birmingham."

"Oh." Asha made a note. "No, I didn't realize." *But I bet you knew I was English before I said a word.*

"My first preference was a French nanny, not based on anything more than some romanticized notion of how refined my child would be. I had grand visions of someone teaching my daughter to speak a foreign language, eat fancy foods, have impeccable style." Hannah shook her head. "It's embarrassing to say that out loud now. I think I was just envisioning the polar opposite of my own upbringing."

She had the unlit cigarette twirling between her fingers and started picking at the paper wrapping the tobacco, letting little bits spill out. Asha was listening but also watching intently, waiting for the contents to cascade out—for both the cigarette and Hannah's mind.

"When I interviewed Katherine, I liked her. She was from a working-class background, not quite sure what she wanted to do yet, but loved kids and had a clear sense of adventure to her. That was part of coming here—she wanted an experience away from home for a bit while she sorted out what she wanted to do with her life." Hannah's shoulders slumped with the weight of all that happened.

"None of this sounds unreasonable." Asha tapped her pen. She could suddenly relate to Katherine.

"The thing is, if someone asked me why I picked her," Hannah sucked her teeth, "I made sure to let them know my nanny came from the same agency as Tom Cruise and Nicole Kidman's nanny. You know those two, they were a huge deal at the time. So maybe I was lying to myself—maybe I picked her because saying *that* made me feel so goddam special. Now the FBI was asking all these questions that I didn't have answers for, and every 'I don't know' was burning the fuse on a ticking time bomb. Questions about background checks and who her friends were and where did she go in her off time and was she dating anyone..."

Hannah watched the rest of the cigarette spill out onto the table, "...and all I knew about the person raising my child was *I found her at the agency.*"

Asha remembered the third degree her own mother gave her father when she was in primary school and he found a local teen willing to sit with Asha for a few hours before they returned home in the evening. *Who is she? Who are her parents? Does she take the tea?* Asha's mom said *tea* instead of marijuana, and the way she asked the question made it sound as if she were more concerned with the transportation of it rather than the smoking. "Was there anything about Katherine, in hindsight, that seemed a bit off?"

"When Tom asked us if she was dating anyone I answered *no* and Rick said *yes* at the same time." She scoffed. "It was like an extra gold star for my shitty parenting award when I didn't know something as basic as that. Katherine had apparently told Rick there was some American guy she was spending time with, that it might be getting serious. But it was one of those situations where she intended to go back to England eventually so she wasn't sure how much time she should invest. She didn't say more about it, like she was a little embarrassed or something."

"He didn't ask?"

"No, but I understood that. I mean, the adult male employer of the young nanny starts asking lots of questions about the nanny's sex life?" Hannah's voice raised an octave. "With his background, he knew that certain questions could look bad, even if the reason you're asking them is innocent."

"And did that information play any important role in the investigation? Would this turn out to be...?"

"Of course it would," Hannah's expression clouded over for a moment, just a half second, before she smiled at her. "But it won't make any sense out of order so you've got to give me time to get there. Besides, in my old age I'm more likely to miss something jumping around."

Asha sighed and ran a hand over her hair. "You're hardly old, Hannah. But Asha was beginning to worry *she* would be old before she got anything new out of her. "What about her family? Were they able to provide anything useful?"

"When I met her parents I learned there was something important about Katherine I did not know. But first things first." Asha bit her tongue so hard it might bleed.

Hannah got up from the table and walked over to the enormous island. "The first press conference. I'm trying so hard to stay in order here, and so much happened in those first 48 hours, it's getting all jumbled up."

Hannah pulled an iPad out of a drawer. "This was late that first night. The FBI had me make a statement while people were still glued to the television. It also dominated the networks the following day. Replaying it, evaluating it, evaluating *me*." She wiped her hand across the screen and looked at Asha. "This won't be quite as bad as the first, but I understand if you can't do another one of these today."

"This is my job," she said. Asha was touched by the comment, even a bit worried about Hannah's feelings. "I think the question is can you take anymore? I can always watch later."

Hannah sat down and handed the iPad to Asha, running her hands over her braid. "I guess we'll find out."

Chapter Sixteen

6 HOURS: 44 MINUTES MISSING

"You can do this. I know you can do this for Gracie and Katherine."

Rick stood behind Hannah and squeezed her shoulders while she wished that was enough to make the weight of the world come off of them.

She reached back to grasp the hand that rested there and was hit with the wave of frustration that flowed from him being held back from a public statement. "Our guy will be focused on Hannah. The world is focused on Hannah. Not only because of celebrity, but because mothers are always more sympathetic," Tom had explained, and Rick had reluctantly agreed.

No one said it out loud but Hannah saw the slight twitch towards Joanne every time the word "sympathetic" was uttered, as if she was the living antonym. Hannah groaned as she imagined the colorful headlines they would dream up for her driveway incident. The secondary goal of this first press conference was to appeal to the public's sense of desperation.

The primary was to give the kidnapper what they wanted—Hannah's anguish.

"You keep on top of the investigative details," her voice cracked and she dabbed at her eyes. "Make sure everyone is doing everything possible. You understand that stuff much better than I do."

"And you," he turned her around to face him, "you make people feel things. Make them feel for Grace and Katherine. Make it so that anyone who knows something will implode if they don't tell someone."

"I will."

"I know." He pulled her in tight, desperation gluing them together.

Hannah took a deep breath and Rick let her go as she was escorted by an agent into a black SUV, only to shoot his hand out to stop the door from closing. The sound of helicopters thundered overhead while the spotlights that circled around them made her home feel like a warzone, a reminder that this was nothing less than a battle for their family.

"This is what you understand better than anybody, Hannah," he said, his hair flying as the chopper hovered above them, trying to get a better view in the dark. "This is where the person who thought they could do this to our family made their mistake. Make them forget the psychic and see only the mom."

"The mom." She nodded, sure she was going to be sick.

"Sir?" Someone reached out to shut the door and Rick let go, sardining her in with Tom and other nameless officers and agents.

Unfortunately for Hannah, what Rick had said wasn't accurate. Letting people see her wasn't what Hannah did. Her skill was reflecting people back at themselves and making herself invisible in the process. When telling someone that their pet still curled up at the end of their bed at night, she needed them to see that encounter, not Hannah—feel the truth of it instead of wondering how she knows it.

This, she realized as she was pushed up against the door of the vehicle overflowing with dark suits like a law enforcement clown car, was the kind of situation that up until today she had been good at avoiding. She was shocked that Rick, along with everyone else, seemed to be relying on her media savvy to fix this, when keeping herself out of the story was her real skill.

"Ms. Smoke?" An agent turned around from the front seat and handed her a pink stuffed bear. "Someone from behavior suggested you hold this."

Hannah looked at it. The toy was Grace's, but it wasn't a favorite. When she didn't reach for it he said, "We chose something that was reminiscent of a little girl. Mr. Parks told us it wasn't one she loved." He held it out to her again. "But no one knows that. We find it helps people focus on the child and not on how they feel about the adults."

Hannah nodded and took the bear, tears brimming her eyes because when she held it up to her face it didn't smell like her, and she suddenly wished it was a favorite. To smell her would have been searing ecstasy as she resorted to parlor tricks trying to get her back.

The drive to the dirt road at the end of her property was shrouded in complete darkness until blazing lights punching their way through the trees announced their arrival. As Hannah stepped out of the car, Tom took her elbow to assist her.

The crowd of reporters, who had finally hushed in her presence, waited to hear from Hannah herself. It almost felt reverent, until a snicker made its way through the mass when an unidentified person in the crowd said, "Well, if she wanted to be more famous, she sure is now."

"What?" Hannah stopped in her tracks, not in anger, but unsure of what she'd heard. Unsure if she had heard it at all, or if it was just a voice in her head.

Tom squeezed her elbow and whispered in her ear. "Let it slide. Those tabloid assholes will say any number of vile things to get a rise out of you. You must let it go. Not another spectacle, this will be dignified for Grace and Katherine." Hannah nodded and kept her eyes straight ahead as she made her way into the heart of the sea of sharks.

"What's that on your clothes?"

"Have you reconciled with your mother?"

"Is that blood? Hannah, is that your daughter's blood?"

Hannah grimaced and a ripple of admonishment went through the crowd. She would have preferred to believe it was a rebuke of cruelty, but suspected it had more to do with the journalists' desire to get what they came for, a comment from Hannah herself.

Tom gripped the sides of the podium set up on the dirt road in the middle of the woods. Hannah stood just behind him, only glimpses of her visible through the police that flanked her. As he spoke, the sound of cameras whirring and flashbulbs popping was so loud that it became difficult to hear him outside of the audio from the microphone. Hannah wouldn't know exactly what Tom had said until she saw it replayed on TV later.

"I am agent Thomas Wolinsky of the FBI. We are here tonight, in cooperation with the Bedminster police department, investigating the disappearance of Grace Smoke and Katherine Willard. I would like to thank the press for their cooperation in this matter. I would ask for your continued cooperation as two lives are at stake. The life of eighteen-month-old Grace Smoke, and the life of twenty-year-old

Katherine Willard. You were all a witness to the events as they unfolded, and there are some details I can share with you at this time. First, is that we have reason to believe that Grace and Katherine were not at this residence at the time of the call."

"How do you know?" a reporter shouted from the middle of the crowd.

Tom gave a withering stare. "This will be a statement only, as there is not a lot of time. Questions are for another day." He let that sit for a beat.

"There are indications that Grace and Katherine had, in fact, been gone for a good stretch of time when the call came in. So, we are asking if you have, or if you believe you may have seen them in the last 48 hours, please call the number on your screen. Even if the sighting is before they were taken, it helps build our timeline of events, so it is still valuable. The photo on your screen was taken within the last two weeks, please take a good, long look at it."

Hannah knew the photo well. An agent had suggested it not just because it was recent, but because of the feeling it evoked. Grace sat on Katherine's lap, her chubby toddler arms reaching for the sky and Katherine's face lit up with laughter as Grace tried to catch the bubbles that Hannah, who was not in the frame, had blown seconds before.

Bubbas, Hannah thought. *She called them bubbas because she couldn't say bubbles* and Katherine had laughed and kissed her wispy honey-colored curls that smelled of sweet baby shampoo as she said it.

There is no way that Hannah could see in her heart, that the same woman who was so quick to laugh with her child and scoop her up in her arms to catch bubbas could ever have set out to harm her. She wasn't looking at it, but her chest hitched at the moment in her head, and an unknown hand reached and landed on her shoulder to steady her.

Hannah had no idea who it was, but was grateful for the reminder that she had a job to do.

"Please," Tom went on, "if you know something and hesitate to call, understand we cannot undo the danger Grace and Katherine are in. The sooner they are returned to their families, the better. Now, I will step aside so Hannah Smoke can make a brief statement. I am going to request that the press in attendance remember what she is facing today, and honor the request being made by the FBI and Bedminster Police Department for no questions."

He stepped away from the podium and held his arm out to indicate Hannah should come forward.

Hannah took a deep breath and struggled not to squint under the glare of the lights. The snapping of cameras was deafening as she approached, and she was grateful to have the bear to hold. It gave her hand something to do besides shake. She clutched the prepared statement in her other fist.

"My name is Hannah Smo...."

"We can't hear you!" voices rang out like a wave of rage towards her and she stumbled backwards a step. Tom held his hand up to calm everyone down, and guided Hannah closer to the microphone. "It's alright," he said, so that only she could hear. "You can get through this. Stand a bit closer."

Hannah nodded. She looked down at the piece of paper she was holding with her prepared statement, and her face started to crumple. The pressure was mounting with everyone there waiting for her to say something, anything.

Hannah's mind flashed an image of Grace, crying in darkness, looking for someone, looking for *her*.

She folded the paper and put it in her pocket, sending the flashbulbs into a renewed frenzy.

"When I found out that I was pregnant, I spent the next week in a stupor, just staring off into space for days in complete disbelief. Grace wasn't planned, and I had no room for a child in my life. Then her father, Richard Parks, said something to me that helped. He said, 'Hannah, it's a baby, not a nuclear bomb. You'll be fine, and so will the baby. We will all be fine together."

A low chuckle went through the crowd at the nuclear bomb comment.

"When she was born, it was like all of that went away." Hannah's voice cracked, and she sniffed before continuing. "She was here, and it just was. There was no going back. It was hard, the hardest thing I've ever taken on, but I was lucky. Grace is not only a healthy little girl, but a happy one that is quick with a smile every time I mess up, which is a lot."

Hannah nodded and brushed away the tears trailing down her cheeks. "I think whoever has Gracie will find that she's not too hard to keep happy. So please, I beg you, keep her happy. Don't hurt her. It won't be necessary. I'm prepared to do anything to get both Grace and Katherine back. Katherine has helped care for Grace in our home since the day Grace was born. Katherine is family and makes Grace feel safe, and if you leave the baby with her, she will cooperate. There is no reason to hurt either of them."

Hannah took another steadying breath and reset herself. There wasn't much left she had to say, but what was left was incredibly important. The most important thing she needed to say.

"You asked me to prove myself to the world, to find my daughter. I assure you that if I had any idea where she had been taken I would be with her, and returning Katherine to her parents who are sick with worry. All I do know is that Gracie is alive. And I am begging for your compassion, not for me, but for Grace and Katherine. I don't claim to deserve it. I am working with the FBI to try to help them, but no, no spirits or ghosts or any manner of mystical being have told me where to find them. I pray that if you have proven your point, you will tell me what I can do to get my daughter and Katherine back."

Hannah started to step away from the microphone, and then shook her head and went back to say one more thing. "And I'm not asking for privacy. I don't give a shit about privacy right now. Only that you all let the FBI do what they need to do. I'm begging, if any of you have seen anything out there, please, be the miracle Grace and Katherine need."

She turned away for the final time and silence turned to bedlam.

"How do you respond to the accusation that this is a hoax to sell more books?"

"How is this different from investigating other missing person cases?"

"Why don't you know anything?"

"Do you think Katherine is involved?"

"Are you saying you do not have psychic powers? That it was all a lie? How does it feel to have your child pay the price for your fraud?"

Tom stepped in, holding up his hand and blocking the view of Hannah climbing back into the SUV as reporters threw questions like knives.

"Katherine's parents are confirmed in flight, ma'am," an agent said as she wedged herself in. "They will be giving their statement live during the morning news cycle."

"Oh, good." Hannah realized she had never spoken to them before. She had sent a basket at Christmas because she was *so nice*, but they hadn't actually spoken. She'd had the opportunity. When Katherine had rang them up to wish them a Happy Christmas, Hannah could have easily grabbed the phone to send her best wishes and tell them how wonderful Katherine had been. It would have taken only a minute, but she hadn't. She'd been busy doing, something. She couldn't quite remember what. *Too busy not bothering because you didn't care enough...*

Chapter Seventeen

"That's reprehensible, the way people shouted those things," Asha said, putting the iPad aside. What she'd seen in this video had been completely unethical, yet on-brand for what she knew about paparazzi in the nineties. At the time, footage of celebrities acting crazy was ratings gold but the part where it all started with something awful being said by someone "just trying to earn a living" never saw the air. No wonder Hannah didn't talk to the press. "Did anything at least come of it? Any useful information?"

Hannah raised a hand to rub at her temples. "I had pictured in my head some person about to be plucked out of obscurity because they provided the lead that brought Grace and Katherine home, but that didn't happen. Not that people didn't watch, it was the highest rated broadcast ever after 11pm."

She tapped her finger on the iPad, the home screen glowing with various apps less offensive than what they just watched. "What it did do was galvanize people, which gave me hope. People all over were doing everything from passing out flyers to organizing searches. It felt like people cared, and I knew that was key. But I also knew I was going to have to keep talking. That's how these things work. People are horrified at first, then go on with their lives as you pray your kid gets a passing blip on the evening news. I'd seen it countless times."

Her voice dropped low. "Things don't feel real anymore while you watch everyone move on. They go back to the to-do list that is their lives, and your baby is still missing and you wonder when was the exact moment that your child moved down below laundry and sitcoms on that to-do list. The practical side of your brain understands that it doesn't mean they don't care anymore, but that doesn't do much for your heart." Hannah looked past Asha. "Yet here I am, insisting that you take all this in now."

"I don't think any parent in your position would blame you for using any special access you had to keep the coverage going."

Hannah let her fingers trail over her lips. It looked like she was trying to keep the wrong words from escaping. "In my career, I purposely avoided more serious work." She sat up, taking a defensive posture. "I don't want to be misunderstood—if I had some kind of information that could help someone, I never withheld it. But when it was optional to consider such a thing, let's just say I had many arguments with my agent over money lost for all of the things I was declining to take part in."

"Why?"

"Because it didn't do me good to dwell on tragedy. Not just in adulthood, even as a kid. I was plagued with nightmares of having to tell a mother one of her children killed their sibling." She shook her head. "The mother changed but the nightmare didn't. She always blamed me in the end."

Asha put her pen down and looked at Hannah, her own childhood traumas seeming suddenly miniscule as Hannah went on.

"God, I remember being desperate for sleep. I was an observant kid, so it's no surprise that I figured out the couple of glasses of cheap wine that did such a good job knocking my mother out might work for me. Joanne caught on real quick and even she wasn't about to let that go." She stopped to look at something Asha couldn't see. "I think she actually rose to the occasion on that one. Sometimes she did that. Sometimes I wasn't just an investment."

Hannah sighed. "But I was still expected to work through it all. I often wondered about other parents. I mean, was this way out of line or does everyone have their own mess and this one was mine?" She looked straight at Asha, as if trying to see inside her. "Like your parents. What did they do after you had that incident with your friend in the water? That's traumatic."

"I..." Asha shrugged. "I don't know exactly. But it was not the same. He eventually would be okay."

But Asha wondered, since okay was not equivalent to the same as before.

"It wasn't discussed much, except to talk about how he was getting on, how we weren't to go to the lake unsupervised anymore, that sort of thing."

Even so, Asha remembered waking during the night and seeing her mother watching her sleep from the doorway. "I think in my case, they kept a close eye on me for a bit. Perhaps they didn't want to talk about it for fear of upsetting me. It's possible they counted on youth to protect me from the severity of what had occurred."

"And the boy? How did he fare after?"

Asha shook her head. "He was fine I guess, but we lost touch as children do." She would have been happy to leave it at that, but Hannah's silence insisted on one bared soul for another.

"I did see him occasionally going to and from school. I remember the look on his face whenever we passed that pond." Asha folded her hands on the table, steering her mind away from the whole truth of the final time she saw Rory. "He would stare straight ahead with this look of determination, like if he didn't look at it he didn't have to acknowledge what happened. I realize now that he wasn't avoiding the pond, but his fear."

But Asha grew to hate that pond too. Rory would recover, eventually find a few boys he had things in common with. Asha would see them running about from time to time. If not for that stupid pond, maybe she would have been able to join them. If not the group, maybe she would have still been friendly with just Rory. Even that would have been enough. But he wouldn't look at the pond after that day, and it would be years before he would look at her.

Hannah raised her eyebrows in appreciation. "I understand his tactic. When I got older, I wasn't better at dealing with missing people cases, but I was damn good at avoiding them. The stories still circulated about me, tabloid headlines claiming I demanded $10,000 to find someone and a bunch of other garbage. But that was your standard psychic rumor, the kind of thing that these days gets posted on social media where anything passes for fact. I don't think that these lies would ever have been told by the parents of the missing—too much real horror on their plate to manufacture bullshit. Hannah shook her head. "I didn't need a measly $10,000 to save a kid's life. I'd like to think the number of humans among us who wouldn't save a kid for free is quite low. But it was easy to just throw that out there, because the worst makes a better story."

"There were, however," Asha hesitated, "parents that were upset with you."

"Yes. And they had every right to be."

Chapter Eighteen

The sun was making itself known as Hannah trudged her way towards the kitchen. She could feel herself slipping further into a cloud of exhaustion, her thoughts getting progressively more jumbled and murky. She longed for the kind of weary that came with an early morning wake up, the *just need my morning cup of coffee* kind.

But there would be nothing normal about this morning.

Hannah looked down at her rumpled suit, less than 24 hours ago pristine, now covered in wrinkles and swipes of fingerprint dust. She hadn't been able to take it off yet, like there was a line she was crossing when she did so. *Gracie was here when I put this on, and...*

More disjointed thoughts tangled in her head. She spent the overnight hours wandering the halls, answering questions when needed. Her mother offered sleeping pills, but Hannah wouldn't even dignify that suggestion with a response.

She stopped to put her ear to the door of the guest room, where fragmented snoring told her whatever cocktail of liquor and pill her mother had taken was working. Hannah was grateful rather than resentful, because the truth was she just couldn't with her mother right now, as she was certain she probably just couldn't with anybody. She would need to rest soon, no matter how obscene it sounded, resting while her child was missing.

"I just want her home first," Hannah said out loud to no one in particular, making the silence of the voices in her head echo louder, and she wished they'd come back and help her sort this out.

Hannah's breath caught at the sight of Katherine's parents. They had never met, but psychic powers were not necessary to figure out who the round-faced middle-aged couple standing in her kitchen must be.

"Mr. and Mrs. Willard, I'm Hannah." She held out her hand like a robot, a reflexive gesture for the one shred of polite she still had functioning. "I'm so sorry we're meeting this way." She looked around, unsure of what to do. "Would you like some coffee or..."

"Coffee? Are you joking?" Mr. Willard demanded and Hannah flinched. "As far as we are concerned, you are responsible for this mess!"

"I'm sorry..." Hannah blinked as a few officers, who had been so quiet Hannah hadn't even registered they were there, placed themselves between her and the Willards.

"Mr. Willard..." Tom flew in from the door that was open to the backyard.

Mr. Willard ignored him. "For both of them!" he shouted. "You're responsible! If Katherine and Grace die, their blood is on your hands." His jowls quaked in fury. "You're so busy, flitting here and there."

"I..." Hannah choked.

"Oh, Katherine told us how you were always gallivanting about, instead of home with Grace. Now you and your snake oil business may have gotten them both killed!" A small bit of spittle launched towards Hannah. The razored edges of his honesty sliced through her, and the tears she had been certain must have run out built up behind her eyes once again.

"I want my daughter back, you monster!"

"Phil," his wife grabbed his arm

"Shut it, Martha! Our daughter is gone because of *her*!"

"Excuse me." Tom stepped in between Hannah and Katherine's father. "Mr. Willard, if you and your wife would follow me, please. We'd like to update you on what's happening and ask some questions." A wall of agents firmly guided them out of the room. "Questions?" Katherine's father could be heard grumbling as he was guided into another area of the house. "You're the goddam FBI! Where is my Katherine? That's *my* question." At the word *Katherine*, Hannah could hear his voice break, and it was enough to plunge her into a new swell of grief.

Hannah didn't budge from where she stood, but she trembled in a way that made it look like there was an earthquake happening beneath her feet, while everything else remained still.

"Ms. Smoke?" An investigator leaned towards her, concern on his face.

Hannah's eyes stayed on the floor. "He's right. He's just the first one to say it out loud. It's my fault. I should have known something could happen."

"No." Rick reached out to her.

"It's my fault." She slapped his hand away without looking up, her voice as flat as the dead and for the first time, Rick looked afraid of Hannah. She pointed at herself with a limp hand. "It is. My job is to know things. It's your job to find out the things I don't know but it's my job to know the rest and it shouldn't take a fucking psychic to see the danger they could be in, the danger they were in because of *me*."

"Hannah, babe." Rick pinched between his eyes.

Her head snapped up. "Don't babe me."

"You're exhausted and you're not thinking straight. You can't blame yourself because some psychopath comes along and…"

"Goddamnit, Rick!" The explosion made everyone flinch. "It. Is. My. Fucking. Fault. It is!"

Hannah swung her arm wide and knocked a glass off the kitchen island, sending it crashing to the floor. She stepped back, startled.

She stared at the bits of expensive crystal sparkling back at her, winking like they were all in on some secret, and Hannah knew damn well what that secret was. Such a hot shot she was, with her expensive glassware and her fancy kitchen. The envy of so many—and hadn't Hannah enjoyed being the envy of others? Hadn't she secretly liked to see people's eyes go wide when they first caught sight of her home? Hadn't she enjoyed the way they oohed and aahed over the large fireplace in her kitchen? Her fancy plates and glasses? She had.

And if she hadn't been greedy, if she had just quit when Gracie was born like she'd planned before the book money came along, Grace and Katherine would still be here.

"And even if it's not my fucking fault," a wave of anger came over her, immense and hot, "she's still gone!" She swept her arm across the marble island, swiping the remaining glassware that sat there, so intact, so fancy—the hallmark of a vain person who had deluded herself into believing it was all okay because she didn't hurt anybody, not really. With one gesture, she ended its mocking sparkle, sending it all to a satisfying crash to the floor.

Now, all of this stupid expensive china and crystal was broken, just like her.

"Hannah." Rick said as her head turned on a swivel surveying the damage, and his breath caught. She was searching for more to destroy. He spoke as if she were a bomb set to explode if he went just a decibel too high. "We will find her, but you need to keep it together."

"What if we don't?" Hannah collapsed forward onto the island, resting her elbows on the surface and wiping her hands over her blotchy face. "Jesus. They've been gone almost a full day now, and that's so long. What if those reporters..." She looked at Rick and pointed towards the street. "What if they're right? What if I really sold my child out for money? Not literally, but with greed and neglect? What happens to them?"

"Ms. Smoke," a woman's voice cut through Hannah's breakdown. "I promise we're doing everything we can."

Her head whipped around to find a lab technician standing there, looking at Hannah with a maternal sort of concern that would have been sweet under normal circumstances. But the fresh-faced woman standing there had thick shiny hair and skin that seemed to glow from the inside out.

And when Hannah's eyes drifted downwards, she saw the obvious bump of her third trimester, mocking her with all of its joy, hope, and full knowledge of where this baby was at this very moment. The technician's mouth popped open as the mistake registered with her, and she dropped a reflexive hand over her belly.

"I mean, we're all..." The woman stammered, trying to recover. "We're all fighting here with you." Her voice faded, and for a moment Hannah understood that this woman was exhausted herself, had likely been here overnight. But those thoughts were shouted down by the voices that screamed *she knows where her baby is* in her head.

"Shut up." Hannah spat at her as an agent grabbed the woman by the arm to escort her out. Hannah walked across the sea of glass on the floor towards her, anger and grief numbing her to the biting at her feet. "I want her back now! Not your platitudes, not your expert analysis. I want Grace. Get me Grace or you and your baby get out of my house!"

"Your feet..."

Hannah disregarded the gasps as she continued to walk through the shards, leaving a trail of smeared blood behind her. "I need her back." She wobbled like a top. "Too long too long, he's had her too long. It's dangerous."

"We're going to get her," another agent said carefully.

"You're bleeding..." she heard from behind her, but didn't turn back.

"What if she's scared?" She said in a hushed voice. The fire was out. Hannah's body slumped and her voice croaked. "What if she's hungry? What if she's hurt? You're not doing enough if I don't have her. I don't want her back dead." Her voice cracked, her posture threatening to sink to the floor, Rick seized the opportunity and swooped her up. "I want her whole. I want to hold her and feel she's okay and have her little arms hold me back." She broke down sobbing as he lifted her, placing her on the kitchen table.

A local officer had come out to the kitchen when he heard the commotion. His eyes went wide at the sight of the broken glass and blood on the floor. "I'll call a doctor."

Chapter Nineteen

Katherine Willard's hand glided across sandpaper.

She held it still for a minute, letting her fingertips take in the surface as if reading braille. Her head filled with images of tiny sand grains dancing across the sea floor with the waves.

Words escaped her at the moment, but the sensation of the gritty surface was pleasant and took all of her attention.

At least it did until she registered the throb parked at the front of her skull. In another disjointed thought, she pictured the pain as a frog, just sitting there, pulsating and ribbiting inside her head. She dragged her hand across the sandpaper and brought it to her forehead.

Her first coherent thought, one built of words and not pictures, was *I feel awful.*

Her eyes fought through the thick gunk that had painted them shut in her sleep. When she could finally see, she registered that it was dark and she was relieved because it was still night and Gracie would still be sleeping. Katherine must be coming down with something, and with the baby to take care of and Hannah still away she needed the...

Adrenaline shot through her as she flashed a memory that was little more than a remembrance of dread. She tried to sit up but her head screamed when she moved. The taste of blood inside of her mouth told her the memory wasn't just a bad dream.

Oh, God.

She ran her hands in the dark around her, now understanding that what she thought in her fogged state was sandpaper was actually the floor. The floor, but *what* floor? She didn't know where this floor was. Her heart pounded and her head followed by pounding harder with it, threatening to tumble her back to blackness. She tried to remember where in the house was a dirt floor. *No, not dirt*, she thought, *but cement, maybe?* Unfinished cement, that's why it was gritty and cool.

Her eyes started to adjust. The room wasn't completely pitch black, and the outline of a child-sized mound materialized not far from her on the floor. The mound was still.

She willed her arms and legs to move, scraping along the floor because she could only manage a doggie paddle-style crawl. She didn't exhale until she put her hands on the mass and felt it rise and fall in time with shallow breaths. It wasn't the same as Gracie's peaceful sleep breathing, the kind that Katherine knew well from when the toddler crawled into her lap for a snuggle and drifted off for a nap, but she was breathing.

She remembered some of it now, but it was still murky and she was only getting flashes that taunted her with the knowledge that there was a lot more to grasp, like trying to spot one fish in a muddy lake that was teeming with them just under the surface. A memory would show itself then dart away before she could examine it.

She knew it had all happened quickly, the way it had spun from tranquil to terror. Her mind cleared enough to understand that they had been drugged, and she dragged the child closer to her, hoping the scratches caused by the floor were minimal.

"They'll come for us, Gracie," she stroked her curls and whispered. "They'll come."

Chapter Twenty

Hannah tapped a coffee basket against the garbage can to dump out the used grinds, and proceeded to stack the parts in the dishwasher. "I understood Mr. Willard's anger. People for years have told me that it was misplaced, but I can't agree that is a hundred percent true. I wasn't purposely reckless with their safety, but I could have been more careful."

"I don't know." Asha hesitated. "Everyone can always be more careful, but when dealing with the irrational, I don't think careful is ever going to be enough. My father used to say *You can't rationalize the irrational.*"

Hannah looked over her shoulder and smiled. "Your father sounds like a smart man."

"He is," she said. Asha thought of his call last night and felt a small stab of longing.

Her father was not only smart, he was usually right. And as much as she told him he just didn't understand how it works when he suggested the big move to America didn't seem to have the payoff she had hoped for, she had to admit she hadn't planned on being a few years in and in big trouble instead of moving up the journalistic ladder.

Asha sat up straighter. The opportunity to give something to all of them—her father, her boss, even her mother, had dropped in her lap today. The proof that all of this was worth it.

Asha imagined her mother, walking through town flaunting a copy of *The Metropolitan* with her headline on it, Asha's name underneath in bold. Giving Louise something to brag about to all those women who gave her the sad eyes over Asha not being married yet, the whispers that Asha might be one of *those* so poor Louise might never be a grandmother.

Asha promised herself that she would give her mother a gift, a gift of an accomplishment so huge it couldn't be denied by anyone. *That's just how it is with mothers*, Asha observed. No matter how tense things got Asha wanted to make her proud.

And for every second of pain the local gossips had heaped on her mother, Asha was determined to make them choke on it.

"Are you close with your parents?" Hannah asked, startling Asha as if she caught a peeping Tom looking at her thoughts.

Asha's mouth dropped open for just a second. "Sure," she shrugged.

Hannah sat back down and tugged at her braid. "Do you want to talk about it?"

Asha laughed. "Um, not really."

"Well, I do, it's a break from talking about me. What's the situation?"

Me and my big mouth. For this moment at least, Asha was grateful Charing couldn't see her doing the exact thing she was warned not to do. "It's nothing serious."

Hannah folded her arms.

"Fine." Asha grunted. "I'm an only child and my mum didn't want me to abandon her for the U.S. She envisioned a future of me living just down the road married to some well-to- do academic making her grandchildren." Asha put a hand over her heart. "I envisioned journalistic glory." She put the hand down. "But you need exactly zero hands to count how many of us got what we wanted."

"That doesn't sound too bad though," Hannah mused. "Somedays I'm convinced the things we want are just attractive illusions meant to force us out of bed in the morning, getting them isn't always the point. And I know a thing or two about mother issues."

"Well," Asha knew she should stop but couldn't help herself, "I had to cancel a vacation with her to start my job here, and when that happened she didn't speak to me for six months. Does that sound normal to you? You know," Asha gave her head a frantic shake, "just your regular mother-daughter stuff?" Hannah flinched, and Asha felt like slapping herself. "Oh God. I'm sorry."

"It's all right. What was it your father said? You can't rationalize the irrational?"

Asha nodded, tucking a piece of hair behind her ear. "That, he did."

"A mother's love is rarely rational. This morning, the same mother who is so displeased as to cut off communication with you for months had breakfast and wondered if you're eating breakfast every day, having something healthy, taking proper care of yourself with all you're working on here." She looked at her hands and flexed her fingers as a darkness passed over her face. "I would know."

"Then you must know your guilt isn't rational. You loved Grace, you can't have done anything that bad." Asha prodded.

Hannah cocked her head to the side like she was considering this. "Someday, if I were to cross paths with your father, I'll agree that you can't rationalize the irrational. But I'll argue you can shake the tree that grows the irrational fruit, and I'm pretty sure I shook the shit out of it. This thing that I did for money... It's a weird line of work. You have so many people who despise you and what you're doing, but you only see the fans. Some of that was Rick's doing for sure. He knew that if I had ninety-nine fans in the room and one angry person I'd forget all about the fans. I was living in a bubble."

"And Katherine's parents? How did that turn out with them here?"

Hannah turned her face back towards her. "This part never made the papers. They didn't speak to the press much after, well, after everything went bad. As far as I know, they never shared this part."

She returned to the table and sat down. "They had a doctor come in to look at my feet, and more importantly, knock me out for a bit with a sedative." She mimicked a shot going in her arm. "Apparently, they thought I needed a time-out before I would be useful to the investigation again, and they were not wrong. I woke up, I think it was a few hours later, disoriented at first. Martha Willard was sitting at the end of my bed..."

Asha's head picked up in alarm. "The woman who blames you for her daughter's disappearance was sitting at the end of your bed when you woke up?"

"...and asked if this was a publicity stunt to sell books."

"Oh."

"Yeah." Hannah looked down. She then said that my connection to Katherine wasn't purely through her caring for Gracie."

"It wasn't?"

Hannah shook her head. "Katherine had a cousin that went missing when they were in elementary school. She thought I knew about it."

"You didn't?"

"No idea. They had been eight, playing in the back garden, when she vanished. Like that," Hannah snapped her fingers. "Katherine never got over it, not just because of the loss or the survivor guilt, but as she got older, that unshakeable feeling of how it could have been her."

"But," Asha's face screwed up in confusion, "she never said anything?"

"I know. It was weird to me too. I can't remember any reference to it, and by now I've mined every memory, probably even created a few false ones. Martha said that a relative, one here in the U.S., had been familiar with me. Apparently, I was asked to take a look. I don't remember it at all, and there would be no record of it since I don't take money for such things."

Hannah sighed. "I still can't believe she didn't tell me. I mean, she was eight at the time but Martha said she brought it up when she accepted the job. Maybe things would have been different."

"What would have been different?"

Hannah just looked down.

"Did she—Katherine's mother, I mean—tell the FBI?"

Hannah nodded. "Yes, which was investigated heavily until...Well, I think we got a clearer picture of where Katherine stood eventually." Hannah wiped away a tear.

Chapter Twenty-One

Making her way downstairs, Hannah attempted, with limited success, to tread lightly on her bandaged feet. Every sharp jab she felt was a reminder of her stupidity. *You could have cut open a damn blood vessel you fucking idiot. That wouldn't be helping Grace.*

Putting more weight on the outer edges of her feet helped, and she found she could almost walk down the plush carpeted hallway with a degree of efficiency when she heard Joanne hiss "It was your *job*, Rick. Hannah paid you to protect them," from the spare bedroom.

Hannah froze, not entirely certain of why she didn't want them to see her.

"Thank you, Joanne. Do you need a reminder that I'm not just an employee around here, but also Grace's father?" Hannah held her breath as Rick paused. "Because I promise you that will go a much longer way towards making me feel like a helpless pile of shit when my daughter is missing than calling me employee."

"Do you need a reminder that I'm her grandmother?" Hannah rolled her eyes, she could hear her mother open a drawer and start rearranging things. Joanne's hands got busy when she got mad, or, more accurately in this case, petulant.

"Yes. For as much as you've been here Joanne, maybe I do."

Joanne gasped. "I don't think my Hannah would like..."

"Joanne," Rick interjected. Hannah could hear the weight of him move across the room. "I take back what I said, okay? We're all exhausted and stressed and... But I need you to listen. What Hannah would like is irrelevant. This is about what she needs."

Hannah flattened herself against the wall, trying to scurry back around the corner so she wouldn't be seen if either of them looked out the doorway.

"I watched the mother of my missing daughter, yes, your Hannah, a person whom I've only ever known to be cool and rational, lose her mind and walk across glass like some sort of fucked up motivational challenge!"

Joanne took a shaky breath. "She's not well, is she."

"Of course," Rick paused and Hannah could hear his voice get closer as he looked out the door, "of course she's not well. I don't expect her to be. But I do expect that everyone in her orbit, when they're not doing something for those girls, are trying to help Hannah keep it together." Hannah's face burned at the humiliation that she had proven Rick right, she was a liability that needed management.

"I... I would never hurt her or Grace." Joanne sniffed. Hannah could hear the creak of the bed as her mother sat down. "It was never personal with you, Rick."

"None of that matters anymore. But Grace is everything to us. And Hannah's going to have to keep it together when she doesn't know where the fuck Gracie is, but she damn well knows that she and Katherine are in danger because of her celebrity. She's going to need to play an active role in getting them back, we won't get them back if she can't hold it together."

Hannah could hear her mother whimpering and sniffling in response.

"Joanne," Rick's voice grew softer. "I need to make sure you understand all this seeing as you haven't been around as much as Hannah would have liked."

Joanne cleared her throat. "She said that?"

"And me too. You're Grace's grandmother. I'd like to have you here more too." Rick's voice was kind and Hannah felt a new wave of tears threaten to overwhelm her.

"I saw her shoes, the pink ones with the stars on them." Hannah could hear her mother was on the edge of losing it. "In your mudroom. She's gotten so big and all I could think was how I stayed away so long and now..."

Hannah could hear the muffling of Joanne's voice as Rick hugged her.

"You're right." Joanne cleared her throat, resolve breaking through her tears. "And you could all come up to visit me as well. When this is all over. I want to take my granddaughter someplace fancy. Tiffany's or someplace. I'd like to spoil her in a way I couldn't with Hannah."

"We would too." It got quiet then, the unspoken *God willing* lingering heavy in the air.

Hannah scurried back to her room. It was time for Hannah to join Rick in being an adult, Grace was depending on her. And if those two could get along, she should have no problem keeping her shit together for her daughter's sake.

When Hannah was sure she wouldn't be suspected of eavesdropping she re-emerged downstairs. The room paused, once again so briefly that only Hannah would find it perceptible. All breakable items had been removed from the countertops, so she couldn't have another disturbing version of a Greek celebration. *Crazy Hannah can't make another appearance, not when there's still work to be done.* She sucked in a breath while her feet protested as she stepped towards Tom and Rick, deep in conversation.

"Anything?" she asked, unable to squash hope even though she was sure if something had happened it would have been brought to her. Rick gave a slight shake of his head. Hannah turned to the window and saw the bright light of afternoon. *Still plenty of time in this day to get her back*, she prayed. Rick held out a cup of coffee, she tried not to notice it was a paper cup, while her mother thrust a muffin at her. "Sugar, you should eat something," She said.

"I'm not hungry."

"Force a few bites down, then." Rick prodded, the exhaustion heavy in his voice. Hannah took the muffin, placated that they had worked out a truce because had she not overheard their conversation, she would have been certain their agreement about anything meant they were hiding something awful.

A voice came from behind and said, "They're right. You're not helping Grace or Katherine by running yourself into the ground." Hannah looked over her shoulder to find a stranger, looking disheveled despite the suit. Her business lawyer, Doug, came in before she had the chance to ask who the hell this guy was coming from out of nowhere with his advice.

"Hannah," he said, nudging the stranger aside to reach out to her. "I am so sorry."

"Doug." She blinked. "What are you doing here?"

"This," he nodded at the stranger, who looked like he was playing dress-up in his father's suit, "is Randall Newman. He's, um, well, he's a partner at the firm and I thought he could help." Doug sighed and looked around them. "The police and FBI are putting an amazing effort out here, but with you being a celebrity, it's complicated."

"What kind of lawyer is he?" Hannah gave them a pointed look.

"Well," Randall raised his eyebrows, trying not to exchange a glance with Doug and not being successful, "I have experience in family law. My purpose here would be solely to act as a facilitator when you need it. If there's information being held from you, I'll make sure you get it. If there is unfair coverage of you, I'll make sure the media remembers libel laws still apply. I'll do everything I can to protect your interests while making sure not to interfere with the investigation."

Hannah eyed him through the steam coming from her cup. "Uh huh. Family law. And how much criminal law experience do you have?" He didn't answer. "Doug," Hannah said, her eyes still fixed on Randall, "I'm getting a vibe here that family at best means mafia family, and I can't help but wonder..." She turned her gaze to him. "Why do you think I need a criminal lawyer?"

"Get used to this, Randall." Doug patted him on the back. "This sort of thing happens when you represent a professional psychic." He looked back towards Hannah. "I want to make sure you are protected from the beginning and that when Grace and Katherine are found—and I do believe they will be—that there isn't some dirty legal trick pulled on you. But if I'm acting in your best interest, I have to recognize I'm not the best qualified in this situation—hence Randall."

"I can also take care of Rick as well." Randall nodded toward where Rick stood. "I'm here for both parents."

Joanne rubbed her arms. "Won't that look bad, lawyering up?"

Doug shook his head. "They're not officially lawyering up. Randall is a partner at my firm, Hannah is already represented by me. If asked, we will tell the truth, that we are here to make sure our longtime client and friend is getting the best investigation possible."

Hannah studied Doug and saw what she needed to see. "You don't think I did this."

"Jesus," he choked. "Hannah, of course, I don't think…"

Hannah held up a hand. "I've heard about some of the coverage. It's not *of course*, but it is appreciated." She looked at Randall. "So, I guess you just wait around until we need you?"

"Ms. Smoke?" Tom approached. "If you're ready, we'd like to do that polygraph now."

Randall shrugged. "Guess I'm not waiting long."

Chapter Twenty-Two

I DAY: 0 HOURS: 37 MINUTES MISSING

Hannah stared out the French doors leading to the pool house and rubbed her arms for warmth as the soft hum of the air conditioner vent gave her goosebumps. *It was supposed to have been easy,* she thought. *I'm a devastated parent.*

So why do I feel like a criminal?

Because, a voice in her head that sounded too much like her mother mocked, *you sure didn't give the truth, the whole truth, and nothin' but the truth so help you God.*

Hannah glanced back towards the hallway, the one that led to the office where Rick was now submitting to his own lie detector test. She wondered what she was in for when they asked him, because she knew it couldn't *not* come up. And not if but when it spread like wildfire, which it was guaranteed to do, how many of these people would feel as sympathetic? How many would start to forget that this is about Grace and Katherine?

It had been going as expected.

Is your name Hannah?

Do you live on Farm Hollow Road?

Do you know what happened to Grace?

Do you know what happened to Katherine?

Did you cause Grace or Katherine's disappearance?

Have you told me the truth?

Simple enough. Then she was hit with the question *Is Richard Parks Grace's biological father?* Hannah looked away from the hall and out the back door.

Is it possible that another man is Grace's biological father?

That seed of doubt had died a long time ago.

But...

It wasn't important. Not with Grace missing. But as Hannah chewed on her impeccable nails, she was painfully aware it could send the investigation into a whole different direction, away from whoever had Gracie. And just like her fame made her baby a target, her whorishness would make people care less about her baby. Grace couldn't stay missing, not because of one night of bad decisions that came to an end when Hannah woke up wearing nothing but regret and one shoe.

An audible click and creak told her the office door had opened behind her, and she tried not to think too much about being past 24 hours missing. A detective had shared that she and Rick would get to access the pool house soon, since evidence collection and documentation were wrapping up. Maybe they would see something the others didn't.

Rick came up behind her, putting both hands on her shoulders.

He knew.

They would have to talk about it, but for right now, it didn't matter. They could fight about this another time, when she was home safe in her bed, the one that was a low to the ground and looked like a princess carriage. Hannah had protested when Rick brought it home saying it was tacky, but it was over when Grace caught sight of it. *Go nigh nigh* was how Gracie would announce she was tired, and Hannah muffled a sob at the thought of her being home, safe and sound, and her and Rick quietly arguing over something so stupid.

Hannah did choke on her coffee as she turned towards the television, and came face to face with Mr. Big Mistake himself, chatting away with Barbara Silver. The runner on the bottom of the screen read, *Is Scott Antonio baby Grace's father?* A detective whispered something to Tom, who glanced in Hannah's direction. She gestured with her hand to turn up the volume.

"Hannah and I had a brief but very intense relationship a little over two years ago." He thought about it for a beat. "A little more than that maybe? We met at the Golden Globes. I was nominated that year, which was very flattering. You know a lot of people didn't think I would ever work in..."

Barbara cut him off. "Are you claiming to have been intimate with Hannah? Are you saying Grace Smoke, the child who was so dramatically kidnapped on live television, could be yours?"

"Well," Scott tried to hide the smirk on his face but couldn't, "I'd be lying if I said she couldn't be. I mean, you've seen the pictures, can anyone say she's not?"

Hannah had almost forgotten about her mother when she gasped and Hannah turned to see her jaw hit the floor. "Hannah?"

"That piece of shit." Hannah seethed. It was one thing to be thrown into a public tragedy, it was another to enjoy it. "He's using this for publicity."

"We're going to get him here," Tom said, nodding at Rick and Hannah while everyone ignored Joanne's wide-eyed stare. "We'll do the DNA, it will take a couple of days, but I want him here in the meantime."

Tom raised his voice and gestured to another agent. "I don't appreciate that he found a reporter about this before anyone in law enforcement. Get someone in LA on picking him up and escorting him to us now."

"Yes, sir." The agent scurried off, and Hannah hoped that whoever was about to pay Scott a visit was large and not prone to answering questions.

"What would you say to Hannah right now?" Barbara asked in her gravest *look at me, I'm a serious news reporter* voice.

He took a deep breath and shook his head, like a character caught in the defining moment of a Lifetime network drama. "I don't know. I don't know what anyone says to her. She's not easy for a guy to talk to. Cold, unfeeling, very career-oriented, not really the mother type."

"You motherfucker," Hannah whispered, and Rick squeezed her hand.

Joanne grasped Hannah's arm, her eyes on fire. "Is this real?"

"Not now mom," Hannah hissed.

"You're saying career women can't be mothers?" the reporter deadpanned.

"Listen," he stuttered. "Don't put words in my mouth. I'm going through a thing too right now. I mean, if Grace is gone, can I even be tested to see if I'm the father? I don't know that science stuff. I guess that I hope whoever has her is watching because you might not like her mother, I get it. But don't blame the baby, ok? The babysitter Kathleen too."

"Katherine," Barbara corrected and he rolled his eyes. "If Grace is found safe, what are your plans?"

"I will get that DNA test. And have a long talk with Hannah about my rights."

"And in the meantime?"

"Talk to the police or whatever." He looked into the camera. "Tell them everything I know about Hannah Smoke."

Chapter Twenty-Three

1992

Two years before the kidnapping

The front door slammed and the sound of designer shoes click-clacked their way into the foyer.

Hannah braced herself for the hurricane that was about to hit.

"Sugar?" Her mother called up the stairs. "I got the loveliest fruit at that posh little farmer's market on the way here."

The click-clacking stopped and Hannah heard the rustle of plastic bags as Joanne opened one, "not that I know what half of it is. But I thought..."

"...oh, you're down here." She shifted gears seeing Hannah sitting at the kitchen island, an amused look on her face. "Well, good." She dropped the bag with an unceremonious thud and took a drag on her cigarette with her free hand.

"Anyway," she leaned in to kiss Hannah on the cheek, "they had some exotic fruits I thought you might like, 8.99 a pound but don't ask me what it is."

Hannah laughed and pulled the bag closer. Her mother had insisted on spending the Easter weekend with her even though her idea of religion these days was praying at the altar of Gucci. "Why did you even buy it?"

"Well I know you like those healthy smushies…"

"Smoothies, mom."

"You like that healthy smoothie shit, whatever." She scanned the backyard to the pool house where she would spend the weekend. "Is my sauna working yet?" Her eyes glittered at the idea.

"Up and running just in time for you to sweat out the nicotine. And you know I prefer you don't smoke in the house."

"Crap. Yes, I know. I'm an old lady and changing my habits is hard." The old lady click-clacked her way in stilettos to the door and Hannah tried not to cringe as she snuffed her cigarette out on a paver. "I wouldn't want to stink up your fancy house."

"Your house is plenty fancy mom and besides," Hannah grabbed the bag of fruit and dropped it next to the sink, "it's bad for the baby."

"Whose baby?" Her mother picked up the squished cigarette and leaned over Hannah to wet it in the sink before throwing it in the garbage.

Hannah, her hand still on the bag, turned to give her mother a pointed look. Joanne White was not known for being quick.

"Whose baby Hannah? Rebecca?" It wasn't until she noticed Hannah wasn't responding, and she looked up to see Hannah was perfectly still, that it sunk in. "You're…" She pointed a too long but perfectly manicured nail at Hannah.

"Yes."

"Huh." Joanne bit at her nail and looked at the floor. "Are you sure?" She crinkled her nose.

Hannah tried not to show her disappointment, she knew how this would go so she shouldn't be disappointed when mom gives a perfectly mom reaction. "Well they say that today's pregnancy tests are quite reliable."

"Oh," Joanne shook her head and headed towards where Hannah kept the adult beverages, "I wouldn't trust something that's stocked on the shelves by some pimply teenager trying to pay for his video game habit, Hannah. I mean, those things have expiration dates and whatnot."

"Well, there's also the doctor."

Joanne went still. "A doctor said you're pregnant?"

"Yes." Hannah turned around to look at her mother, her hands on the counter behind her.

Joanne nodded and reached for some Chardonnay, thought better of it, and grabbed vodka instead. "Well, that is a thing isn't it."

"And there's this." Hannah reached into a drawer and pulled out a black and white sonogram.

Joanne kept her chin up but let her eyes roll down to look at the picture. "Oh, yes. I see." Joanne whispered. "So, I guess that means..."

"I've decided to have it."

Joanne's hand went up in a series of gestures that indicated her mind was racing from one thought to another, they just were knocking each other out of the way before they reached her lips. "Okay, I can see it."

"You can?" Hannah went to stand next to her.

"Yeah, yes," she gave an exaggerated nod and smiled. "Sure. I can see it working. You're going to be a mom and I'm going to be a grandma and single moms are so accepted these days," she tipped her glass at Hannah, "as long as they can afford their kids which you obviously can so no harm done to your career. It could be good, maybe even great for your career. Yes," she nodded, as if some invisible tribunal had convened and decided. "It's going to be better for you than it was for me."

"So, okay?" Hannah held out her arms.

"A baby!" Joanne toasted no one then hugged her, but quickly gasped and pulled away. "Oh my God, whose is it?" Hannah's mouth started to open and Joanne stopped her. "No, no, no, let me guess."

Hannah made a pained face. "Ew, no..."

"Johnathan Mine."

"Mom." Hannah was certain she had never been in the same room with the A-lister who starred in a blockbuster spy series.

"You can't blame me for aiming high. Oh, what about what's his name?" She snapped her fingers. "I know you've met him."

"Mom..."

"The one from the bad teenager show," she clapped her hands, "Scott Antonio!"

Hannah felt the blood drain from her face. "No. Jesus mom, not him either. Do you think I've slept with everyone who's ever been on TV?"

"Well if I was in your place..." She chuckled and took a sip of her cocktail.

The sound of footsteps in the mudroom interrupted them. "Hannah?" Rick called out. "Joanne?" Joanne's eyes grew wide as his footsteps got closer.

"Look at this," he pulled a giant chocolate bunny out of a bag. "Sort of a waste for you Hannah since you always eat so healthy but I'm sure I can get Joanne to help me."

"You son of a bitch." Joanne plunked her drink down on the counter.

Confusion passed as quickly as it came over Rick's face and he put the bunny on the table. "I see she knows..."

"After all I did so you could have it better, Hannah."

"*You* did?" Hannah scoffed.

"Joanne…" Rick interjected.

"Shut up." She held up a hand at him. "You've done enough. And you," she pointed at Hannah, "I don't claim to have been perfect but I also know I raised you to be so much more than I could ever be. If you were going to get yourself pregnant," she said through clenched teeth, "it should have been by somebody who was your equal."

Hannah crossed the room to stand beside Rick and gave her mother a quiet look of defiance. "I guess that's the beauty of what you've done mom. I have enough money to get pregnant by whomever I choose."

Joanne huffed and shook her head as she grabbed her purse. "Yes, Hannah Smoke, you have plenty of money. Plenty of money but not enough sense to know that you fuck the hired help, you don't let it knock you up."

Chapter Twenty-Four

"*Second Chance High*!" Asha snapped her fingers.

Hannah grimaced. "Ugh, how would you even know about that?"

Asha laughed. "We get all of your big shows in syndication. So," she pursed her lips. "I guess he wasn't the broody bad boy trying to turn himself around that he played on television?"

"God, no." Hannah shook her head. "I was so pissed when he showed up. Not about being embarrassed—in another life I would have died from shame but they could have flogged me in the town square for all I cared. The FBI fast-tracked a DNA test and said it didn't matter. But of course it did, because I knew this would be a *thing*. That now the story would be that I was a whore, or a liar, or a lying whore, but not about where those girls were. And I knew it couldn't be Scott who took them—you may as well ask him to build a rocket ship to the moon before you ask him to coordinate the kidnapping of two people, one of whom was a grown adult."

Hannah picked up her water and looked to the ceiling in thought. "But now, he would have to be looked at and any time spent looking at him was time wasted. And the media looked at him, of course. They couldn't get enough of him and all the wonderful things he had to say about me. It was another notch in my shitty mother belt."

She propped her elbow on the table and started counting with her fingers. "One, I let my daughter get taken. Two, the media attention we needed was now going to Scott because I made the unfortunate decision to sleep with him." She took a sip of water, "I mean, one could argue that tequila made that decision but, at that point it didn't matter."

"Alcohol makes all sorts of unfortunate decisions." Asha winced. "And how did Rick take it?"

"He was better than I deserved, especially after having to pretend he was just an employee for so long, only to be served up this new humiliation. He said we could fight about it when Grace was home." Hannah hesitated. "We actually never got to have that fight," Hannah shrugged. "Because when it came to deception, he would soon find out I was capable of much worse."

Chapter Twenty-Five

I DAY: 3 HOURS: 34 MINUTES MISSING

Hannah was hungry for information in a way that wouldn't be satisfied, but that didn't mean she could cope with what little did come her way.

As she stood in the doorway of the pool house, paralyzed by her synapses firing all at once, it hit her that no sign of anyone being seriously hurt didn't mean no sign of a struggle. Walking through the space meant that Hannah understood Grace was scared, and that if she was dead, the last moments of her life had been terrifying.

Hannah grabbed onto Rick at the sight of papers and a cup knocked off a table as if something had been dragged across it. What—*who*—had been dragged? Why would anyone need to drag Gracie? She wouldn't put up a fight, she was just a... Hannah caught sight of a stuffed duck toy and had a vision of Grace, playing on the floor in her little footie pajamas with the ducks on them, looking up with wide light brown eyes as the shadow of a stranger enveloped her.

Hannah bit her fist and forced herself to take deep breaths, reminding herself that she needed to pull it together.

Tom broke through the silence. "The door was left open. You last spoke with Katherine around 7:30 the morning before the 4 pm television appearance, and we're still working on finding anyone that can confirm contact in between to narrow down our timeline, but everything points to them having been gone before the call."

Hannah scanned the room, looking for any small clue that might speed up getting her daughter home. Of the few things still on the table, there was a spilled bowl of Cheerios, Gracie's favorite. The plastic training potty, sitting in the corner never having been used, was there at Katherine's insistence. She wanted to be ready. Hannah had laughed and said she was sure Katherine was ready to stop changing diapers.

No, Hannah decided. *These were not behaviors of someone getting ready to participate in the kidnapping of a child.* You don't care for someone that way, then do this because you don't like their mother's job. *Let me feed you your favorite food and enjoy this cup of tea but hurry up, I've got a high-profile kidnapping to take part in* just didn't fit with everything else they knew.

Hannah's thoughts trailed off as she noticed Gracie's cereal sitting next to a full coffee cup, and then her eyes moved to the spilled coffee cup on the floor.

It was as if Tom peered into her thoughts. "Yeah, that's a thing, isn't it?" He put his hands on his hips as he approached from behind. "The cups. If she's here by herself with a baby."

"It's not just that," Hannah said, the heat rising inside of her. "Katherine never made coffee for herself. She would buy fancy coffee drinks when she was out but at home, it was always tea."

"Always?" Tom lifted his eyebrows.

Rick and Hannah exchanged a look. "Always. Someone was let in," Rick said.

"It sure looks that way. Did Katherine have guests often?"

"Never." Something died inside of Hannah, something that lived and believed in Katherine. Of course, Katherine had a life, but she knew how much Hannah and Rick valued the privacy of their home. It wasn't a place for acquaintances to breeze in and out. Katherine knew it. Respected it.

Until now.

Hannah turned on her heel to put her back to the cups to try to think, which was impossible with the voices arguing in her head.

Why would she have someone here without telling me?

How do you know she didn't tell you?

It's not like she doesn't get time off to socialize.

Maybe she did tell you. Maybe you were so wrapped up in your career that you didn't even hear the words coming out of her mouth.

She knows why this is important to us. She knows why we protect our privacy.

You protect your paycheck.

"Hannah!" She jumped as Rick put a hand on her, then she followed his eyes. Hannah's heart sunk at the confirmation of betrayal. "Someone was here. Someone expected." Tom paused, giving her an opportunity to explain. "The purses." Hannah pointed to the bags neatly hanging from the hooks and braced herself, knowing how stupid this would sound. "They're perfect."

Tom's face crunched. "Isn't that where they would go?"

"No." She turned to him. "Grace had a thing for purses. It was an imitating mommy kind of thing..."

Hannah trailed off, thinking about how she was actually imitating mommy walking out the door, since she did that sort of thing a lot.

She pushed her guilt aside. "She was always grabbing bags and dragging them around, that's why the hooks were so low." She pointed to the rack that had been installed just below where a few of Katherine's coats hung. "Those are just for her. They're filled with toys and such so she could drag them around and empty them out on the floor without getting hurt." Hannah choked on the word *hurt*. "There was always a bag on the floor around here somewhere once she learned to walk."

Tom was listening. "I understand, but at some point Katherine must put them back."

"Rarely. Katherine could sometimes get her to hang them up, but that was a game to Gracie." Hannah paused for a second, feeling her voice break. "She thought it was funny. You know, you tell the baby no, it's not purse time, then they look at you and do it anyway." Hannah could hear Gracie's giggle, see her curls bounce as she craned her neck to see if Katherine and Hannah were watching her mischief.

"Alright, this is good." Tom put his hands on his hips and nodded. "Tells us the cups weren't a fluke. If you had to guess, how frequently was everything neatly hung like this?"

Hannah exhaled. "Once a week. Wednesday mornings to be exact."

"Exact?"

"The cleaning people always came on Wednesday morning," Rick said, giving the rack a hard stare as if it might tell him where Grace was.

"Yes." Hannah turned on her heel to look at him. "And even then, the bags were like this only if you happened to get in here before Gracie. Someone was here. Someone *invited who she knew was coming* so she had tidied up. We have to track down this American boyfriend."

Chapter Twenty-Six

Hannah gazed out from the colonial revival office building that had previously served as a satellite office for publishing magnate Maxwell Finnegan. Maxwell had lived on the same dirt road as Hannah until his death, though they had never met.

Her neighborhood wasn't the kind where people knew each other, unless they crossed paths in a boardroom or at some well-heeled event.

After Maxwell's death, his son had moved company operations closer to his own home but still owned the building Hannah found herself in now. She appreciated how he had agreed to allow use of this space as the headquarters of the investigation, ideal since it was close to both the local police and Hannah's home, and also provided ample space for the FBI.

Besides being a kind gesture to help find the girls, Hannah was also grateful because it meant that Scott Antonio wouldn't darken the doorway to her home, where she would have to watch her mother gaze at him and wonder *what if?*

"Are you ready?" Rick stood in the doorway behind her as a black SUV pulled up.

She crossed her arms. "To meet my kidnapped baby's spurned father? Sure. I've got all sorts of time for this right now."

The door of the SUV opened and he appeared, a star in the flesh. Hannah noticed that he looked around for the press, but they were not permitted access beyond the driveway entrance, which wasn't visible from the building. She picked up on the slight frown that came over his well-maintained face when he realized his picture wouldn't be part of the media updates tonight.

This is a problem of your own creation, a voice only she could hear admonished as the entourage entered the foyer down below and she turned to take a seat at the conference table.

"So, Hannah," Scott said when he breezed in moments later. "This must be awful for you. All this," he paused to gesture in the air, "attention."

Rick grit his teeth and pushed past him to take a seat. "This isn't some cheap soap opera, you dick." Hannah knew that whatever happened from this day forward, she couldn't possibly not love Rick.

But they needed him, at least for the moment. And in discussing this interview, Tom had pointed out something Hannah had never thought of before: even in the likely event he wasn't the father (Hannah had appreciated his kindness in saying likely), he could have been an unwitting target of someone trying to gather information on Hannah. Someone who could be associated with the kidnapping.

"Let's stay focused here," Tom laid out some papers on the table in front of them. "You're claiming possible paternity of Grace Smoke. That means we need to talk to you."

"Of course." He gave a megawatt smile. "Anything for my maybe daughter."

"Jesus…" Hannah started.

"The DNA collected will tell us in the next 24 hours if she is. But regardless, because of your history with Hannah, and your," Tom turned his nose down, "affinity for the spotlight..."

"What did she tell you?" Scott demanded. "You've not been telling lies about me, darling, have you?" He leaned back and Hannah got a whiff of that cologne she was grateful was not impregnating her house.

"What do you have to say, Scott?" Tom dropped any pretense of patience.

"Just that you shouldn't trust Hannah. She has a tendency to stretch the truth, even if just by omitting details." He looked at Rick. "And despite yourself, I think you know that." He paused, waiting for Rick's reaction.

When none came, Scott leaned in like it was just he and Rick. "Listen dude, I get it. You're the main guy around here, I mean in so far that she didn't even tell anyone you were a couple. But that's not a surprise. The thing about someone like Hannah is, you can sort of know her, but you can't ever really know her, can you? Too many demons fighting in there that she was deep in a relationship with before she met either of us."

Something curdled inside of Hannah at the thought he wasn't entirely wrong, then Rick reached under the table and squeezed her hand, reminding her why Rick was the one, demons or no.

Randall pinched the flesh between his eyes. "Agent Wolinksy, I'm going to advise we go straight to Scott's individual interview. Maybe he'll be more helpful in that setting, and not as combative towards the mother of a missing child."

"Sure." Scott scoffed. "*Missing* child."

"Excuse me?" Hannah gripped her chair so she didn't strangle him.

"Come on," Scott threw a hand up. "This chick who tells ghost stories for a living has you all snowed. She'll do anything, or anyone, for publicity." He gave Hannah a pointed look. "I would know."

"We're done here." Randall stood up and took Hannah by the arm. "We have people who will be happy to show him how serious this is."

"Are you going to interview all of her lovers?" Scott laughed. "Because from what I know about her time in LA, you're going to need a bigger building."

Hannah's face burned as Rick got in between her and Scott. "Let it go Hannah. It doesn't matter. He just wants the reaction so he can run to the press with it."

"You can wait here until we get someone in to ask questions." Tom looked at Scott and stood up. "Get Agent Brown on it, it will be good practice for him" he said to an agent standing by the door.

"Wait. Aren't you, like," Scott gestured at Tom, "the lead guy?"

"Yup," Tom answered without looking back and left.

"Ouch," Randall said as Rick and Hannah left the room. Once they were out of earshot he poked his head back in the door, looked at Scott and said, "Aww, looks like you're not the lead story."

Chapter Twenty-Seven

"I just realized," Hannah grew taller in her chair, "I have a question for you."

"Oh?"

"I've been working under the assumption that you don't have children of your own. I mean, I imagine you're at an age where even if you don't have any, your friends start having kids. Do you? What about your friend with the lake, Rory? Is he a father?"

Asha's stomach lurched at the thought of Rory, and all she didn't want to say but she could feel Hannah digging for it. *She knows damn well he's not a father, she just wants to bring him up again.* Reaching around in her mind to get the details of whatever she couldn't find for the file she no doubt had sitting around that detailed Asha's life. "No children for any of us." A lie by omission. *Today is about Hannah's secrets, not mine,* Asha reminded herself.

"Well, I was younger than you when I had Grace, so, it dawned on me it was possible. Significant other?"

Asha's last real relationship had fizzled out shortly before she left for the U.S. She might have said it ended *because* she left for the U.S., but both she and Lily knew, in a place that wasn't so deep down, that wasn't

140

true. Asha had started out quite pleased with herself the night it ended, she had rushed out of work to make it to a couple's dinner that Lily would have otherwise had to attend alone.

The look that greeted Asha when she appeared in Lily's doorway made it quite clear she would prefer to attend alone.

"There's nothing, Hannah. No significant other, no children, no pets, not even one of those sponsor a poor child memberships."

"Well you're accomplished, you're pretty, and I'm sure any…"

"Right," Asha surprised herself with the boldness of her own interjection. "When the DNA came back and proved Rick was the father, that at least took the distraction of Scott out of the picture." She tapped her pen on her notepad to bring Hannah back to her questions. "But I get it, the damage to the case had already been done. Tell me about Theodore Shieves."

Hannah exhaled, bending to Asha's sudden change of subject. "I still can't believe how long it took to put it all together. Teddy Shieves was the break—the link was right there but we just couldn't find it at the time."

She dropped her chin in her hands. "I can't tell you how many times I've gone down that path, the one where we figure it all out when we get Teddy. You can make yourself crazy thinking about it. But… Jesus, Theodore Shieves should have turned out to be the problem that the kidnapper couldn't plan for, the one that put him right under our noses."

Asha checked that the recorder still had plenty of memory available, and Hannah picked up on the slight nod of satisfaction she gave to it before she asked. "I read he was a search volunteer, is that correct?"

Hannah twitched. "Yes. The police didn't have enough manpower to search the acres of woods and fields surrounding the house, so they coordinated a volunteer effort. It's pretty standard. You want your experienced law enforcement focused on leads, but area searches take time. So, they put an officer in charge of a search effort, and that person organizes the volunteers."

"Who were these volunteers?" Asha asked while scribbling away again. "How many did they have?"

Hannah drew in a breath. "I'm not sure how many. I only caught glimpses of them through the trees, with their bright orange vests. The who was anybody who showed up and volunteered. There's no screening process per-se, but there is a sign-up procedure that requires identification. They also keep track of the plate numbers of the volunteers' vehicles, details like that."

"Because sometimes, they come back," Asha said.

"Yes. It started when an officer in charge of the volunteers noticed one of them was asking a lot of questions. Questions about Grace, did they have any leads, did they think she was still alive, how was I doing, would I be out there searching with them, stuff like that." She held up a finger. "No questions about Katherine. That isn't so unusual, sometimes people are more worried about a baby. But what alerted the officer something was off was that this guy was more preoccupied with asking questions than searching his assigned area. As time went on, he started wandering off on his own."

She pointed out the back door towards the woods beyond the wrought iron fence. "The way I heard it, the officer had already asked someone to look into this guy, you know, see if there were any red flags, when Theodore caught sight of me walking from the pool house back to the main house and said, 'I need to talk to Hannah.' When he tried to get through the gate, they grabbed him and there was a struggle. *That* I did see."

"What were you thinking at that point?"

Hannah's face went slack. "Dogs had already been through those woods and hadn't found any sign of Grace or Katherine, but when I saw officers running towards *something*, I was sure it would be bad and I ran back inside." She dabbed at her eyes. "I shouldn't have done that."

Asha scrawled on her notepad. "I haven't had experience directly with this sort of trauma, but I'm guessing there is no right way to react."

She shrugged. "It was about 20 minutes later when Tom came back to the house. I remember looking at the bag in his hand and thinking, *it's not big enough to be a body*. But it still wasn't good. It was Grace's blanket and it had been found in this guy's car."

Chapter Twenty-Eight

The blanket that had caught Hannah's eye when she was pregnant had been picked up during an impromptu visit to a warehouse chain store, the kind that had locations in multiple countries and sold every kind of baby gadget imaginable. About nine weeks into the pregnancy, a month before Joanne stormed out of her house, Hannah hadn't fully accepted the boom that was lowering on her life, and when she saw the store taunting her across the parking lot, she gritted her teeth and went in, like an adolescent accepting a dare.

The blanket was a small patched-style quilt, with puffy animals sewn on it. Hannah tried to think back, tried to remember if she'd liked animals as a baby. She decided that she did, snatched the blanket from the shelf and marched out of the store victorious in battle, even if the battle was only in her head.

And it was because of this unplanned battle at Babies R' Us that the blanket was one of likely thousands, not anything custom or handmade, so Hannah, Rick, and a few officers scoured her property to see if this was just a coincidence.

But the blanket wasn't going to be found, she knew that, because they had already found it.

Their lives depend on you getting this right. Hannah braced herself for the ugliness that would be required to finally get some answers against the hope that finally, they had something.

"His name is Theodore Shieves." Randall briefed Hannah and Rick.

"Officially, he was a foster care kid and that's the end of the story. Those who dig deeper will find from the age of 11 to 21 he lived in various mental institutions." He looked up at Hannah from his file. "Diagnosed schizophrenia and depression. If the paperwork we've managed to get our hands on is painting an accurate picture, he's never demonstrated violence towards others, but has been plagued with thoughts of self-harm. That explains why after all those years in the system, no one tried to take him in."

He let the folder drop on the table in front of him and rubbed his eyes to bring the focus back into them. "It's not unusual for that to happen. Foster kid with mental health issues requiring acute treatment goes to an institution for a short stay, then ends up spending all of their formative years there because there's no place else for them to go. Pair that with the constant state budget changes, these kids get moved around from one hellhole to another."

"Which," an agent looked up from his own notes, "doesn't do much to help with the issue that landed them there in the first place."

"If he's not dangerous," Hannah said between clenched teeth, "then he had better have a damn good explanation as to why he has Grace's blanket."

"He does." Tom came in and threw another file on the pile that was growing. "The landscaper story checks out." He had claimed to have been a landscaper that worked on Hannah's property a few times, the most recent time two months prior. He admitted to stealing the blanket during one of those visits.

"We're not saying it ends there." He held his hands up towards Hannah. "Just that the landscaper claim is true. He's worked for the same company for years, before you even were in that house. According to his boss, he was, quote, "a weird guy" but never in a way that was alarming or caused any trouble."

He sighed. "Whether that remains the case... He trailed off and looked at Hannah. "Are you sure you want to do this?"

"If he wants to talk to me, we're going to let him." Hannah shook her head and locked eyes with Tom. "Not only because I'm desperate, but because I promise it is fucking hard to manipulate or hide things from me." She pushed nasty thoughts away, voices that peppered her with questions about Katherine's missing cousin and mystery boyfriend as she said it.

Tom nodded at Hannah. "You remember the plan? Keep it simple."

"Right," Hannah agreed.

"ABCs simple, Hannah." He sorted papers that didn't need any sorting as Hannah studied him. "He hasn't said too much to us, which could mean he's really, really crazy or really, really smart. Don't give—"

"I've got it." Hannah interrupted. "This is me. This is what I do." She took a deep breath. "This might be where I can actually help."

Tom ran his hands over his hair, then slapped them on the table as he leaned forward. "This isn't the same as telling some rube from the boonies that Grandpa loves them. This guy—" He was cut off by the rumble of people approaching, a rumble that they all knew meant *he* was coming.

Hannah closed her eyes and implored the voices to be orderly. She fought back the bile threatening to come up at the thought she was trying to find the girls this way, this way of all ways, but it wasn't as if she had a choice.

Blanket man—Theodore, she reminded herself—made his way into the room, forced into a shuffle because his wrists and ankles were shackled. He was small, as far as a grown man can be small, and his slightness indicated his time institutionalized would not have been easy. Hannah felt a flash of pity and disappointment. She knew in the way she knew things that this wasn't their kidnapper. This man knows something, but they hadn't caught Him. Theodore's eyes lit up like Christmas trees through greasy dark bangs when he saw Hannah.

"Oh, Ms. Smoke," he breathed. "I'm so happy to meet you. It's such an honor." He gave her a smile as officers helped lower him into a chair.

She folded her hands on the table. "An honor?"

"Of course." He bowed his head. "And with everything that you have going on. I was only trying to help, you see, and—"

Tom interrupted. "Mr. Shieves, we have some questions we'd like to ask."

"Yes." He tried to sit up straighter but his body seemed to reject an assertive position and reverted back to slouching, Hannah noted. *Definitely would have not done well in an institution.* "You have no idea, Ms. Smoke. I've been trying for days to get someone to listen to me. They ignored me at the roadblock, then at the police station, the FBI hotline, so I volunteered, hoping I could talk to you."

"You can talk to me now." Hannah spoke like a school principal. "Please tell me where Grace and Katherine are, Theodore."

"Call me Teddy." He smiled, revealing crooked teeth.

"Alright. Teddy. Call me Hannah." She slowly rubbed her palms together. "Tell me where they are and I'll give you whatever you want. I'll make sure the world knows that you're a hero."

He struggled to put his elbows on the table to rest his chin in his hands but after fussing for a bit realized he would never reach. "A hero." He sat back and sighed. "That would be nice. No one's ever treated me like anything good before."

"You'd be better than good, if you help me."

"I can't help that much. I don't know where they are, I told the FBI. That's not a lie, I wouldn't lie to you."

"Why do you have Grace's blanket?" Hannah spoke as if they were the only two people in the room.

He shrugged. "I'm sorry. It was there, on one of the chairs in your yard. I took it." He got agitated. "It wasn't perverted or anything, I swear, I just wanted a piece of Hannah Smoke. Thought you wouldn't miss it." He looked at his knees. "I didn't even know it was a child's blanket until I got home and got a real look at the thing. I thought it was a beach towel. I cleaned up the flower beds around the pool that day, I hope you liked it."

"They looked beautiful, thank you." Hannah scrambled to remember if she noticed anything with the flower beds to help her pinpoint a timeline, see if she noticed anything else unusual, but came up empty. "Teddy, do you believe in what I do?"

"Oh yes, of course!" He sat up straight again and smiled at Hannah. "And you don't have to explain it to me, I know how these things go. You don't control what you know and when you know it, that's why, well, it's why I'm here."

"Right." Hannah forced a smile. "So, you know that I know that what you've told me is true. I do understand that the story of how you came to be in possession of my missing daughter's blanket is true." Hannah surprised herself with the evenness she was able to maintain in her voice. It had only been five days, but it felt like years since she had sounded so sane, felt so confident in setting things right side up.

"Oh, thank you." He exhaled. "It is the truth!"

"Good." Hannah sucked in a breath. "Because it means you also understand when I say, Theodore Shieves, I know you haven't told me everything you *do* know."

He recoiled as if slapped. His face contorted with the battle that was happening in his mind. "Yes, yes, okay." His hand shook as he rested his wrists on the edge of the table. "But I don't know where Grace is. Really, I don't. I don't have anything to do with taking her, and I didn't even know she would be taken."

"But you know something. It's why you volunteered. Not to find them, you *knew* you wouldn't." Hannah's voice was starting to show the desperation inside of her. "You know something and it's important."

He trembled. "I can't lie to you, Ms. Smoke. I can't." He paused, deciding how to proceed. "But I think Grace is alive, and that you can fix this. I just don't know about Katherine. She might have helped? She might be dead?" He shook his head. "But she's not important like Grace."

"Helped how? Did you know Katherine?" Hannah knew she shouldn't rapid fire too many questions but couldn't help it. "How do you know Grace is alive? Why Grace? Why is she important?"

"I mean," he giggled. "You heard it." He rolled his eyes like they were teenagers sharing secrets. "You were there, duh. I believe in you, but the kidnapper doesn't, and he's real angry about it."

"He," Hannah gripped the edge of the table and everyone in the room leaned forward. "Who is *he*?"

Theodore's face crumpled, and he leaned forward to bite at his shackled hand. "I shouldn't say," he said with a finger in his mouth.

"Someone stole them, stole them from their home," Hannah fought to keep calm as the tears flowed down her face. "They could be hurt, or worse. We need to know who *he* is."

"I—"

Hannah jumped up "Just say it!" She lunged at him across the table as officers tried to restrain her and Theodore leaned back in alarm. "Tell me where my baby is! Who has my baby?"

"Nonononononononononono..." Theodore shook his head and started to rock back and forth. "I don't know, I can't, please don't be mad I just came to tell you I don't think he will hurt Grace! I'm sure of it! That's all! That's all I know!"

"You know WHO!" Hannah bellowed as she continued to struggle against the hands restraining her. "I know you know who! Give me a name!"

"I don't know a name anymore!" He shrank back. "I don't know, I don't know anything except that I just wanted to help." He started to weep. "Now everyone is mad. This was a mistake." The rocking intensified, and he started to grunt. Hannah leaned toward him as the officers held her back, using every ounce of self-restraint as she spoke to him through unkempt hair that fell across her eyes. "Listen to me. Please.

I don't know what happened to you but I think you care about children. That's why you're here. Do you care about children?"

He cowered back in his chair. "I don't have any friends."

"If you tell me what you know, I will be your friend."

His crying accelerated and a ribbon of snot tried to make a bridge to his shirt. "Nononononononono, I have no friends."

"What about the kidnapper? Was he your friend?"

"Nobody's enemy. Nobody's friend."

Hannah pulled a picture out of her back pocket and waved it at him. "She's eighteen months old. Her name is Grace and she loves Elmo and animals. She loves to go to the playground even though she's so small compared to the other kids." Hannah's voice cracked, thinking about how she worried that a bigger kid might run into her, as if that was the biggest threat in the world. "She's just a baby. If you help a baby, everyone will want to be your friend."

"I screwed it up, I screwed it all up." The tornado of emotion that was ravaging his face disappeared, and he went blank. "My one chance," he said to Hannah. "I thought I could be useful to both of you, but I'm not. I thought I could help you fulfill the purpose, make everyone happy, but I can't."

"You can still—"

Teddy Shieves didn't hear what Hannah had to say.

He propelled his body up and brought his face crashing down into the glass tabletop.

It would be determined later that there must have been some sort of defect in it, either in the manufacturing process, or a nick that happened during its many years of use. Because the glass smashed after the first impact, and Hannah understood his intentions. She saw the determination and had calculated it out before the officers could stop him.

Before he launched himself down a second time onto a jagged edge, ripping his neck open.

"Noooooooooooo!" Hannah couldn't hear anything but her own scream.

Everyone else heard the sound of a bedsheet tearing, and the splat of the blood as it poured down onto the plush carpet below.

Chapter Twenty-Nine

Asha felt herself blanch, as if all of that blood had poured out of her instead of a stranger decades ago. "I um, I hadn't anticipated that."

Charing tutted in her head, *get it done Asha, if it bleeds it leads.* It didn't fit for a hardened journalist, but Asha would get woozy at the sight of a skinned knee, and now had to fight through the haze that threatened to overtake her as she imagined a curtain of torn flesh with a wave of blood spilling out. *Don't you dare faint,* she scolded herself.

"May I please have some water?"

"Oh Asha, I'm sorry." Hannah jumped up to get some. "I kind of underestimated how disturbing that is." To this day, when Hannah squeezed extra water out of a sponge, she remembered the squish of the officers' shoes on the carpet as they tried to lift him up and stop the bleeding. "I, of all people, should have known to be more careful in my description."

Asha felt her stomach flip. Hannah must have noticed, because she offered a sympathetic smile. "Let's take a break, Asha. We can take a break, or even stop for the day and pick it up tomorrow?" She placed the glass in front of her. "That was intense." Hannah sighed. "I know, I was there."

Asha thought of the reaction of not just Charing, but of her bosses, if she were to turn up at the office and say, *Sorry, I didn't get anything new because I needed a break.* She knew what was at stake here. "I take it this is not the new development that has you talking now? I mean it may be new to the public..."

Now it was Hannah's turn to blanch. "No."

Take a Tums and man-up, Asha. "Then, I'm fine." She forced down a sip of water. "I don't understand how..." She shook her head, not out of doubt but to shake off the fog.

"How they kept that quiet?" Hannah offered, trying to push Asha past her queasiness. "The official story was that the person of interest—that's what they called him—died after trying to attack some officers during questioning. There were scattered rumors here and there that the death had been especially violent, but for sure no one who was in the room that day was eager to relive what they saw, so I guess that helped. It also helped that the man had no family. No one to press the press, in a manner of speaking. It would have been all over the news in that case. They would have loved it."

Asha twirled the glass on the table, then stopped and looked at Hannah. "But why not report what really happened back then?"

Hannah grunted and Asha could see the frustration on her face as she thought of Theodore Shieves and his suicidal stunt. "A few reasons. First, it was agreed that, if he really was involved this was what the kidnapper wanted. That sending him to us was meant to create a splash." Hannah winced. "Bad choice of words. I don't mean literally, but you don't send someone like that and plan on it not being interesting. I mean, I was there and I still have trouble believing how he killed himself. I have trouble believing it and I also have trouble forgetting it."

She grabbed a kitchen towel and wiped some water off the table, and her face darkened. "He was so tortured by whatever lurked inside his mind. But there was another idea the behaviorist had, the one he felt in his gut was closer to the target and I have to say, I tended to agree. He believed this guy wasn't really part of it. Maybe he imagined he knew the person and was just inserting himself, and once he took over the headlines, the real kidnapper could act out to reclaim it. If someone unplanned was allowed to take the kidnapper's spotlight, we feared the consequences. Turns out we were both right and wrong on that account."

"How were you?"

Asha got a glimpse of the desperation of that day as a spastic wave passed over Hannah's face, her voice getting thick. "Frantic. I knew that *if* Grace and Katherine were alive, we were running out of time."

Chapter Thirty

Katherine could fill an ocean with everything she didn't know.

Among the little fish of mystery were scattered big fish named *where they were*, *how they got there*, and *how long they had been there,* since time didn't function reliably in her current state.

She knew time existed, but couldn't get her hands around any measurement of it. Every time she tried to come up with some kind of estimate and found herself lost, the small ember of Katherine that still functioned coherently inside that fog would get angry. It burned a bit brighter every time an *I don't know* swam by, just close enough that she could almost grab it, then darted away leaving her with nothing.

It was all there in her head, yet out of reach.

She had figured out some things in the six days since the kidnapping, though the concept of either six or days was currently unmeasurable to her. The one fish she caught and turned into an *I know that* was they were being drugged. It could have been the water or the food, but it was happening. Not enough to render her or Grace unconscious full-time, but enough to keep them heavily sedated.

But they were alive, and despite the effects of the drugs and the horrors that lived both in her mind and in reality, Katherine could recognize that being alive was somehow significant.

In the dark, she could feel omnipresent eyes boring into her, watching to make sure that the drugs were working to keep her numb. She would have thoughts like *The drugs are key*, but then spend an unknowable amount of time watching keys dance behind her eyelids. And she knew that was wrong, that the thought was right and the dancing was wrong, and the ember would glow a little brighter.

In moments that approached lucidity, she suspected a crack in an upper corner where two walls came together, but she knew she didn't have a snowball's chance in hell of investigating it, and if she did, being seen looking for a camera would defeat the purpose. She kept her back to that corner as much as possible, facing it only to get the water or food left under it.

But when the ember inside glowed she gave that corner the finger.

The door opened.

Footsteps. Stable, undrugged footsteps.

She sat on the floor with one leg splayed out to the side as Gracie rested her head in Katherine's lap in an endless doze. Katherine rested her head on the raised mattress in front of her, and she could feel him near, the sound of his breathing getting louder and louder like a train barreling up from behind until it hurt her ears.

She was hallucinating. She couldn't hear his breathing any more than she could hear Grace's, but at least she could *feel* hers and know she was alive. She felt him touch her ankle where the metal of the cuff that chained her to the bed was attached.

"Too tight," he said. She felt him use something to loosen the cuff, slightly but enough that it wasn't digging in anymore. *Why?* she screamed in her head.

"Wouldn't want you to die of gangrene," he answered. "Wouldn't serve the purpose."

And then she remembered *him*. She remembered how she used to share a small studio in the city with the other foreign nannies on her day off, how she had that favorite coffee shop she loved right downstairs.

She remembered how he knocked into her in that coffee shop one morning, causing her to spill her expensive latte, and insisted he replace it. She remembered being reassured by the generous tip he gave the barista when she said she'd replace it for free.

She remembered how she felt that this older man was interested in her, but suspicious of his distant nature.

She remembered she had written him off until he called a few days ago and asked if they could meet for coffee and talk.

The ember burned hotter at the thought of him and her foolishness contributing to this mess. Words did a mocking dance around the ember — *planned, used, gullible.*

A wave of adrenaline surged through her. He had answered her. The *why* she thought was internal she must have spoken aloud. She could talk. If she could talk, she could do other things that were purposeful, like go long periods of time without eating or drinking so she could clear her head. *You bastard,* she thought, and the ember's glow pulsated, and Katherine stared into it, watching its light fade and brighten, fade and brighten, as it told her what she had to do.

Chapter Thirty-One

Barbara Silver's eyes locked into the camera, giving it her very best *I'm a serious newswoman reporting on an important event and not sensationalizing a kidnapping to further my career* face. Hannah would have liked to feel a little less alone in her questioning of Barbara's motives since she seemed a tad obsessed with reminding people that Hannah had a book coming out, that Hannah's own nanny made the first call, and that there hadn't been a single demand made since. And there was the question of paternity. She had reveled in that, single-handedly reviving Scott Antonio's career.

But Barbara always ended segments with her "prayers" for Grace and Katherine, which Hannah knew didn't count for shit since she was a bundle of prayers over the past six days and had gotten exactly nowhere. They especially didn't count when the true intent of Barbara's prayers was to absolve her viewers from the sin of tragedy voyeurism.

"Andy Waters," Barbara shuffled her notes like she was about to cross-examine a mob boss. "You say you *worked* with Hannah Smoke. What can you tell us about her?"

The picture changed to a heavyset man with a beaming smile. He adjusted his flashy scarf as he spoke. "Oh, Hannah. You must realize we don't all get to be like Hannah."

Barbara's eyes flashed with hunger. "So, you knew her? Personally?"

"Of course." Andy looked down at Barbara, seeming positively bored with her excitement. "Anybody who is anybody is bound to cross paths in this business, and while she is more famous now, I was more famous then. I first met Hannah when she was still a child. This would have been around the same time you first interviewed her, Barbara. We both worked the occasional psychic fair, but only the big ones." He smiled at the camera. "At that point, we were both too famous to do any event that wasn't big."

Barbara nodded. "Ah, you were competitors then."

"Oh heavens, no." Andy laughed as if Barbara had just suggested he might give birth to an alien. "I liked Hannah, even helped her out. I introduced her to the right people so she could get invited to private events. People pay big money for the flamboyant gay man who is loads of fun and psychic to show up at their well-heeled soirees. I knew a pretty and sweet little thing like Hannah, who maybe wasn't ready for a cocktail party, could do well, say, with a daytime event. Very different kind of character than me, but a character nonetheless, and in this business character is 90% of the job."

"Okay." Barbara leaned forward. "But what was she like?"

"Oh lord," he sighed. "She was so pretty, and forget about psychic because pretty is a power all its own. I think the innocence of youth was part of it too. That's appealing to clients in our line of work."

"Oh!" His eyes lit up. "I remember the very first time I met her. She was cute as a button, so worried that no one would come see her." He leaned back and laughed. "Then we took a peek through the curtain and the line at her table was 20 deep in a few minutes. That she became a star later was no surprise to me."

"So," Barbara was jotting something down, "she didn't know anyone would come see her. But if she's a psychic..."

He rolled his eyes. "Shouldn't she know that? That's not how this works. Think about a sense you understand, take sight for example. Even you aren't keenly aware of everything that you actually can see with your own eyes right now in this moment. Imagine if you were. Imagine if you actually had to consciously recognize and deal with everything your senses could detect at this moment, you'd be overwhelmed." He tilted his head. "It works the same way with us. It's not just that we're sensing things you don't, our brains are tasked with sorting them like any other sense, that's the difficult part. The sorting." He adjusted his pocket square. "It's not my fault if you don't get that."

"Okay." She held her hand up, using limited time as an excuse to cover her disappointment with Andy's version of Hannah. Hannah loved him for that. "We'll move on. Would you describe her as ambitious?"

"You know," he sat back in thought, "I wouldn't describe her as ambitious as much as I would say she was a hard worker. But unlike a normal adult with a job, I don't think she was making a choice to skip other things for this work. She didn't seem to have anything else. It made me a little sad." He shrugged. "But I always thought that was me just picking up on the feelings drifting off from her. I think Hannah was a little sad."

"Yet you liked her?"

He sighed. "In the psychic arts, there's a few rules you need to follow to keep the money flowing. Never tell anyone anything unpleasant, never let a mistake throw you, and never do anything for free. Hannah broke all those rules. At first, I thought it was because she was just a kid, and well, there you go, more money left for me, right? A few years after she came on the scene, I overheard her consoling someone who was bawling at her station. She apologized to the rest of the line and said there was going to be a delay because a client needed some professional help."

"Professional psychic help?"

He shook his head. "No, not psychic, like *help*, help. The person had just opened up that she had been sexually abused her entire childhood. Apparently, Hannah had said something about masking pain—a standard phrase in our business since who isn't masking pain, right? —and this woman completely fell apart. Hannah told me all this later saying she couldn't just pat her on the head and let her go. She wouldn't let her leave until she had given all of her information to a therapist. The therapist was some highly regarded person, someone who she met at one of those high-end parties she was paid to appear at. Listen, Hannah was tenacious as hell. She couldn't have been more than eighteen at the time, but tracked down the location of their office and insisted this person have an appointment. She said this should be normal, in a way I suspect put the rest of us adults in our place. She felt that when we encourage people to reveal their deepest darkest secrets to us, we have a responsibility to actually help them."

"That's the Hannah I knew." He smiled. "Hannah didn't have the happiest childhood, I suspect, but she struck me as one of those people that came out kind despite that. I was so pleased when she and Rick had a baby. I met him a few times, he's a nice man."

Barbara looked at him in surprise but before she could say a word he added, "I know that was news to ya'll, but everybody in the business knew about those two."

"And what would you say now?" Barbara could barely contain the smugness on her face. "A psychic's baby gets taken, and there are accusations that Hannah knows more than she's letting on. Some people are even suggesting that motherhood got to be too much for her."

Andy narrowed his eyes and gave Barbara a cold stare. "Too much for her so, what, she sold her child on the black market? Or maybe she stuck her in a microwave? That this, along with the nanny, is all an elaborate cover-up? Say what you want about my line of work, Ms. Silver. Say I'm a fraud, a liar, the worst of the snake oil salesmen. At least you can't say I'd throw out the ugliest of all accusations you could lob at a mother because it will get me ratings."

"Now hold on a minute. I didn't mean to—"

"Hannah wouldn't let a client leave because she wanted to make sure she got help. There were no cameras around when that happened. As far as I know, this is the first time that story has even been shared. The idea that the same girl is now faking kidnappings or even worse is ridiculous." He turned to look into the camera directly. "I believe in you, Hannah. I got to see who you are, and I can't explain why, but somehow, I know it will be okay."

Chapter Thirty-Two

The once-welcome glare of the lights now made Hannah feel like a cornered animal. It wasn't that she couldn't escape. She knew she could get up, march past the cameras and the microphones and walk right out. No one would blame her, at least not anyone from her own team, who all had some valid reservations about this interview to begin with.

Except for Rick. Rick would blame her, he already had, and now he was gone. Off to *do something that actually might help*, as he put it. While Hannah *stayed behind to poke a rabid tiger in the eye and get...*

"Say it," Hannah had whispered when he stopped short.

He leaned in and pointed at his head. "I know you *think* you know what you're doing."

She grabbed at him and he swiped her hand away, so she took a step closer and leaned in. "I have no fucking idea what I'm doing, Rick. But in case you haven't noticed what everyone else is doing isn't working yet, and it's not like we can sit around and wait forever."

He looked around him and ran his fingers through his hair. "Do you think I hadn't noticed Hannah? She's my daughter too! I've noticed, and I've *managed*, a lot this past week." he said through clenched teeth.

"And what is that, exactly? My meltdown?" Hannah's eyes demanded an answer. When he tried to look away she grabbed at him again, this time he didn't fight it. "I am also trying to help, and since we both know damn well this started with me, I am going to have to be part of the thing that actually helps. So, if you have a clear idea of what will "actually help," Hannah let him go to make quotation marks with her fingers, "I'd appreciate if you'd let me in on it."

"You know I didn't mean..." he started.

"The hell you didn't."

"Hannah," Rick sighed and looked around them, at the people pretending not to notice the bickering but knowing full well there would be news reports about the tension between them later. He took a deep breath. "I'll be back," he said, kissed her on the top of her head, then bolted out the front door, minding the cables and equipment that webbed their way through her home in the process. Hannah had spent enough time around grieving families to know that tempers flare up, but was surprised to realize she thought it would be different for her and Rick.

But he wouldn't say it, Hannah thought, her heart racing and hands tingling as she made her way to the chair set up in front of the camera. He didn't because you can't say poke a rabid tiger with a stick and get our daughter killed, at least *he* can't, not yet. If this didn't work, she now knew he would soon go over the cliff where he would say that and worse to her.

She also knew she will have been the one who pushed him off that cliff.

Hannah took her seat, struggling inside to keep her head above water in the deep well of memories of her last interview. Everything brought her back to that moment. The worst was the black hole created by the bright lights that surrounded her. When she tried to look beyond the television lighting currently taking over her living room, she could see only dark and hear Katherine begging her to find them. She forced her eyes into her lap.

Every member of Barbara Silver's production crew had tripped over themselves to congratulate Hannah on being strong. She hadn't appreciated before how good Tom and Randall had been about sparing her inane platitudes like *hang in there* and *you're doing great* and *I don't know how you keep going.*

She fought the urge to scream and yell, remind them of her predicament. It wasn't strength that had her sitting here, ready to do a live television appearance that itself was reminiscent of the events, and with her worst critic at that. Today was a Hail Mary done out of necessity.

Strength, Hannah thought to herself, flexing and relaxing her hands on the arms of her chair to work out the tension cresting inside of her, *was the luxury of people that had a choice.*

It had been over a week, and no one had an explanation as to why the kidnapper had not reached out. It didn't take a psychic to figure out the possibilities, especially when rooms filled with chatter went reliably silent with her arrival, faces working overtime to not look at her. The only thing Hannah knew for certain was she needed to prove a point or satisfy a longing. She wouldn't be hearing from the kidnapper until she figured out what that was. Today was an attempt to do that.

She closed her eyes and hoped that, somewhere, Grace and Katherine knew she was coming, knew she was doing everything she could. Gracie, who no doubt had asked for *Munny,* because she tried to imitate Katherine saying Mummy, *countless* times.

Her heartrate picked up as she pictured her asking Katherine for *Munny*, and the thought crossed her mind that if Katherine was still alive, she might be working under the assumption that the authorities had already written them off as dead, and she flinched.

They're alive they're alive they're alive and you're going to find them she scolded herself to get it together. Tom approached, crouching down next to her chair to meet her at eye level.

"Hey. We'll make it quick, I promise."

Hannah gave him a false smile and patted his shoulder. "I'm fine," she lied. "Anyway, I don't think Barbara is accustomed to taking orders from the FBI." She sat up in alarm and looked at him. "Don't cut her off, Tom, even if it gets rough."

"Alright." He nodded in agreement.

"I plan on using her today even more than she uses me." Hannah studied her hands, hoping that the mild sedative pumping through her veins was a good idea. She had decided it was, considering she didn't want to wind up with a live TV version of her smashing incident. Whatever "the purpose" was, Hannah knew it wasn't that. But she did know that a polite exchange between her and Barbara wasn't going to work either. "It's got to get rough, doesn't it, if we want this to work."

Tom's eyes reflected regret. "I think so. But this doesn't all fall on you," he said. "We have a job to do too."

She considered this. "You look tired, Tom."

He smiled at being seen. "You too."

A commotion interrupted them as Randall got into it with a producer, some disagreement about where he would sit during the interview. "I know you have your reasons, but we have our own to worry about." He stomped past someone from Barbara's camp and plopped a chair beside Hannah. "This isn't entertainment!" he yelled over his shoulder. He turned and winced when he caught Hannah's eye. "Sorry. These media types get me worked up. I don't trust them. First, they say I shouldn't be sitting next to you. That it's distracting."

"I need someone sane by my side." Rick's angry face as he stormed out flashed in her mind. Deep inside, Hannah knew it was probably for the best. Had he stayed for what she had planned it would have been a disaster. She wondered when he would look back and notice that she hadn't begged him to stay with some tears and some please don't goes.

"Then," he adjusted his suit jacket, "they wanted me to put on makeup."

"Try not to lose it over a bit of face powder and remember why we're here." Their eyes locked. In the space of a few days, they had gotten adept at unspoken communication, and Hannah knew that even if Grace were found that instant, she'd be keeping Randall on as her lawyer. "I will never lose sight of that. As your lawyer or as a human." He turned serious. "This plan is rather delicate. Delicate is not my area of strength."

Hannah turned her eyes to watch the scurrying around them. *Yes, the sedative definitely had been a good idea.* "You don't say?"

Randall touched her arm. "What if she doesn't ask?"

"She'll ask. I've been a psychic long enough to know. She's the type."

"But what if it doesn't work the way we planned?"

Hannah's mouth tightened. "My whole life has become a big *what if.* I have to try something."

A flurry of activity descended upon the room, with Barbara Silver herself in tow. "We're live in one minute!" a PA shouted somewhere.

Barbara was flush and breathless, looking like she'd jogged the last mile to Hannah's house. "I'm so sorry we have no time for a proper hello.

Getting through the press outside was madness, absolute bedlam! Then there's everything I need to prepare and..."

She trailed off when Hannah responded with a blank stare and didn't engage her pleasantries.

"Well, I thank you for doing this." She sat across from Hannah, not acknowledging Randall. "To be frank, I thought I was on an undercover camera show when they told me you said yes." Barbara broke into an uneasy smile. "We of course have to ask but I didn't expect you'd ever accept."

"We are live in ten!" a disembodied voice shouted from behind the lights.

"Thank you for coming." Hannah looked away from Barbara, towards the camera.

A producer came in front of them. "In 5,4,3," then silently flashed 2,1.

"Good evening. I'm Barbara Silver. Tonight, a special live edition of News in America that you won't want to miss. The kidnapping of Grace Smoke and Katherine Willard has gripped the nation for eight agonizing days. But despite this roller coaster ride, there are still more questions than answers. Tonight, we are live from the home of the woman at the center of the tragedy, Hannah Smoke."

She nodded in Hannah's direction. "Our audience should know there are some conditions that were agreed to for this interview, most notably the presence of Randall Newman, Hannah's criminal defense lawyer. While everyone has their own opinions about Hannah's profession, tonight we ask all Americans to keep an open mind, but more importantly open eyes and ears. We will have a phone number at the bottom of your screen throughout the entire broadcast. If you have any information that may lead to Grace and Katherine's return, please call."

"And now, we bring you 'Smoke Over Fire,' the interview."

Hannah visibly twitched. *Smoke over Fire?*

"Hannah, thank you for agreeing to do this." Barbara mustered up a friendly smile. "If you remember, we met several years ago when you were just a child."

"Yes, I remember."

"I am so sorry that when we meet again, it is under these circumstances."

"As am I."

"We have limited time, so we should get right to it. How are you holding up these days?"

Barbara was good, Hannah mused. After all of the things she had said about her, night after night claiming that the whole thing would turn out to be a scam, she looked at Hannah with genuine concern.

"I'm operating on a single track, one purpose. Every day, I wake up and try to figure out what I can do to find Grace and Katherine. I look for anything I haven't thought of or tried before. No matter how crazy it seems."

"Hence this interview." Barbara leaned forward and put her hand on top of Hannah's. "And I know what people are saying, that I shouldn't do this because I have questioned what happened, but I promise I am here because I knew it would bring attention that might bring these girls home." She turned towards the camera. "America must not rest until the girls are found and the important questions can get answered."

"Right." Hannah startled as if she remembered something, pulled her hand away and sat up. "There's one other thing I'd like to mention."

"Please."

"I currently have a little over three million in liquid assets. That's all the cash I have. I mean, I'm pretty sure I have more in stocks but I don't manage that and..." Randall reached over and touched Hannah's shoulder, bringing her back to the script. "I guess I'm getting off track. My attorney says I have three million that's accessible." She took a breath. "If somebody calls with information leading me to Grace and Katherine, I will happily turn that money over."

"You're offering a personally funded three-million-dollar reward?"

"Yes."

"Has a ransom demand been made?"

Hannah frowned. "No."

"That's unusual."

Hannah clasped her hands in her lap. "From where I sit, there's nothing about this that is usual."

Barbara held up a hand. "Not that you'd offer a reward, I expected that. And I would pray it spurs someone into making that call, even if they've seen something they're unsure of. What's unusual is the amount, and that it's entirely personally funded. How did you end up with that kind of money? Will that wipe you out financially?"

Randall interjected, "This generous reward is being offered, I think that's all that needs to be said about the subject."

"I'm sorry, I was just getting into the questions that people have about money. It's noble to offer your personal fortune and many parents would understand why."

"If Grace and Katherine are found alive I would hand over every cent I have without a moment's hesitation."

Barbara nodded. "And the lack of a ransom demand seems so strange."

Hannah observed it took longer for a pot of water to boil than it did for

Barbara to go from being occupied by the kidnapping to being distracted by dollar signs and zeros.

"If you need me to say out loud that I won't be paying myself the money because I didn't have anything to do with their disappearance, then, there. I said it."

"Alright." Barbara's palms went up in surrender. "But the psychic business has been good to you."

"No." Hannah shook her head. "The people have been good, but not the business, not if that's what led to this."

"Of course." Barbara sat back and smiled, and Hannah could see the questions she was loading into her Uzi. Her eyes sparkled with the bullets, but she held back.

"I know we have video of Grace and Katherine?" She pointed to someone off camera. "Why don't you go ahead and roll that."

Hannah knew they were cutting to a montage that would include melancholy music and Barbara's voice stating the facts of the case. It was a standard formula in television.

Someone from Barbara's team came over and pulled her out of her chair. Hannah and Randall exchanged a concerned look. There weren't supposed to be any breaks, and this video was only about thirty seconds.

She returned, with just half a second to spare. "Now," she said tapping her notecards on her knee, "I'm going to have to ask about some unpleasant things."

"That's fine."

"There have been questions and accusations about your career, and the timing of all of this."

"There have, but they don't concern me."

"They don't?"

"Think what you like. That I'm a scammer who would try to weasel money out of people facing the worst tragedy imaginable. That I would put my child and nanny in real danger to sell some lousy books. Go ahead and think that I would hurt my baby to make a buck when I have so many in the bank. As long as people call that number if they know something, I don't care."

Barbara switched gears. "Did you have difficulties after having Grace?"

"Difficulties?"

"Issues with exhaustion, depression, dark thoughts?"

"No."

"Because it's very common and—"

"Having a child for the first time is difficult, yes. But I was fortunate in that I didn't suffer from anything more serious than fatigue, emotional and physical. I certainly didn't suffer from anything that would make a baby disappear."

"Over the video break, we got some news. I wish I could say it was regarding Grace or Katherine, but it is regarding another missing person. Does the name Travis Brown mean anything to you?"

Hannah searched her memory. "I don't know."

"Travis Brown, a seven-year-old boy who went missing in Springfield, Missouri, four years ago?"

"Possibly. You have to realize, I get calls about missing people all the time. It's not that they don't matter, but over time I can get them confused."

Most viewers would have missed it, but Hannah caught the threat of a smile that crossed Barbara's lips. "Get your wires crossed, you could say?"

"I guess. What does this have to do with Grace?"

"Travis's mother just got ahold of our production team. She said she sought you out for help about a year after his disappearance."

"That's possible, but I don't recall."

"She said you spoke to her."

Hannah's brow furrowed.

"Are you saying she didn't?"

"I'm saying I don't know."

"Well," Barbara unfolded a paper of hastily scribbled notes, "she says that you told her Travis was dead. That you said he was a smart little boy and that he would call his mother if he could."

"I'm sure he was a smart little boy, but that doesn't mean I said any of that."

"One year after that chat," Barbara reported it as fact, "Travis was found—alive. Alive and, thankfully, well."

Hannah exhaled. "That's wonderful. I wish that for everyone with a missing child."

"That's not all."

"It's not?"

"No. She said that she approached you at an appearance after he was found and that in front of an audience you said you got your wires crossed."

Hannah grimaced. "That doesn't sound right."

"Are you saying this mother is a liar?"

"I'm saying that doesn't sound like something I'd say."

"Well, I'm pretty sure you just said it to us moments ago. And she says she has video proof and that she's sending it to our network."

Hannah stared for a minute. "I couldn't care less. I'm just happy her son was found." Her breath hitched, "Whole."

"This woman," Barbara tapped her notes, "is saying that you said *you had your wires crossed*, that you must have confused him for another kid, no big deal. Like you accidentally picked the wrong shoes out of your closet that morning. Does that happen a lot? Can signals get crossed like that?"

Randall popped out of his chair and came on camera, tripping on a wire in the process. "We're here to talk about finding Grace and Katherine, not whether Hannah's career is to yours or anyone else's satisfaction. It is best to move on to the details that may help us find them."

Barbara tilted her head like she didn't quite buy it. "Here's a quote for you, Mr. Newman. It's from Hannah herself. From three years ago, being interviewed by *People Magazine*. She said she preferred lighter work and that she'd had arguments with her manager over not wanting to take on missing-person cases."

"And what of it?" Randall asked.

Barbara smiled. "Oh, I'm not finished. Hannah mentioned something interesting her manager had said. She told the magazine, and I quote, that he said, 'Well, shit, Hannah, we're going to go broke if you keep turning down work. Then again, you could have your own baby, have it kidnapped, and we could all live off of that forever. Imagine the money!'"

Barbara put down her notes and looked at Hannah. "So frankly, the questions about your wealth in connection to what has happened seem fair, since you laid out this very scenario without prompting."

"Oh my God." Hannah was talking to herself, momentarily forgetting she was on camera. "I remember that."

"You remember?" Barbara put her hands up. "The interview? The statement? That you publicly acknowledged the idea of this scam before Grace was even born?"

Randall put his hand up, stopping Hannah from answering. Hannah touched his hand softly, silently communicating for him to back down.

Barbara wasn't finished. "If there's one thing you *do* know, it's how to sell books. Hannah, it was announced by your publisher that the book release would be delayed, possibly scrapped altogether."

"Of course." Inside, Hannah held on. Praying the kidnapper was getting what he wanted. That this would end it. "I haven't thought about it, but I'd imagine it doesn't get released at all."

"But there is the matter of the presales, and due to the volume of them, your publisher last night made the decision to move forward with the book."

Hannah looked at Randall in surprise. "Can they do that?"

He opened his mouth to answer, but Barbara interrupted. "Before the incident on *The Judy Show*, your book had a presale number that may as well have been zero. In the few days since this occurred, Hannah, do you know how many people trotted off to their local bookstore and plunked down their money, to guarantee they get a copy?"

"No," Hannah choked out.

"One point four million. That's not just a record, that's unheard of."

Randall gritted his teeth and grabbed Hannah's arm. "I think we're done here."

"No, no, no, I apologize," Barbara said with a smirk that was anything but apologetic. "This is about Grace. I'm just trying to address the questions people have. Is this the tragedy we've been led to believe it is, or is it a carefully choreographed money-grab, with Grace and Katherine waiting it out safely in a secret location?"

Hannah was barely keeping it together now, quiet tears streamed down her face. "Whether people think I'm psychic or not isn't important. Grace is missing and—"

"What about those who say you know exactly where they are, and you are waiting until the book money drops in your account to *find* them?"

Hannah had been thrown into a spin cycle and gripped the arms of her chair to push herself up. She gritted her teeth. "Get out of my house."

"One more thing, Hannah, if you please. Will you read me?"

"Lady, you have a Hell of a lot of—" Randall started to say, but Hannah held her hand up and sat back down across from her.

"You want me to give you a psychic reading, right now? You think that's appropriate?"

"If accurate and specific, it could generate a lot of sympathy. Maybe the world was wrong in its horrible accusations against you. Maybe someone who knows something is holding back because they hate you, and maybe that could change their mind."

"Sure."

Randall ripped off his mike and covered Hannah's as he whispered into her ear, "As your lawyer I'm begging you not to fall into her trap."

"Hannah?" Barbara asked hopefully.

"Yes. I'm sorry, Randall, I'll need you to step aside, or you'll mess with my concentration." Hannah couldn't work if Randall was lurking over her shoulder with constant grunts and disapproving stares.

"I must admit this is very exciting," Barbara said. "Except for some crystal ball reader at a carnival when I was nine, I've never been to a real psychic."

"So glad you could pick such an appropriate moment," Hannah replied, hoping someone among the millions watching was fluent in sarcasm and shared her anger.

"Do we need tarot cards, or crystals, or a pyramid, or..."

"I need you to be quiet."

"Oh. Okay." She sulked.

Hannah sat back and closed her eyes. She didn't need to do this, but the longer she sat there quietly the more she could sense Barbara squirming in her seat like she had ants in her pants. The more childish she looked the better.

Hannah opened her eyes and let out a long sigh. She looked at the floor as if she was uncomfortable about something, then gave Barbara a frown.

"Well?"

"I think it's best if we just show their photo again with the number. Please." Hannah's eyes begged the camera. "Three million to anyone who helps bring our girls home."

Barbara's jaw dropped. "What about my reading?"

Hannah held up a picture of Grace and Katherine. "This was taken a week before they disappeared. If you've got Grace and you're taking care of her, she loves those little puffs they make for toddlers that melt to prevent choking. Be careful if you put anything in her hair, like a bow or something, she puts them in her mouth and she almost choked on one once."

Barbara sat back in her chair with her arms crossed, a smarmy satisfied smile plastered across her face, but Hannah pushed on. "Most toddlers her age like milk, but Grace doesn't. I get her these kids' yogurts that don't have a lot of sugar. Thankfully she doesn't have any allergies or medical conditions, so taking care of her is pretty easy. So please take care of her. And please reach out to me. I will do whatever it takes to get her back."

"There is a number on the bottom of our screen." Barbara attempted to regain control.

"Yes, there is. But you found a way to reach out to me before and I'm sure you can do it again. Three million dollars cash if I get them back."

"You're offering the money to the kidnapper?"

"I want Grace and Katherine." Hannah kept her eyes on the camera, Barbara nothing more than a buzzing fly now. "It doesn't matter if it takes money to get them, and I'm not concerned with whom it goes to." She stood up.

Barbara nodded. "You need a break? We can go to commercial."

"No. I'm finished. I said all I needed to say." Hannah looked for the clip to remove her microphone. "You can finish up here, then I'm sure you can see your way out. Randall, you'll oversee that for me, please?" He nodded in agreement.

"You don't want to discuss how you couldn't give me a reading?"

Hannah paused. "I didn't say I couldn't, I said it was best that we don't."

"Don't be silly, Hannah. Of course, a reading will help. People will stay tuned in." She clutched at Hannah's skirt to stop her from taking another step. "Every minute they stay tuned in is another minute that somebody could remember something and call in an important tip." Her eyes blazed at the opportunity to finally expose the fraud to the world. That's why she didn't look worried when Hannah sat down and said, "Yes, I guess maybe you're right."

"Excellent." She smiled.

A calm came over Hannah, the likes of which she hadn't felt in days, and she had been through a lifetime in those days. "I want to thank you for agreeing to this."

"Of course."

"A rule in my line of work is to keep things positive, so I need to thank you, because I don't think this will be pleasant." Hannah closed her eyes again. But slowly, slow enough that she caught the look of worry that came across Barbara's face.

"I'm sorry, I don't understand."

"Being a psychic is ultimately running a business." Hannah was in her own world now, with the voices that lived in her head. Barbara felt far away, like she was trying to talk to her from underwater. "I know you're very concerned with my business, so it's fair you should know how it works. In my business, you don't want to share anything bad. Making people feel bad is bad for business." Hannah opened her eyes and stared into Barbara's. "When I locked into you, it was not good."

Her face tightened up, "Oh, well that's a surpri—"

"I got the sense of the spirit of someone who died rather young around you. Her name begins with an E. I can't hear her, but as she mouths the name I can see it starts with an E."

Barbara shifted as if her seat suddenly grew several uncomfortable lumps. Hannah knew she was stalling to gather her thoughts. "Yes. I lost my sister Ellen when she was four years old. We were both children. But that's no secret."

"Hmmm. Right. I can see her, fair and small." Hannah's eyes stayed closed, and a small smile formed on her lips. "She's got this thin hair that gets picked up by the slightest breeze. It's like all of her might get picked up like a kite. But her stare," Hannah's closed eyes squinted, "is heavy. She's got her eyes grabbing into mine, like I need to pay attention."

"Is she speaking to you?"

"No. She's showing. She's showing me her pillow. Her face has turned angry and she's holding the pillow in both hands like this at me." Hannah kept her eyes closed, putting her balled-up fists straight out in front of her.

Barbara's pancake makeup face couldn't hide the ten shades of green she turned. She held her hand up to her mouth as if she were about to vomit. "I don't, I can't." Tears started to make her eyes shine, but they didn't spill over. This being national TV, she was trying to maintain her composure. But Hannah had been doing this long enough to know that she would have bolted had the cameras not been running.

"She's tearing that pillow into pieces now, stuffing them into her mouth, feathers are floating around her."

"I think you were right, I don't want this reading." Barbara removed her mike and was waving to the camera to cut to commercial.

Tears carved lines in the makeup on Hannah's face. "She's covered in them now. The feathers of the pillow stuffing. And her eyes," Hannah's voice wavered, "she's staring at me so hard through those," a trembling hand covered her mouth, "feathers. Those feathers are choking her."

"No more, please—"

"She's crying."

"Ellen, stop!"

"It's figurative. They communicate this way, Barbara. But she wants me to tell you her tears are red, like blood. She said you will know what that means."

"We, uh," the director stepped forward, "we just cut to commercial."

"When?" Barbara asked hopefully.

"Right when I said we cut to commercial."

Barbara knocked over her chair and went toe to toe with him. She wobbled in her heels and wiped the snot off her face with the back of her hand. "The next time I say go to commercial, you go to a fucking commercial right fucking then you fucking understand?"

"What the Hell just happened? What's that smell?" A network executive stumbled in and sniffed. "It smells like the air after lightning strikes..." He snapped his fingers, trying to summon the word.

"It's ozone," Hannah said flatly. Tom brought her a box of tissues to clean herself up.

Barbara turned around like she just remembered Hannah was there. "I don't know what you just did..."

"I did what you asked."

"...but I'll figure it out."

"Be careful what you wish for," Hannah replied, all too familiar with that bit of truth.

Chapter Thirty-Three

Asha dropped her pen, shaking her head to clear it. "What do you mean it was a setup?"

"It had been over a week, Asha. A *week*. Think about it. No demands, no contact. At that point, Rick and I weren't the only desperate ones." Hannah was bent over the fireplace, adjusting logs to stir up the flames. Satisfied, she put the poker down. "Not that he agreed with my methodology."

"Lots of relationships don't survive something so awful..." she started.

Hannah held up her hand. "Lots of relationships don't survive lying either, and we can argue over the reasons but that's not going to change the fact that I did lie to him and it was another broken link of trust. The FBI were certain that whoever took them was waiting for something, some kind of public spectacle." Hannah continued, returning to her seat. "And we gave them one. That story about the mother claiming I was wrong about her son? That was planted. The kidnapping was real, but part of a custody dispute. The mother was a psychologist who worked in law enforcement, so when she was approached to be part of the act, she agreed. It was real enough that anyone who gave it a quick glance would find that there had been a young boy named Travis that had been missing, but they would not have had time to verify if the mother and I had been in any kind of contact." Hannah shrugged. "Barbara wasn't going to wait to confirm the video of me saying—what was it, something about getting my wires crossed? We timed that tip perfectly, banking that she wasn't about to check the source before she reported it live on air, and we were right."

Guess I'm not the only reporter who isn't meticulous with sources? Asha stared at the table as their plan came together in front of her. "So, the idea was if you were publicly humiliated, maybe the kidnapper would reach out."

"Exactly. There were countless journalists we could have chosen, ones who at least tried to act like they didn't believe I had anything to do with this, but it was decided that it would be more effective if the interviewer was likely to turn combative, which," Hannah sat up straighter, "she did in record time. Barbara Silver wasn't wrong when she painted me as a liar in that interview, what she got wrong was what I was lying about."

"What about the reading?" Asha asked.

Hannah didn't answer.

"Was that a setup too?"

Hannah struggled with something internal while the silence ballooned between them.

"I imagine there were a lot of questions about Barbara and her sister after that." Asha probed.

Hannah sucked in a deep breath. "She retired shortly after. She was getting to an age that people wouldn't question it anyway, but I can tell you she was the type who would have worked until she dropped dead if she could. As far as what happened, she said nothing more than what came out on the original broadcast—that she lost a sister when she was young and didn't want to talk about it because it was too painful."

"But that story..."

"The Silvers were an influential family. Johnathon Silver owned a paper mill, the largest one in the United States. It's not a stretch to imagine a parent using his influence to protect his family from a dark incident."

"And how did you know about it?"

"If you're asking if I had Rick do some digging..." Hannah trailed off.

Asha nodded.

"I guess I have to admit that yes, I did. I told him to dig up whatever he could find about her."

"Blackmail?"

"Maybe emotional blackmail. I said I was going to try to appeal to her humanity. Sort of a, imagine if your family were treated the way you are treating mine." She folded her hands on the table. "At least that's what I had to tell him because I knew he would not like what I really planned to do with whatever he brought me."

Asha looked at her notepad where she was sorting the truth from the lies. "You came up with the reading thing on your own?"

Hannah scoffed. "Barbara Silver was part of the problem, seeing that she was only making me more famous. That crazy number of presales? I'd bet that can be directly traced back to her constant coverage of me. But if we both came out of this looking bad, maybe that would be impactful. So," she shrugged "when I learned about their deep, dark family secret I dug up that ghost."

Asha scribbled down *Barbara never stood a chance*. "It sounds like you accomplished that for certain."

"What about you?"

Asha looked up. "What about me?"

"Have you ever had a feeling, like the one that I gave Barbara?"

"What?"

"Because if you have..."

"I haven't." Asha bristled.

Hannah persisted. "I'm just saying if you had, it's not something you should let affect you. You can ignore it."

"Why does any of this matter?" Asha burst out.

"It doesn't. My point was everyone has had an unexplained feeling or experience, that doesn't make what someone like me does more or less real. But just the feeling makes it easier for people to believe. Asha, I'm not trying to trick you."

Hannah flopped back in her chair. "Look, I cheated. Every time Barbara Silver thought she was getting the best of me, she was doing exactly what I wanted her to. And I would do it again. So, make sure you write *that* down."

Asha startled and looked up, and Hannah went on, determined.

"Because before you decide what I did to her was a low blow by dragging her dead sister into this mess, remember we are talking about someone using my child's and Katherine's lives to get ratings. Maybe she thought she was right. Maybe she really believed I had something to do with this, but she damn-well didn't know for certain, she couldn't have, and I wasn't about to let something like being the better human being stop me from getting Grace and Katherine out of that situation if I could."

Asha took in the heat coming off Hannah. "So, the reading, the pillow..."

Hannah nodded.

"Wow. Rick's digging was very thorough."

"It helped tremendously." Her voice dropped down to a whisper. "And when I'm feeling particularly low, I guess that's when I can acknowledge that at least some part of me wanted to break her because I was broken. I wanted someone to hurt as much as I did."

"But you did feel justified."

"Yes." Hannah wiped her eyes. "Everything she did was in the name of ratings. She was mean for a logical reason, so even if it wasn't a good or moral one, I guess I think that's better than no reason at all. Barbara Silver, in all likelihood, was making a career move out of asking the questions that others had but were too polite to ask to my face."

Hannah sighed and dropped her hand. "We both had our reasons. I like to feel mine were less shitty. But there was one thing that she surprised me with that day..." Hanna hesitated.

"What?"

"That quote? The one where I said I could make a lot of money if my own baby were kidnapped? That was real. I had said that a few years before. I had forgotten," she held her hand out, "but I had said it."

"Oh." Asha tried to look indifferent while she fought a sudden wave of nausea.

Chapter Thirty-Four

"Rewind it." Hannah's heart was racing. Three days after the interview with Barbara Silver, they finally had something. "I want to see it again."

Rick's eyes were glued to the screen as he hit the button. They didn't have them back, but now they had hope, or something hope-adjacent.

"It's not the best quality picture," Tom said as they sardined together in front of Hannah's TV, trying to see through the snowstorm on the screen. "We've got people working on it. Image enhancement will help."

"Hopefully he's got a tattoo or something unusual we'll see," Rick murmured. "Dammit. He's not showing us his face."

"No, he won't." Hannah bent down for a closer look. "I'm getting him now." Hannah's fists trembled in front of her. "After all this time I'm starting to finally *get* him. We're not going to see anything this guy doesn't want us to see."

She placed her fingertips on the outline of the man on the screen, obscured by the fuzzy haze that pointed to a security tape that had been recorded on over and over again. "It's *him*. He's not about to throw all that planning away." Hannah leaned in even closer and murmured to the screen. "But we gave you something and you can't help yourself. You had to respond." She stood up straight and let her hands slap against her legs.

Rick shook his head, "Hannah, we don't know that for sure."

"I do. That I do know for sure. I don't know if he was able to sort it all out, but if he didn't, it's not going to be because he's stupid."

Rick peeled his eyes away from the video and looked up at her. "Or maybe this was the plan all along, Hannah. We don't know."

Hannah's lips sealed shut in a tight line for just a moment, not wanting to fight about the interview yet again. "But he does know we were trying to get a rise out of him and this is his answer. What is he trying to tell us?" Hannah exhaled and turned away. She needed to think.

Randall cursed and slapped the side of the television. "What is it with convenience stores anyway? They're a hotbed of criminal activity, but none of them want to install a video camera that can take a decent picture. You'd think this was new technology or something."

Hannah kept her back to them. *What is he trying to tell me?* She knew it was there. This wasn't going to be him just coming up for air. There was a message and he expected Hannah to get it.

"Nobody thinks something bad will happen to them. Not actually happen to *them*." This was a painful truth she knew too well now. "So, they do their due diligence. They set the camera up and then the tape gets reused a million times without replacing it because nothing happens, while the image quality gets worse and worse." She let out a frustrated huff and turned back towards the screen with her hands on her hips. "I'd say we were lucky that they even had a recording at all, but no." She shook her head and pointed. "He knew it would be recording. He *knew*."

"Maybe not," a voice from the doorway said. They looked up to see a man that Hannah had a vague recollection of, someone who worked with the lab technicians. "It appears he left something else, perhaps a just in case the cameras weren't working item?"

"What did you find?" Tom asked, his voice climbing in hope.

"A fingerprint?" Randall asked, pointing back at the screen. "His hands are bare."

"A fingerprint in a convenience store? Sir, we'll find a lot of them. In a place that busy we can expect some criminal hits, but whether or not they'll be related to Hannah will take some time to sort out." He stepped forward, and Hannah eyed the plastic evidence bag in his hand. Her words caught in her throat when she realized it was the backside of a polaroid picture. "Ms. Smoke? Can you tell us if this is Grace?"

He held the bag out to her and everyone in the room fell away. She hesitated, afraid that it would be Grace and afraid that it wouldn't. The plastic felt slick in her hand. Her eyes fell to see a close-up of her daughter.

Alive.

Grace's eyes were closed, but the color of her skin didn't look alarming. An arm gripped around Grace's midsection and Hannah smiled. The slight flex of muscle told her that arm was also living and the freckles on that arm belonged to Katherine.

They were alive. They were still alive.

And he wanted Hannah to know it. That's what he's telling her. Whatever it is that he wants, she's getting closer to delivering it.

There was still time to fix it.

Hannah and Rick collapsed together in a heap of joy and despair.

Chapter Thirty-Five

Despite having no sense of time, Katherine knew enough now that she could make decisions. She could decide to eat or drink what was available sparingly and at well-spaced intervals that allowed her some semblance of coherence. Sometimes she was successful at timing this right, sometimes she wasn't. But the ember that burned reminded her to stay angry and stay careful, because sometimes the drugs had the effect of making her think things were okay when they were anything but.

Once, she had a particularly good stretch where her brain was functioning well enough that it was time to work on a plan, since chained-up people don't live to tell the tale unless they are found.

And she knew, in a way that Hannah would know, a way that she couldn't explain, that they wouldn't be found by sitting there. That wherever *there* was, it may as well be nowhere and Katherine would have to do the rescuing for both of them.

In her intermediate school, they had watched a video about self-defense. In it, Katherine learned that you never let anyone take you to the second location, but she had.

Just like Miranda echoed in her head.

Even if her memory of it was hazy, somehow she knew winding up here was her fault. So, she would have to take on the rescue mission, because she had gotten them into this mess. She would get them out of here and beg Hannah to forgive her. She prayed she would understand that Katherine could never have foreseen, even if she should have, that the mysterious man that had shown an interest in her—the mysterious man she had actually given up on—was mysterious for a reason.

Katherine considered the toilet in the corner of the dusky room. She had the idea at one point of drinking that water as it wasn't likely drugged, but knew she was being observed, so that wouldn't work. Smashing him over the head with the heavy porcelain lid would be not only brilliant but also satisfying, except again, her waiting behind the door with it poised in the air could easily be spotted by the eye in the sky.

A small ray of hope broke through the fog later when, while pulling herself upright and using the metal bedframe for support, she felt it move.

It. Moved.

It was slight, but she felt the metal bars shift in the concrete floor, heard the low sound of a few grains crunching against the metal. She wasn't shackled to this end. The chain was attached to the foot of the bedframe. But this front end had moved, she was sure of it. She moved her hand along the metal, attempting to pull herself upright, hoping the eye in the sky would think that was all she was doing.

She felt it again, the slight shift of metal in concrete, and gasped out loud when she ran her hand over the circle.

She could make out the top of a Phillips head screw, loose inside the bedframe. It took some time, but eventually her mind worked out the puzzle. That the screw was the weak point, allowing some movement between two metal pieces. She knew it hadn't been that way when they were first dumped here, he would have made sure of that. Her constant pushing and pulling on this end likely created that weak spot. The bed couldn't be pulled out of the concrete, but it could be disassembled within it.

Katherine's ember broke out into a full-on bonfire in her mind's eye, so bright it hurt to look at it.

She listened as it told her—using the voice of her primary school teacher, Mrs. MacCarthy—what she needed to do. It answered all of her questions and helped her scrape together some hope. *Because poppet, he may be a monster, but the monster is of a man, and that means you can fight*, the flames told her. *You won't win, but you can fight.*

The baby stirred, and Katherine was grateful to be conscious to take care of, she couldn't remember the name, just *her*. She felt the grit on her hands as she wiped tears off her face and made the silent promise to *her* that she would do whatever was necessary so that they wouldn't be taken again alive. Taken, maybe, but not alive.

Chapter Thirty-Six

Katherine froze as she heard the key tumbling in the lock and it took her inner Mrs. MacCarthy bonfire to scream *Don't do it, don't you move your hand away from the screw* to keep her from panicking. *He'll notice if you move it and then he'll know you were faking sleeping and then you'll be found out. Katherine. Listen to me.* The fire grew with every syllable, as if being fed by oxygenated breath and not her imagination. Katherine could feel the anger in the flames, spittle from the fire singeing her as it shouted commands.

Now you listen to me, Katherine Willard. You keep calm and relax that hand, but leave it exactly where it is. Because the eye in the sky would notice that your hand moved as he opened the door, and that will arouse suspicion.

And she did. Katherine left her hand over the part where two bars were connected by what she hoped was a long screw and relaxed it. *There you go, darling,* the flames said. *Now, my little drugged-up teapot, it's naptime for you. And you know those who don't stay very still during naptime don't get their playtime. I'll be watching.*

The door opened and Katherine was back in primary school, pretending to nap so she would be allowed out for play later.

Nothing happened. Usually, there was the sound of items being moved about, or he would come close to observe them, close enough that Katherine could hear him breathing, but this time the silence that followed the open door pounded in her ears.

She couldn't help but scream when the loud bang and bright flash filled the room.

Chapter Thirty-Seven

"Tonight, on Network of the Americas, an explosive development in the Grace Smoke and Katherine Willard case. The FBI and police are looking for the man seen in this security footage. What you are seeing was recorded in West Virginia about twelve hours ago. The man, who never shows his face directly to the camera, used a credit card linked to Katherine Willard. For more on this story, we are taking you now to Bob Matthews, who is live at the Fill n' Sip convenience store, in Martinsburg, West Virginia. Bob, what can you tell us about what happened?"

"Thank you, Gretchen. This situation is developing by the minute. As you stated, what got the attention of the FBI was the use of Katherine Willard's credit card. Now, we're also hearing reports of another piece of evidence that may have been purposefully left behind by whoever made this purchase, which we have been told was indeed diapers. In the meantime, I am here with Ryan Jacobs, the young man who was working at the time of this event. Thank you for speaking with us, Ryan. I'm sure all this excitement was not what you expected when you came to work today. What can you tell us?"

"Oh, well, I just came in and it was like every other day." Ryan laughed and dragged his foot on the ground, kicking up dust. "Maybe even a little boring, you know? And that guy, well, he seemed normal." He shrugged. "I kinda forgot about him before he even left. But I'll never forget seeing those patrol cars come screeching into the lot and bouncing over the curb. I thought, oh, shi—I mean, oh, no—because I thought maybe I'd tripped the silent police alarm by accident. Then these guys in suits swarm the place, and, uh, it's just me, you know. I told them I had to call my boss and stuff, but they were already all over everything, looking for the security video and whatnot."

"Did he say anything to you?"

"The guy? He just asked where the diapers were when he walked in. That was about it."

"What about his appearance? Can you tell us what he looked like? Maybe something that stood out?"

Ryan exhaled. "Like I said, he was just normal. Looked like every other guy that comes in here. But if the cameras were working like my boss promised they did the police should have something."

"Do you know anything about what else investigators might have found in there? We've had some reports that he may have left something else."

"Man, they didn't tell me jack shi—sorry. They didn't tell me anything. Not that I think they should—I respect the law and it's an investigation." He puffed up his chest. "I was thinking maybe someday I can be in law enforcement, or the military, something like that. But they didn't tell me about what they found unless they had a question about it. You think they're gonna find those people?"

Bob paused, not used to being the one answering questions. "I know we're all praying they do."

Ryan nodded in agreement. "Be an awful shame with so many looking for them if they aren't found, or they ended up dead or somethin."

Chapter Thirty-Eight

The time had come to cheat and lie. Cheats and lies were what he wanted. Hannah wasn't tricking him, she knew that now. He was in on the deception with her, and he needed more deception from Hannah the way people need oxygen.

"As your lawyer, I can't believe I agreed to this." Randall broke into Hannah's thoughts. When another gust threatened to turn his umbrella inside out, he grabbed at the edge of it and winced, looking up at the dark threat of the sky. "And it's not that I don't understand the hurry, I'd stand in a monsoon with you if necessary. But if we just wait an hour this weather is going to clear up and—"

Hannah shot him a look and he shut up. "I promise you won't melt, Randall."

"Will *you*?" He met her gaze directly. "Why is it that I think there's more happening here, Hannah? Ever since that photo you've gone silent. That doesn't make the job of protecting you very easy."

She looked out over the rolling hills of Pennsylvania in deep thought and squeezed her fist around the contraband in her pocket. The way the sharp edges of it pressed into her palm was comforting.

"I'm not a normal client. That's something you have to decide if you're okay with. Even if Grace and Katherine are delivered to me 100% fine today, I will never be a normal client, Randall." She turned her face to him. "So, you will have to decide for yourself if you're comfortable with that or not."

She felt tears threaten to spill and hoped the rain would hurry up and disguise them. She would never again be a normal client, daughter, girlfriend, or mother. Her own mother had made that clear about an hour before.

Joanne's hand had shot out as Hannah was preparing to leave, almost pulling Hannah off her feet as she dragged her into the guest room. "Are you sure about this?"

"Mom! What the hell?" Hannah caught her balance before she fell over. "I can smell you've been smoking in here."

"Nevermind that. I want you to consider what you're doing, because after this you're not going to have Rick to comfort you anymore."

Hannah sighed. "You don't even like Rick."

"He's grown on me." Joanne shrugged. "But he's about a hot second from leaving for good if you go and pull another stunt behind his back."

"I don't know what..."

"You damn-well do know what I'm talking about. I may not know what but I know you are up to something, mothers always know." She pulled out a cigarette and lit it in front of Hannah. "What mothers also know is a man can only take so much." She paused to exhale out a plume of smoke. "Even the most loyal of dogs will stop heeling if all you do is rub its nose in shit every time you call."

Hannah sat on the bed.

Joanne sat beside her and held out the cigarette. "It's going to be bad, isn't it?"

"Yes." Hannah took it.

"You want me to stay?"

Hannah looked at her mother, seeing the years on her face for the first time, and took a small drag. "Yes."

Joanne gave a sad smile and took the cigarette back. "Then go on, I'll be here when you get back."

"How long do I have to decide?" Randall's question snapped Hannah back to the present.

"Not long." She turned her face back towards the fields below, where everyone was waiting for the signal. "Whatever happens next, you have no comment. You will not mount a defense of me, you will not scream about my innocence for all to hear."

"You don't understand what you're asking. Hannah, you're asking me to treat you like I think you've done something."

"I have," she murmured and left Randall behind, him looking after her, worry and confusion fighting for top billing on his face.

The wind whipped around her, lifting her hair and raincoat, making her part of the threatening storm while everyone else tried to cower away from its wrath. At the same time, she rose above it, as if she were built for another layer of the atmosphere. The rain and wind were doing their best to let the earthly beings below—the circus of agents and cadaver dogs—know they weren't welcome. Hannah wondered briefly if it would all disappear when they crossed back into Jersey.

Tom gave the signal from below and she felt a twinge of regret for having deceived so many people who had worked so hard, who only wanted to help.

She closed her umbrella and stood in the wind, letting the first raindrops overtake her hair and clothes. During Hannah's psychic fair days, there had been these spiritual dancers that were supposed to help summon spirits if you were having trouble getting the information you needed. Hannah needed something like that, some odd gestures that indicated she was up to something, but not quite as dramatic. Hannah slowly spread her arms out wide and let her head fall back to look at the heavens, inviting the spirit world and the flashbulbs in. *Time to deviate from the plan.*

Chapter Thirty-Nine

Forty-eight hours later, Rick stormed out of Hannah's front door for the last time. Where she saw opportunity, he saw Hannah getting Grace killed, and there was no middle ground between those two warring ideas.

That was why it was only Randall and his not normal client that sat across from each other at a heavy steel gray table, the silence between them echoing around the barren walls. They both would have preferred the smell of coffee and baked goods that dominated Hannah's home to the stale sweat and cold steel that bounced between the cinderblocks of the local jail. Randall leaned back and glared at Hannah, who answered his unspoken question by jiggling the chain that had her handcuffed to the floor.

The door swung open and Tom took both of them in—Randall looking like a disappointed father and Hannah looking as she had since her arrest, like a miserable Mona Lisa, unwilling to give up her secret.

"I, for one," he said as he took the chair next to Randall, "need an answer to this question, who the hell is this?" He pulled out a plastic bag and placed it on the table carefully, as if the contents were still of a living breathing person that might feel the gesture.

Hannah looked at the fragile vertebrae in the bag and Randall let out a long, slow breath.

"Why did you do this, Hannah?" he asked.

Hannah looked away and refused to answer questions.

Chapter Forty

Asha shook her head and held out her palm. "Clearly you didn't murder anybody, because we're sitting in your kitchen and not some penitentiary."

Hannah gazed out on the weakening daylight. "Once he responded so strongly to that interview and I knew they were alive, I also knew he wanted more. It's not like I was the only one who could figure that out, the behaviorists knew it too. They were the ones who came up with the plan to take it further, to stage a crime scene search. They said it should be a big one, complete with cadaver dogs and a mobile crime lab. The scene should be unrelated to this case, but it would be leaked that I was there to assist in the search efforts."

Hannah's eyes were somber. "Assist, as in psychic assistance. As in I was working again."

"Oh." Asha frowned. "That sounds..."

"Disgusting." Hannah interjected. "That was the intent. The tip was designed to look like an accident, an officer letting my name slip over one of those not quite secure radio transmissions. Not to mention that any blacked-out SUV that left my property was followed, so leading them there would be no problem. The FBI set up lookout, and Tom and I established a signal so I would know when press had been spotted and I could act, I don't know, I guess extra psychic so the paps could capture it on film and create a shitstorm."

Asha scribbled, trying to map all of this out in a diagram. "This sounds like a lot of moving parts, so I imagine they expected there would be a payoff."

"That photo." Hannah's voice fell to a whisper. "They were alive. You can't imagine how it felt to know that."

She took a deep breath, collected herself and went on. "So, it was decided that if they staged a scene and later made a big public spectacle of how I didn't turn up anything useful, or, even better, gave incorrect information, it could get another rise out of him. The goal was to make us all look like fools, me for being useless and the FBI for being gullible. We hoped that by doing so, we were one step closer to satisfying his need."

"Did they have any idea what he might do in response?"

"No. But every time he stepped out of the shadows to communicate was another opportunity to track him. He was smart, but the more confident people get, the less careful they are. We wanted to lure him out and give ourselves another shot. I'm sure he knew that, but if it fulfilled the need, it wouldn't matter. He wouldn't be able to help himself."

Asha tapped her pen on her notepad. "You mentioned two deceptions. What was the second?"

Hannah sat up. "Well, I knew him now. He needed me to be in real trouble. He needed it not to be a game anymore. Maybe it was the way he carried himself, his self-righteousness. In his reality, I was the criminal," She shrugged. "But I knew I couldn't tell anyone for this to work, I had to keep that and my other plans to myself."

"Rick?"

"No." Hannah paused for a sip of water. "By that time we had a daily argument about what to do next. At least we did until he watched them slap cuffs on me and that ended all of our arguments."

"Well, what about Randall?" Asha flicked her head towards the driveway, as if he would still be there to save Hannah from a poor choice she made two decades ago. "Did he know?"

"Nobody knew anything. A few years prior, I had been gifted some bones."

Asha grimaced and Hannah shrugged. "I used to get all sorts of weird fan mail. The letter they came with claimed they came from some tribesman in South America. They were believed to have powers—nothing evil, it was intended for good luck." Hannah shook her head. "To be honest, I didn't think they were real, didn't even open the jar to look at them. They just ended up in a pile of other junk. When I finally went through that pile a few months later... It was *oh, shit*." Hannah shook her head. "I realized they were not only real, but if they were human they were the remains of a child. I had put them aside, planning to contact authorities and give them a proper resting place. Something dignified. My plans changed."

"So, no one knew you were going to drop real bones at that staged crime scene?"

"No. And when a few fragments of young skeletal remains were found by the cadaver dogs, no one knew my fingerprints would be on them. No one knew that the search video, which I knew they'd be taking because they wanted to get a record of anyone who showed up, would show me dropping them on the ground. What would you have done?" Hannah surprised Asha with the question. "If you were me?"

Asha wasn't even aware of it when she started doodling on her notepad. She was too busy turning the question over in her head, trying to see it from all of the angles, trying to see if there was something else she should be asking. "I don't know." She started to chew on her lip and forced herself to stop. "I mean it's completely off the rails on one hand, but on the other it was just you and the kidnapper and no one else got that."

Hannah exhaled. "Exactly."

Asha nodded. "I'm not claiming I wouldn't try to talk you out of it, but I also can understand why you had to be the only one who knew the truth, especially if you thought he may have some innate sense of when he was being put-on."

Hannah's shoulders relaxed and she looked on the verge of getting emotional. "That's the best I could hope for—someone to try to understand. It was desperation and desperation makes you do crazy shit you would never consider in a normal life."

"How long were you able to maintain that? To keep the world convinced that you were directly involved?"

"Only three days for law enforcement. This was the one time where all of our resources worked against me—it just so happened that our state lab had a dedicated forensic anthropologist. Damn brilliant woman was able to determine pretty quickly that the bone itself was very old, so while it could have been a female child around Grace's age, this child had died decades ago. They kept me in the county jail and didn't update the press for a few more days. But by then my lie didn't matter. We weren't in the driver's seat anymore."

"Why not? What happened?"

Hannah went to lift her hand from the table and it trembled. She put it back down, covering it with her other hand. "My plan may have worked, but those bones didn't have the good luck promised. They had bad juju all over them."

Chapter Forty-One

If asked, she wouldn't have been able to quantify it, but it had been about twenty-four hours since Katherine had anything to eat or drink from the supply available to her.

One of the drugs had a side effect of making her irrationally thirsty as it left her body, so she did at one-point risk drinking from the toilet while pretending to vomit. He didn't seem to notice.

From the fire, Mrs. MacCarthy instructed her to pretend to eat and drink, keeping her back to the camera as she did. *Doing so will reassure the eye in the sky that nothing is amiss while you make crumbs and water dribbles down your blouse, Dearie.*

The fog was lifting now, with just enough sedative left in her system to keep her from going all-out insane from the thought of what she had to do. And she thought about it constantly. Step by step, action by action, because the fire told her she had to, the fire said she couldn't just wing it. If she winged it, she'd panic, *and panic*, Mrs. MacCarthy was quick to remind her, *would be the death of both of you.*

When the tumbler in the lock finally clicked, Katherine was lying on her side next to the toilet, back to the door, while Gracie dozed on the bed.

She squeezed her fingers together, feeling the pinch from the threads of the three-inch screw that she had hidden there.

Mrs. MacCarthy didn't speak this time, but Katherine felt her eyes boring into her from the flames. Instead of pulsing with her words, they pulsed brighter now with Katherine's heartbeat.

She heard him enter.

The heartbeats pounded so hard she was sure he would hear them.

Get ready, the flames whispered, as if they too believed he could hear what was happening from within.

She felt him standing over her.

She felt the heat of his closeness as he kneeled down behind her.

And when he turned his head to check the wound from where the cuff bit into her ankle, she catapulted her hand around and drove that screw into his neck.

He yelped and there was a crash. The fire exploded and bellowed, *GET UP, KATHERINE.*

Katherine stumbled from the floor, fighting the dizziness that bounced around her senses. Even as the fire was warped by it, it still instructed her. *Get up! There is time to be dizzy later!*

She pulled herself up using the toilet for leverage, as he stumbled up from the avalanche of baby supplies in the corner.

Katherine caught a glimpse of him, just enough to register the look of surprise on his face as she smashed it in with the porcelain top of the toilet tank.

He collapsed to the floor and was still, but Katherine knew she had neither time nor strength to attack again. Her legs were already throbbing after so much inactivity. She grabbed at his belt, feeling for the key that would unlock her chain and hit paydirt.

Unshackled, Katherine's trembling hands picked up Grace and obeyed Mrs. MacCarthy from the fire when she said, "Now, Katherine, you and Grace get the fuck out of there."

Chapter Forty-Two

"I was willing to sit in that jail as long as it took to get the break we were waiting for. Instead, we got heartbreak."

"Was that when...?"

Hannah nodded. "The day after I was released, we got the news that Katherine..." She squeezed her eyes shut. "That her...That she had been found in the water a little over an hour from here." Hannah rushed those last few words out, like she had to say them before she had time to ponder them.

Hannah stood and turned her back to Asha, fumbling through a drawer for something, and Asha suspected she didn't even know what she was looking for. But then Hannah gasped and pulled something out, smiling as she gripped it in her hand.

"I got this for Katherine when she first came to live here with us." She gave a sad chuckle and bit her lip as she held up the coffee mug with The Union Jack, the flag of the U.K. emblazoned across it. "We joked about how we were going to make her one of us, lure her away from proper English tea to crappy coffee."

"Did you?" Asha asked.

"No," Hannah said as she placed the mug on the counter with a soft thud.

"You cared for her."

"Very much." Hannah sniffed.

Asha paused, not wanting to trample Hannah with her next question, but she needed to ask. "After she was found, was there ever any closure on Katherine's involvement?"

Hannah didn't answer right away. Instead, she went into another cabinet and pulled out a small tin.

"She never did drink my coffee, preferred those fancy drinks from cafes when she opted for coffee, but she did drink tea from her mug all the time. This was her tea." Hannah caressed the box like it contained expensive jewelry instead of leaves that had gone stale decades before. "I only mention it because, at times, I've thought, maybe I should send them to her parents." She put the tea down next to the mug. "Not because they were valuable, but because they were hers."

She kept her hand on the counter next to Katherine's treasures and turned her eyes back to Asha. "I didn't. I can't decide if it was because I didn't want to upset them any further, or if it was just because it's my happy piece of her. As to your question, officially, Katherine was never put entirely in the clear. First, there was the missing cousin she had never disclosed. There wasn't a single investigator that felt that was a likely coincidence—it felt to them like potential motive. But there was no one who could speak to her having anger towards anyone except whomever took Miranda, no visits to chat rooms for people angry at psychics or anything else off. Then, there was the matter of a someone, a man." Hannah shook her head. "One American in her nanny group said she thought of it as being like a George Glass situation."

"George Glass?"

Hannah smiled. "*The Brady Bunch*. Jan's made-up boyfriend's name? I'm sorry, it's an American pop culture reference."

"Oh." Asha's eyes darted side to side. "Right. I think that one we had, it just wasn't as big as other American shows."

"When that fisherman, that poor man," Hannah shook her head, "when he found her body..." She trailed off, then sat back down, gripping the mug again, studying it.

"As I said, it was soon after I was released, which was its own media storm. I was sitting at this table with Randall when Tom came to tell us her body had been found." Hannah sighed, looking out the back door, where the twilight gave the yard an almost magical look, as if the outside world wasn't part of reality. "It was sunset then too, because just before he came I remember looking out this window, thinking about how another day had been lost, that another day had gone by and they hadn't been found."

Asha watched as Hannah paused a moment, taking in the twilight of another day not found.

"Then Tom walked in and I knew it was bad. He is not well-suited to announcing death, even though I'm sure he does it all the time as part of his job." She turned back to face Asha. "He had this blank slate face happening, the kind of face you make when you're trying not to show any emotion but screams a million terrible things at you on its own. He told us a body that appeared to be Katherine had washed up on the banks of the Delaware River, not far from the Delaware Water Gap on the border of New Jersey and Pennsylvania." She paused and anger rose from her once again. "That she had been shot in the face and it would take DNA and dental records to confirm it was her."

Hannah's eyes welled up and she clucked her tongue. "And that Grace was nowhere to be found."

"That didn't absolve her?"

Hannah shook her head. "Conspirators turn against each other all the time. If the dead body of a criminal turns up, the first people you look at are the ones they work with. But I know that's not how it went with Katherine. She told me. And in doing so, she blew everything else open. When Katherine went, it was with a fight. A fight for her and for Grace."

"She..." Asha trailed off, then gathered herself and folded her hands. "She *told* you?"

Hannah nodded, picking up Katherine's mug again and turning it in her hands. "She can't talk to everyone these days, but the dead do talk, Asha. It doesn't always take a psychic to hear them if they're loud enough and by the time her body was found, Katherine was screaming."

Chapter Forty-Three

Twenty-six days ago, the idea of Hannah collapsing into Rick's arms when something was upsetting would not have been noteworthy. Even if much of the outside world didn't know it, they were Rick and Hannah and Grace, they were each other's people. But as Hannah collapsed into Rick's arms upon seeing him at the state medical examiner's facility the full force of how much things had changed in such a short time was evident. The only thing uniting them anymore was their grief, even though to anyone who knew them before, much looked the same.

But a weed sprouted in Hannah's subconscious as Rick rubbed her back and tried to soften the blow of what they were about to see. It occurred to her that this could come back to be her fault, leaving her a grieving mother, horrible employer, *and* despised ex. The thought bloomed and she realized that if Rick had to make a list of the top 3 mistakes in his life, Hannah would have to be in there.

"Are you sure you're both ready to do this?" Randall looked between Hannah and Rick as they gathered next to the door. It was locked, Hannah mused, to keep the living out. It wasn't as if anyone behind it could get up and walk out. "Water," Randall sighed and put his hands on his hips, joining them in staring at the door as if they could change what was on the other side of it, "does ugly things."

Hannah wiped the tears from her blotchy face and thought of Katherine's parents—her kind mother, her father who had been left with only a bag of rage to carry his grief in, and nodded. "If she is, um," she swallowed, "difficult to recognize, it needs to be us. They say she is dressed?"

"Yes. That is my understanding."

"If she's so bad off that we only recognize her clothes," Hannah paused to grab a tissue and blow her nose, "I don't want to put her parents through that."

"It's only a preliminary ID," Rick said. "If it is Katherine, I'll speak to the lab people about special arrangements." He grabbed more tissues and handed them to Hannah. "Sometimes just wrapping the body up tightly in a sheet, covering the worst, can make it," he scoffed, "better. As if that's possible."

Hannah looked at the floor. "I know what you meant."

The door opened and they were ushered into another room, this one empty save for a glass window covered by a curtain. The lab tech that let them in was a petite woman who looked barely old enough to drive much less to be ushering in people to identify victims of grisly murders. She left them with a polite nod, not saying a word, and Hannah felt like it was a tactic decided upon through experience, not awkwardness. It appeared that the business of death was no longer the exclusive purview of old, rotund men.

The curtain slid open and Hannah gripped the window frame. A covered body was just below them on the other side of the glass. The sound of her breathing was the only thing she could register and even that felt rude under the circumstances. On the other side, a worker covered head to toe in the same white coveralls that investigators wore in her pool house gave another polite nod. Hannah knew the suit this time was to prevent any contamination of evidence yet to be discovered on the body.

The worker pulled back the sheet, bringing it all the way down past the victim's feet. The exposed skin was discolored, pale with a marbled network of what had once been hidden highways of blood vessels. A smaller green surgical cloth covered the face, from her upper lip to just above her eyelids where the skin turned into an angry and gnarled purple line.

"They can remove the covering if necessary," Randall said. "But the damage is such that an ID from her face is not likely, that's why she is covered." He looked at Hannah. "I told them to see if you could identify her without seeing that first."

You mean what remains of her face Hannah bit back and swallowed the bile of grief and anger that rose inside her.

She rested her forehead on the glass and let her eyes wander over the light brown hair that Grace used to pull; the shirt that Katherine had picked out a few months earlier when they had been out shopping, now painted with broad strokes of faded blood stains; and her fingertips, where she spotted one chip of that nail polish with the glitter in it that Hannah hated but Katherine and Grace loved. Grace would grab Katherine's hand when she wore that polish, grab it and lightly run her tiny finger over the glitter to study it like it was the most fascinating thing in the world, as toddlers do.

"Oh, Katherine." Hannah put her palm on the glass as quiet tears slipped down her cheeks.

"Are you sure?" Randall put a hand on Hannah's shoulder and for a moment she couldn't answer. She was consumed with all she was unsure of. *What had happened? What did Katherine know? Did she get in too deep before they were taken? Why didn't she come to me for help?*

Rick's brow furrowed and he stepped out of the room for a moment. Hannah nodded and the technician nodded back, covering Katherine's body once again, hiding all of the memories underneath it. Rick came back in and sighed, eyeing Hannah from across the room. "Are you okay?"

Hannah was never going to be okay. Even if Grace was delivered to her arms, perfectly fine as if nothing had happened, Hannah knew okay wasn't hers to have ever again. "Where did you go?" Before he could answer, the young technician appeared again, the one that had ushered them into the room, this time on the other side of the glass and covered in the same type of gear as the other.

"Oh, I had a thought, about..." He looked at her. "Maybe you and Randall should go. Make some phone calls to Katherine's family. They will have questions about how we know it's her."

"Right, of course. I'll..." Hannah stopped talking when she caught Rick's eyes make the slightest twitch towards Randall and she realized he was prompting him to intervene and get rid of Hannah. She turned back to where Katherine was. The technician was busy folding a pile of green surgical drapes, saying something Hannah couldn't hear while the other technician looked back and forth between them and the body.

Hannah's breath caught. "What's happening?"

Randall looked at Rick, his face blank with confusion.

Rick sighed and pinched between his eyes. "Sometimes, I can't unsee things I wish I could. Things I've seen during investigations in the past."

He cringed as the technician bundled the drapes into one package that she could carry in both arms.

About the size of a small child.

"There was this case I had worked on once." Rick went on as the technicians moved towards Katherine again. "A woman, holding her young son, God— he couldn't have been older than two — trying to escape her drug addict boyfriend. The blood stains, they..."

He trailed off as the technician pulled the top sheet back again, uncovering Katherine and the memories once more. And now Hannah could see it, the voids. The places where the bloodstains were *not*. And when the technician laid the bundle on Katherine's chest, it filled the void, along with the voids of her inner arms as the technician placed them so they circled the bundle.

And Hannah collapsed and clawed at her ears, as Katherine spoke to her for the first time, about how she'd clutched Grace to her chest, protecting her as she died.

Chapter Forty-Four

27 DAYS: OO HOURS: 23 MINUTES MISSING

Tom flipped through papers in Hannah's kitchen, shaking his head. "I'd be surprised if she was able to stand up."

The final toxicology report wouldn't be available for several weeks, but the preliminary report they had now indicated a cocktail of sedatives that Hannah knew made the pills she was taking to get through the day look like tic-tacs. The small relief that passed through Hannah with that finding—because willing participants don't need to be drugged into a barely conscious state of cooperation—was welcome but hollow.

The Willards could mourn without the cloud of suspicion hovering over their daughter. Hannah could forgive herself for relying on *the* agency and letting them take care of all of the legwork of selecting a nanny. But Katherine was still as dead as ever and Hannah struggled with the mental gymnastics of what that meant for Grace.

The image of Katherine clutching Grace so tightly to her body that blood didn't get between the two of them when she was shot in the face, mouth open, her fear, her fight, the little details of those last horrible seconds, were burned into Hannah's mind.

The dead, however, did speak, and Katherine continued to reveal, chapter by chapter, the events that happened after they were taken. Some answers came quickly, like the conclusion that Katherine's death had been unplanned, at least in the manner that it happened.

"This doesn't fit. So far, he had planned every moment down to the nanosecond," Tom said, putting his hand on Hannah's shoulder. "Shooting her and dumping the body in a river, without even breaking it down first..."

Hannah pushed away thoughts of a butcher with a carcass as Tom spoke.

"...it's desperate and sloppy. This is what we see in spur-of-the-moment killings, crimes of passion and such. This isn't our guy, or at least, it isn't what he planned."

"When?" Hannah asked.

Tom paused. "When what?"

Hannah's heart sank. She knew he was stalling and she knew what that meant. "When was she killed, Tom?"

"The final autopsy report will take some time. There's things that need to be—"

"Oh fuck-off, Tom." Hannah gave him a pointed look. "You know what I'm asking."

He looked away. "Right now, it looks to be about two days before she was found."

Hannah looked to the sky and threw her hands on her head. "Right after I was released."

"We have no way of knowing if these things are related."

"Of course, it's related." Hannah sank to the floor. "It's all related." She let her head rest on the wall and closed her eyes. "I know I gave him what he wanted. I know I did." Tom sat on the floor beside her. "But I fucked it up too."

"Hannah, this is where he will have made mistakes. We are going to stop him." He kept his eyes straight ahead but didn't answer when Hannah wondered out loud if it was a mistake made too late for Grace, as it was for Katherine.

Chapter Forty-Five

"Diatoms." The man in the white coat made the announcement to the group more than three weeks after Katherine had been found.

They were gathered around a conference table at the state crime lab, which was sharing resources with the FBI. This lab technician—Hannah didn't quite catch his name, she thought it might have been Greg—had been flown up from the main FBI laboratory in Virginia to bring all teams up to date on the most recent findings. Tom had suggested he also meet with Hannah, Rick, and Randall to bring them up to speed.

Hannah had no idea what to expect, only that there had been some *significant findings* that put butterflies in her stomach.

Diatoms. He said it like that would be self-explanatory and she wondered if he had been through this speech multiple times already.

"They haven't been briefed on any of this yet," Tom explained to Greg. "I thought you had the best shot at doing it without confusing them."

He nodded to the group. "My apologies. There were diatoms. The victim's remains were loaded with them. Sometimes they can tell us a lot, other times it doesn't reveal much. But in this case, it helped us pinpoint where the victim was placed in the water and since the Delaware river is three hundred miles long..."

Rick's head perked up. "That's huge."

"We know where she... I'm sorry." Hannah shook her head. "Diatoms, I don't know what that means."

Tom gave Greg a nod and he went on. "That's understandable, ma'am. We're just starting to use them in investigations so it's not the first thing people think of. The simplest way I can describe them is they are single-celled plants that live inside of fancy glass houses. They have ornate outer surfaces made of silica."

"Fancy glass houses can tell you where she was put in the river?" Randall asked.

"As I mentioned, diatoms were all over the remains, but this by itself is not any special news. It's not something that people would even have looked for in an investigation like this until recently because they are everywhere. Saying you fished a body out of the water," he went pale, "pardon the expression. I mean, finding them on any victim is like saying you went outside and found air. Diatoms are in all bodies of water and soil on the planet."

Rick locked his eyes. "But soil characteristics can be specific to a location."

He nodded. "Yes. And so are diatoms. Some are quite specific in fact. There are over 100,000 species identified. And they are so picky as to where they live you can have one species of diatom enjoying one corner of a lake, while another corner of that same lake is populated by a whole different species, just because of a slight difference in something as mundane as pH or temperature. We took several samples from the area where Katherine was found. For the sake of simplicity, let's say that area is dominated by diatom A. But her body also had significant amounts of diatoms B and C." He shook his head. "Diatoms B and C are partial to an area of the river about 50 miles north of where she was found, where the waters are slightly cooler and the current moves a lot faster."

"So, you think that area, where B and C live, that's where she was put in the water?" Hannah asked.

Greg and Tom exchanged a look. "A lot has happened in the past 48 hours," Tom said.

Greg pulled out a map and unrolled it on the table, pointing to a red circle as everyone stood and leaned in together to get a closer look. "The victim was found here." He traced his finger along the winding blue line of the river, several miles upstream. "But we found diatoms inside of the tissues and clothing that led us here. "Now," he turned around to grab another sheet, this one a transparent satellite image, and laid it on top of the map. "What do you notice about this area?"

Hannah looked, scanning the waterway for something, but besides the river it was an endless green blob. "I see, trees?"

"Exactly." He nodded.

"Exactly?" Hannah responded.

"When the lab came back and told us about this area, that she had been there, it was important." Tom added his fingers to the map. "There's nothing here, no houses along the river, no public parks, just woods. And to say this rather indelicately," he paused and Hannah nodded that he should go on, "if you have to dump a body quick, are you dragging it through the woods?"

"No," Hannah's eyes widened as she understood. "I'm picking a spot I can drive up to."

"Right. Now there are a few smaller drive-up boat launches, all privately owned. Many of them locked at their entry point. But there is one public boat launch with a small parking lot just up the road, so we checked that out."

"And?" Hannah asked.

Greg frowned. "Nothing."

"That was," Tom interrupted, "until some local guy saw people with badges snooping around the boat launch and stopped to ask questions. Asked if it was anything related to someone trespassing his property a few weeks prior."

Everyone turned to Tom and he went on. "That was our people's reaction. Apparently, this guy who approached our investigators was all worked up. He owns a small cabin, not a permanent residence, more like a hunter's cabin, just up the road from where we were searching. When he arrived last weekend, he said the chain on his gate had been cut. The local police took a report, but that was all since the cabin appeared untouched and the chain was the only damage."

"And this gate?" Rick started.

"Guards a dirt driveway that goes past the cabin and all the way to the riverbank." Greg stood back and couldn't help but smile. "This guy was more than happy to let the FBI scour his property if it meant he might catch, as he put it, *some goddamn hippy squatting on his piece of the river*.

"Our team found some tire tracks which were definitely not those of the property owner, but they weren't well-defined, so that was about all we could say for sure. That a vehicle that didn't belong to him had been driven on his property up to the riverbank. That wasn't much." Tom shrugged. "It still could have just been a *Goddamn hippy*."

"But it wasn't." Hannah pressed.

"Well, we thought it likely was, until he mentioned he still had the severed chain in the house." Greg placed an evidence photo on the table of a thick chain with a smooth cut in a link, the large padlock still attached and closed, securing nothing. "Now the first thought when you find something like this is to look for fingerprints. But even then we were not hopeful. He's been too careful so far, so it would be unrealistic to think that he doesn't remember to throw on a pair of gloves or wipe down everything he touched."

"You found something anyway." Hannah's heart pounded.

"Yes." He pulled out another photo. "We found this, caught between two links that were kinked together. I think he got pinched by the chain."

Hannah squinted at the photo, struggling to understand what she was looking at without any context. The evidence photo showed a clear substance that looked like a crumpled shred of plastic wrap, but she wasn't sure. "What is it?"

"Have you ever heard of liquid bandage?"

Hannah shook her head no.

"Oh my God," Randall muttered, the pieces falling into place for him faster.

Greg continued. "It's exactly what it sounds like. It's a liquid that you paint over a small cut to protect it. It dries into an invisible but flexible coating. That's what that is." He tapped the photo.

"It was a bit beaten up," Tom said. "But it was very clear, before they even flattened it out in the lab that there was a print on it."

"I've heard of this," Randall said. "I've heard of people doing this with crazy glue."

"Ms. Smoke, he wasn't wearing gloves," Greg said. "We think it's possible he *never* wore gloves, that he wears this stuff on his fingertips 24-7. It's like he's wearing invisible gloves all the time, so he doesn't arouse suspicion while hiding his identity."

Hannah took this in, the mental calculations of what all of this meant falling into place so fast they took her breath away.

"Dumping the body in the water was an attempt to eliminate evidence and it was a smart move because water will destroy so much. But this time it backfired because we were able to find out exactly where she was dumped. Now, we've got a print. We think he's been walking around covering his fingertips in this stuff the whole time not because he's a stranger. He's going to be someone you know, and he's hiding his prints because he knows we would find him in a database. And now we have that print. It's a matter of time."

Chapter Forty-Six

Hannah placed a lid on the box of Katherine's belongings that she was preparing to send back to her parents, taking a moment to run her hands over the top. It had been months since Katherine's remains had returned to her home country, months since her funeral, which, as was reported to Hannah, was packed with people who had known her going all the way back to primary school.

She wished to have been there, to share with everyone how wonderful she knew Katherine to be and how she died a hero no matter what the media implied, or, when they skipped the *imp* part and just outright lied, but she would never put such a burden on her already devastated parents. It wasn't necessary anyway. When that many people show up to say goodbye, it means they know. They didn't need Hannah to tell them.

The sound of pebbles crunching on her driveway tore her away from the box of memories, as Hannah glanced out a window and frowned at Tom's arrival. She was confident she knew what he was going to say, because it was exactly the kind of conversation you politely call ahead to make an appointment for when regular updates had fallen away.

There hadn't been any news, not for several months. Despite all that Katherine had told them, despite the deep wound in her ankle that showed she fought to survive to tell them, despite the incredible find of a mappable fingerprint, neither Grace's kidnapper, nor her remains, had been located.

All of the national fingerprint databases had been scoured. Criminal, military, civil— and when they didn't turn up anything, they searched it again. Greg, the lab technician, had called Hannah personally, promising he wouldn't let this go.

"Something's off about this that I haven't figured out yet, but he's in here somewhere. I *know* he will be." Hannah, in a daze of valium and wine at that moment, could barely muster a polite "sounds good."

And that had been it.

The holiday season had come through in a painfully slow march, which, like that phone call, was managed with a mix of pill and bottle. While Hannah and her mother could hide away from it all in her house, sparing them from the decorations and cheerful hustle and bustle, they couldn't avoid the television. There was a necessity to keep up with the news coverage and every commercial was a stabbing reminder of all of the big happy families and their big happy celebrations and their big happy lives going on.

"I should have been here."

"What?" Hannah was reading an article about fingerprint databases for the thousandth time, like maybe today of all days she would discover something new and make a true Christmas miracle happen. She looked up to see her mother frowning at the glass of Cabernet in front of Hannah. An interesting switch from her youth but at this point Joanne knew better than to say anything.

"I sent Grace a gift, but I didn't come. Maybe if I had, we'd be closer. Grace and me. And then maybe I would have been here, or she would have been at my house when..."

"Mom, please." Hannah rubbed a hand over her eyes.

"I know. I guess I'm just kicking myself for not showing up until things turned to shit."

Hannah turned to look at the woman who she had managed her whole life, and saw a shell of the scrappy social-climber who once inhabited her. But she had been there, and at this point she was the reasonable one. "That's not why the bad things happened, mom." *But if someone could tell me why, I'd be all ears.*

The disconnect between them and the world was made clear later that night when a news anchor made the efficient transition from reporting there were no new developments in the search for Grace Smoke, to a snappy story about how kids could track Santa's progress with a toll-free phone call.

Santa was still delivering magic to kids around the world, despite Katherine being confirmed dead, and Grace, well, nobody had to say what they were thinking about Grace. It was a recovery, not a rescue. And while she was grateful that the investigators tried to spare her from the worst of those discussions, she still knew what the worst involved. Evaluation of weather conditions in the area where Katherine was found, current patterns in the Delaware River, the fast rate of decay with a smaller body mass.

A tiny body missing in a big, big world.

Peeking through the curtain, she watched as Tom opened the car door and extricated himself from it so slowly she wondered if the SUV was trying to hold him in. Hannah opened the door before he had to ring the bell.

"How are you, Hannah?" He put his hands on his hips and said it with that tone of *I know you're shitty, but how shitty are you?*

"I'm, here." She gestured towards the kitchen, failing to mention how she considered not being here as a viable option these days. "Coffee?"

"You always had great coffee," he said without a trace of cheer.

"I guess you're going to miss it then," Hannah replied, turning her back on him to get a cup.

He sighed, a sound so familiar it had become a part of the soundtrack of Hannah's life for the past six months. "We're not closing the case, Hannah. That I promise you. This does not end until she's found. And even then, I still want him."

"I understand." Hannah stared into her own mug, because if she looked at him she'd crumble into tears. Since the pain between her and Rick had dissolved their relationship, Tom had been the adult in her life. She could count on him. Now he was leaving too. "The FBI is pulling back its resources."

"There will always be someone working on this case. And believe me, the second any physical evidence is found, our lab will be all over it, but..."

"But you can't have an entire staff sitting around here indefinitely with no new developments." She slapped her mug on the counter, hard enough that some coffee spilled over the top.

The disappearance of Grace Smoke would go on the back burner among the cases like it that had come to a series of roadblocks. It would exist in a dead zone where it only got picked up by fleeting media interest on a milestone birthday or the anniversary of her disappearance, or someday when Hannah was old and gray and some ambitious young agent between cases wanted to roll the dice to solve the unsolvable. Grace would be the modern-day Lindbergh baby.

Hannah huffed and grabbed a paper towel to wipe the spill. "My head understands that, Tom. I wish someone would explain it to my heart."

Tom stared at the untouched coffee in front of him. "All of the files are coming with us back to Virginia. The local also has people still on this." He put his hands on his hips. "I won't leave this one behind. And that print—"

"Tom."

"I know that damn print means something."

"Tom!"

He looked up in surprise, having been pulled out of his train of thought. "What?"

"Just say the investigation is being shelved. You'll call me if you find anything new."

"No, Hannah. I'll call you just to check in." He nodded at the stack of documents on her table. "What are you up to?"

Hannah ran her hands over her hair and sucked her teeth. "I've decided to go to Switzerland. Geneva, actually." She inhaled and shoved her hands in her back pockets. "And I am scared shitless."

He took in the files. There was no response needed. You don't say "have a nice trip" when someone is going to look at a database of photographs to see if their child has been exploited and her images are now being used in online child pornography. Investigators in the FBI's cybercrime unit had identified chatter on the internet about videos of the psychic baby and the only way to see images of these children was to travel in person to see the database.

"I know it was to be expected. That sickos would use her name." Hannah crossed her arms. "But even if it's not Grace, it's somebody, you know?"

"There's no winning with something like that, even in the likely event none of them is Grace." He nodded. "Promise me you'll be careful. Looking at all of that, knowing what happened to all of those kids, is like standing there and letting someone blast you with bullets you can't see."

"I will."

"No, you won't. You forget we've met." He scoffed before he took another sip of coffee. "You'll dive in the shallow end head-first, determined to save every kid whose picture you come across."

Hannah chuckled. "Probably. Then you'll have to rescue me." Hannah shrugged, "Again."

He looked out towards the pool house. "How is Rick?"

"Struggling same as me, I assume."

"It's a stressful thing for any relationship. Most don't survive it."

"All the things I did, I think it just sped up the inevitable. It's the painful reminders that are the real problem."

Rick saw Grace when Hannah stared at something in concentration; Hannah saw Grace when Rick used his hands while he talked.

Hannah often got lost as she pondered over what a strange crossroads it was to be at, to want so desperately not to forget something, but find it unbearable to be reminded at the same time.

"We stay in touch to share information. I'm still debating telling him about Geneva though." Hannah drummed her fingers on the table. "I still haven't decided if I want to chance him insisting on coming with me, which I am pretty sure he would do."

"I would prefer you don't do something like this alone." Tom nodded. "I'm going to suggest you tell him."

"Right."

"How's the press been treating you?"

She smirked. "As long as it's radio silence on my end, they seem to follow suit. But on a slow news night, the people in my survivors' group have told me that the tabloids will go back to raking me over the coals. Thank you for that, by the way." In the months since the evidence trail went cold, Tom had suggested she try a victim's parent group. It helped, only because horror is a path better walked with company.

"Yeah well, it's unfortunate that I have to know that it's helpful. Anyhow, the press will get distracted by a shiny new case and then will be over you."

Hannah grimaced because she would prefer to remain the target if it meant this wouldn't happen to anyone ever again.

He walked around to empty the mug in the sink and put the cup in her dishwasher. "If anything turns up, you'll be the first person I call."

"Are you on your way to see Rick? Is he going to get his Dear John letter in person too?"

"It's not a..." He sighed. "Yes. I'm headed there now."

He started towards the door, then stopped and asked, "Did you ever do anything about security here?"

"Yes, Dad."

Tom put his hands on his hips and glowered.

"Really, I did. I've got the whole perimeter of the property wired with cameras now. I had an idea for a new second gate at the stone wall, that's going in next week."

"Recordings? Motion alerts? Panic buttons just in case?"

Hannah opened what used to be a coat closet in the entryway. It now housed a series of monitors showing different locations around the property.

"Good. Too many crazies out there and too much attention on this case to be lax about security."

"Rick oversaw the installation of all of this stuff." She put her hands in her pockets. "Like I said, it's civil."

"If you ever need manpower, I've got some good resources for you. Real professionals. Not that mall cop shit. Hell, if you need anything."

"Thanks again, Tom." There was only one thing she needed and no one had been able to deliver it.

"Take care, Hannah." He held out his hand and she shook it. "I'll talk to you soon."

"Go catch some bad guys," Hannah said as he walked to his car and he saluted. She closed the door with the sense that she wouldn't speak to him for a very long time.

She was wrong.

Chapter Forty-Seven

"You were in a serious relationship, and something about it still bothers you."

"Relationship...What? Who cares?" Asha looked up in confusion from her notepad. "I want to know about what happened after Tom left."

"I can see it every time I talk about my relationship with Rick coming apart at the seams. You react like you know something of it." Hannah nodded and reached to snuff out her cigarette, putting the stamp on what was, in her mind, established fact. "I'll get to what happened, but I want to know about you too. Think of it like a break for me."

"I don't..." Asha sighed as she remembered denial was pointless, in the age of social media it wouldn't be hard for a stranger to dissect her life. "It wasn't the same. We didn't have a child."

"I'm not saying it was the love of your life, I'm just saying there's something about what it all meant, or didn't mean, that bothers you."

"Maybe you're right." Asha shrugged. "Not love of my life, but admitting it still stings nonetheless is a bit bothersome."

After Lily walked out for good, Asha would see couples who appeared to still have the butterflies and wonder how they did it. How they stayed together without letting each other down and losing themselves in the process, or were they happy to lose themselves, condemning Asha to be a spinster because she knew she could never. Lily may have been the one who grew acidic towards the end, but Asha knew it was because Lily had wanted more and had grown weary of doing all the heavy lifting alone.

"Was Rick the love of your life?"

"Romantic love? Absolutely."

"And," Asha held out her hand, "does *that* bother *you?*"

"Of course it does. I'm just saying, too much has happened to me but for you," Hannah pointed and Asha rolled her eyes, "it's not too late. Don't work overtime convincing yourself love is not for you. She just wasn't the one." Hannah stared at Asha, then frowned. "But that's not it." She shook her head, saying it to herself rather than to Asha. "Something else."

"It, what?"

Hannah's mouth stretched into a slight smirk. "Something you not telling me. There's something you're not telling me and it's on purpose but you want to. You can, you know."

"I thought the whole reason I was here is so you can talk of things you hadn't spoken on before."

"Of course, sorry." Hannah returned to the present. "Old habits and all that... Anyway, of course I went and told Rick about my trip. Tom was right, I actually ran to the phone and did it before he was even out of the driveway, so I couldn't chicken out. I knew I might if I thought about it too much." She looked at Asha and paused. "For me, it's usually a toss-up between over-thinking or acting rash that leads to bad choices. I tend to mess both up."

"And you were going to Geneva to look at pictures of exploited children?" Asha asked, and Hannah nodded.

"The internet had a significant presence at that point, but was still young enough that it was the wild west. Before Amazon was even selling books, there was already a vast network of suppliers selling *people*. Now most people can conceive of the dark web, but back then there was just the web. So, when I heard there had been chatter about," Hannah broke eye contact, "child sex videos of the psychic baby…"

"My God." Asha rubbed her temples. The full picture of the resulting casualties from one tragic event had emerged in Asha's mind as Hannah was forced to plunge into the trauma of not a single worst-case scenario, but every worst-case scenario, over and over again.

"Yeah." Hannah could see the merry go round of horror spinning in Asha's head. "I should be clear, the FBI thought this was likely nonsense and I tended to agree. It was expected that somebody would use that name just to make their filth more valuable and it in no way matched the profile of the kidnapper. But the international center for missing and exploited children maintained a book of pictures. Pictures of children that they had evidence of being victimized but had yet to identify. It could only be viewed in person by the parents or investigators working on a specific missing-child case. The center, to their credit, had recognized that while traveling to Geneva put a burden on anyone needing to view the photos, it was the best way to protect them."

"Still, I understand why you had to go."

Hannah turned to the window, where the light was almost gone, and let off a shaky exhale. "As a parent you don't know what to wish for—find their picture because maybe they're still alive, or hope that they are gone so they can be at peace. And all those kids who are being hurt, even if it's not your kid, it's someone's kid, or they were unwanted but it's a kid and you're just so angry and so helpless. Tom said looking at those photos would be like being hit with invisible bullets and he was right."

Hannah cleared her throat and turned back towards Asha. "That's something to write about. There are people who look directly into the depths of evil, real evil, every day to try to rescue these children. To try to stop the monsters who are hurting them. I don't know how they do it." She shook her head. "But thank God they do. We talk about the first responders, the police, the firefighters, but the people who hunt predators don't go to work thinking they might see something bad—they *know* they will. And then there are the parents. There's no stone you leave unturned for your child, even when you're not sure what you want. What to feel if you see them or not. I used to pray for Grace to send me a sign if she had passed so that I'd know she was okay, that she was still with me."

The lights in the backyard lit up, setting the black night ablaze in light and color. Asha startled out of her seat. Hannah turned to see the lights behind her and chuckled. "They're on a timer."

Night had officially fallen, and Asha knew that her time was running out. Even Hannah seemed somehow unsatisfied, like she was still carrying a burden that was hanging by its last frayed ends. Asha saw it was becoming more likely she would have to use what she was hiding to cut those final threads. It was the only thing she hadn't tried.

She cleared her throat. "Did Rick go with you to Geneva?"

"He went with me as far as we were able to get."

Chapter Forty-Eight

"Hey, man," a young guy behind Rick in the security line said. "Don't I know you?"

"No," he replied, while Hannah watched from a few passengers back. They entered the security line a few minutes apart, calculating that they were more likely to be recognized as a pair.

"No, no, no," the stranger shook his shaggy head. He looked to be about college age and Hannah hoped he was as slow as he appeared to be. Rick had already shown his passport to another agent earlier in line, so he discretely slid it into his pocket now.

"No way, dude, you look so familiar. I know you. I've met famous people in the first-class line before." He chuckled with lazy eyelids while Hannah clenched her teeth.

The family in front of her was ushered to another line, and Hannah was about to be directed to join Rick. An agent opened her passport and boarding pass and started asking the standard questions:

"What is your birthday?"

"Where are you flying to?"

"How long are you staying?"

"Okay well, enjoy your flight, Ha—"

Rick snuck a peek back at Hannah, who just shrugged at him as the TSA agent stood, mouth agape, looking at Hannah's passport.

Or, more specifically, the name on her passport.

The whole line was being held up behind her, with only seconds left before they recognized the delay and its cause. The security agent didn't finish saying Hannah's name. She closed her mouth and Hannah's passport, handing it back to her with a nod. "Have a nice flight, ma'am."

But the guy pestering Rick had noticed, so before he could say another word, Rick turned to him and deadpanned, "My name is Richard Parks and I've been on TV because people I loved were kidnapped and murdered."

Hannah came over and threw her belongings on the belt.

"Holy Shhh... sorry." He stammered. "Are you *the* Hannah Smoke?"

"Gee, I don't know if I'm *the* Hannah Smoke," she answered, tossing keys from her pocket onto her bag. "I mean in a world of six billion people there must be another, don't you think?" The boy, whose disheveled style went well with the stench of yesterday's alcohol gave her a wounded look. She sighed. "I really just want to get through here without attracting any atten—"

"Sir, I am going to need you to step over here." The same woman who had checked Hannah's passport was pulling the young man out of line for a more thorough screening. Hannah made a mental note to add her to her prayers.

Later, in the peaceful bubble of the dimly lit first-class lounge, Hannah nursed a glass of wine and tried to shake her unease over their TSA incident.

"How long before that guy goes to the press?" she asked, pausing before taking another sip. "Because I'd like to at least be in the air before that hits."

"I think it will run on the front page of the next issue of *The Enquirer*," Rick answered. "I don't think he could keep his mouth shut with two hands and a staple gun."

Hannah sighed. "I guess it doesn't matter."

A dull ping came over the intercom, the kind usually signaling an announcement for a boarding flight. "Good evening first-class passengers, we have a phone call for Richard Parks. Will Mr. Richard Parks please come to the first-class concierge desk, there is a phone call for you."

Curious faces started to look around.

"It's probably a prank," Rick said, not looking up. "That shithead is telling all of his shithead friends we're in here and now they're messing with us. Bastard."

"Are you going to," Hannah nudged her head towards the desk, "go see?"

"No. The only person that would be looking for me is sitting right here." He gave Hannah a sad smile.

She smiled back but shifted in her seat with nervous energy. "I mean, just in case?"

Another soft ping. "Will Hannah Smoke please come to the desk? There is an urgent phone call for you."

Now everyone in the lounge picked their heads up, a few nudged their companion and gestured in Hannah's direction, her baseball cap not making her a master of disguise. "You have a cell phone, Hannah," said Rick. She pulled it out of her bag to open it and her face fell. "I don't have a signal here, do you?" He fished through his pocket and glanced at his phone.

"No. I don't."

They held each other's gaze as the murmurs grew in the lounge. Hannah ripped off her hat and strode to the desk. "I'm Hannah Smoke."

The woman smiled pleasantly. "Oh, good. It sounds quite urgent. Here you go." She held out the receiver.

Hannah grabbed the phone and was greeted by static.

"Hello?"

"Hannah!" Tom boomed over the line.

"Tom? What's happening? We're about to—"

"We have a name."

Her heart skipped a beat before she realized it was probably someone she should meet with overseas—of course Tom was still helping. She grabbed a pen and a scrap of paper.

"Okay, go ahead, I'm ready to write it down."

"You won't need to." And then he gave her the name—not the name of someone who could help, but of the name of the person who made that fingerprint. The one that had been found on the cut chain where Katherine's body was dumped in the river.

And the world fell away and suddenly made sense, all at the same time.

Chapter Forty-Nine

Rick maneuvered Hannah's car around the rush-hour congestion on the turnpike, finding spaces to slide in where they existed and creating them by force when they didn't. Hannah couldn't hear the angry honks directed at them because the voices in her head were in full chorus, drowning them out. She was perched in the passenger seat, directing Rick where to go. Tom had sent some agents to pick them up at the airport, but Hannah wasn't about to sit around and wait. She needed to deal with this now.

"This is all my fault, Rick." She pounded her fist on the dashboard. "Take this exit." She pointed and he darted into the exit lane, driving on the shoulder to pass the traffic towards the Lincoln Tunnel.

"It sounds like you have a plan." He gave her a quick glance before pulling back into a proper travel lane.

"Just drive." Hannah wouldn't have much time to organize her thoughts. Once they were enclosed in the tunnel and hidden from chaos under the calm surface of the Hudson River, Rick sped through the tube, lights rushing by them as Hannah explained what she was about to do.

"I think this will be my only chance."

Rick was silent, considering what Hannah told him about her intentions until they blasted out of the tunnel into Manhattan. When he finally let himself respond, he kept it simple. "Tell me where to turn next."

"Rick?"

"You're right this time."

She hoped so. Because what Hannah knew now was that her baby, if she was still alive, was in the hands of someone she'd crossed paths with before. Someone who wouldn't hesitate to kill, at least not anymore.

Chapter Fifty

6 MONTHS: 18 DAYS: 21 HOURS: 27 MINUTES MISSIN

The guard leaned into his hands on the security desk and looked between Hannah and Rick warily. "Who did you say you were?"

"My name is Hannah Smoke. Please." Hannah fought the urge to bolt right through, reminding herself she wouldn't need to and doing so would only cause more delay. "There's the phone." She pointed behind him. "Pick it up. Please. Call up to Jack Talbot. He will see me."

He sighed and gave a look that indicated he had this conversation on a regular basis. "You want me to call the head of the news department. Right now?"

"I'm Hannah Smoke." She dug out her passport and shoved it into his hands. He opened it, looking less than excited. "I used to have a TV show, *The Psychic Next Door*, but then my child and nanny were kidnapped." She took a breath. "I don't know if you know my story but…"

Hannah felt relief when the man's eyes got wide with recognition as he examined the identification, recognizing her real last name that had been so widely publicized after the kidnapping and he held up a hand for Hannah to stop talking. "Wait." He turned around to pick up the phone and had barely hung up when Jack trotted out and extended his hand.

Hannah flooded with relief that the security guard hadn't been calling the looney bin to come pick her up.

"Ms. Smoke," he grabbed both of her hands and ushered her and Rick into the waiting elevator. "What can I do for you?"

Chapter Fifty-One

"Why did it take so long to identify who made the print? Hadn't they had those computer programs back then? The ones that match them?" Asha had stopped taking notes.

Hannah gave her a rueful smile. "You're not the first to react that way, if only you could find where they made the mistake, you would somehow be able to travel over two decades into the past and fix it. Juvenile records are sealed. And when that juvenile is later acquitted, forget it. You have to also remember that not everything was computerized back then. Today, when they collect fingerprints, they just roll your fingers over a scanner that creates and stores the image. Back then, it was still ink on paper cards. There was a lag between those paper cards being collected and those images being uploaded. Once he was acquitted, his prints should have been removed from the system, but as it often happens, that paper card still existed. With his name pulled out of the system as criminal, his prints wouldn't be found in any of the standard databases. That lab tech I told you about, Greg, was stubborn enough to keep on it. Afterwards, he said he knew it had to be somewhere, that you don't go hiding prints in plain sight for no reason. He had searched the criminal databases, federal and state, then when that didn't produce a match he moved on to the non-criminal records. Military, police, teachers, etc."

"But even those were a dead end."

Hannah sat back. "Right." She sighed. "He said later he had an idea when someone used the old expression, 'where there's smoke there's fire.' It got him thinking about how that's often true in justice as well. That for people who had been accused then acquitted of crimes, many of them were not *completely* innocent. Maybe innocent of the crimes they were accused of, but not innocent in general. They often have other serious crimes under their belt that they had never been caught for. He figured for someone who had been convicted but later acquitted, a new identity solves all of this, but for their prints." Hannah waved her fingers in the air. "They would know their prints were still out there in the nooks and crannies of the system even if they technically had been expunged. All of this searching specifically for expunged records might not have been entirely legal. The hope was that if he did find a match, that person would also be on that list of names of people who were possibly a threat to me, whom I had history with. It's funny how things come full circle, because that's where we found our mistake and finally hit the jackpot at the same time. The list of names that they had originally targeted didn't go back far enough. In the end, the sins of the past, even if you argue they really weren't mine, came back to haunt me."

Asha's eyes glanced at her recorder. "How do you think they missed his name the first time?"

Hannah shook her head. "Because when someone does something so awful to you as an adult, you don't think it's going to be someone holding a grudge from when you were a kid. Someone who you understood to be in prison." She swallowed. "If I had told the truth, this wouldn't have happened at all. The person who started all of this was me."

Chapter Fifty-Two

"Let me help you." The makeup girl approached Hannah as staff scrambled to rearrange the set so she could go on as soon as they came back from commercial break.

"Oh," Hannah startled. "I'm not here for..."

"I know what you're here for." She didn't wait for permission, she brushed Hannah's hair away from her face and started applying powder. "Nothing fancy, I promise. Let us take care of you." She had kind eyes and Hannah believed she meant it, that she just wanted to help and this was the only way she knew how. So, Hannah let her.

Hannah signaled to Rick that she needed him and he pulled away from Jack, kneeling to be at eye-level with her.

"Can you call my mother?" The full force of how this would affect her would have no bearing on what Hannah had to do, it still needed to be done and it needed to be brutally honest. "Tell her to turn on channel 7 and that there's no time to explain..."

"I'll do it now," he said and pulled out his cell phone. Hannah grabbed his hand.

"Tell her I'm sorry."

He squeezed her fingers one last time then walked away to make the phone call that would break her mother's heart. A few minutes later, Jack signaled that they were ready and jogged over to Hannah to confer with her one last time. For once she had reason to be grateful for her notoriety when that notoriety could get things done fast. "We're going to throw it to you quickly after we come back from commercial. Are you sure you're ready? You wouldn't rather do this as an interview? We could still do it live and help guide you."

"I've got it. And Jack." He stopped directing people and looked towards her. "Thank you," Hannah said as she tried, unsuccessfully, to keep her eyes from filling up. She wasn't nervous about what she was about to do, just nervous that she would do it wrong. Jack gave her shoulders a supportive squeeze, and sat down next to Hannah.

"We are live in five, four, three ..." Disembodied hands reached out from the darkness of the studio and flashed *two, one*. A message blared announcing a break from regular programming and Hannah prayed he was listening.

"To our viewers across America, good evening. My name is Jack Talbot. I am the head of our news division and I know," he shook his head, "you are not used to seeing me on the air. But tonight, there is an unexpected development in a story that has both captivated and devastated people across our nation. Just a short time ago, Hannah Smoke walked into our broadcasting headquarters here in New York City. She has new information crucial to the safety of baby Grace that she would like to share with all of you. So now, I will turn it over to Hannah."

The light on the second camera consumed Hannah, bringing her back to that fateful day on Judy's soundstage, and her pulse raced. *The beginning,* she told herself, fighting off the impending panic attack. *Just start at the beginning. It's his beginning too.*

"Twenty years ago, I wasn't famous. I didn't have a TV show, or celebrities inviting me to their homes, and," Hannah's eyes flicked away for a moment like she was remembering something. "I didn't have Grace."

She paused, taking a sip of water to try to clear the tightness of her voice. "I was just a kid doing psychic readings out of our dingy house on the wrong side of the tracks for five dollars a session. But I developed a reputation. A reputation that had spread just enough that when a little girl went missing in the next town over, I was asked to go to the house to see if I could tell them anything."

The studio, the lights, the similarities to *that* day were striking, so Hannah looked down to bring the cresting wave of anxiety back in control. "I remember being so scared. My mother acted like it was no big deal. I still try to wrap my mind around it—who asks a child to do something like that?" She shook her head. "But no one gave it a second thought. They were desperate and I got so scared to the point of being sick to my stomach. I will never forget how sad the eyes of that poor mother were, how it crushed my soul to have to look at them."

Hannah looked up at the camera. "These days, I understand that sadness and pain more than I ever wanted to. But on that day, I threw up all over the kitchen floor. That was all it took. It didn't happen that way because I was psychic, it was because I was a kid scared to death. Marcus, I think, deep down, they already believed it was you who had murdered your sister. But since the adults in charge couldn't do their jobs, they wanted me to scare you into confessing. Two paths formed that day: on one, I became the child psychic that helped catch a killer, and went on to become rich and famous for it. On the other was you. You were branded a child rapist and murderer that would spend the next few years in and out of various institutions. But what nobody wanted to see was that both of those were lies. I didn't know anything about what happened to Kylie, and Marcus, you didn't kill your sister."

"Marcus Keegan." Hannah sat up straighter, finally able to speak the name of the man who took her daughter. She saw a cameraman's hands tremble as he tried to adjust focus, and somehow that made it easier for her to push on.

"That's his name. I have no idea what name he goes by now or has gone by since, I imagine there are several. But Marcus Keegan was the man in the surveillance video. He was fourteen when he was convicted of raping and murdering his sister Kylie. The fact that he was not actually responsible for his sister's death wasn't brought to light until he had already spent two years incarcerated in a facility that housed some of the most violent juvenile offenders in the country." Hannah scoffed. "Marcus, how much help did you *not* get because of what they did? How much did you suffer because they treated you as the worst kind of criminal until technology finally caught up and showed that someone else, someone who was since incarcerated for another crime, had killed Kylie?"

Hannah's shoulders sagged and her voice dropped low. "And how much did you blame me? The one who you thought pointed the finger at you? I never said you killed your sister, Marcus. I'm not psychic, wasn't then, and I'm still not now. I am a fraud. Spirits don't speak to me—God knows if they did I would have Grace in my arms. The same private investigators and public records that make it so easy for me to look like a living miracle were never going to be enough to get Grace back."

The words came easier now, just as the silent tears that slipped down Hannah's face did. "And I am sorry. When I heard that you were convicted, I didn't know that they had railroaded you because local politicians wanted this done so they could declare the community safe and ensure their jobs. I thought the justice system worked, that if you were convicted it must mean you had done it. But I'm still sorry. If I hadn't been going around pretending to have special powers, maybe it would have turned out different. Maybe somebody would have taken a closer look at the evidence and you would have been cleared earlier. Maybe you would have even been helped." She swallowed. "I suspect that you went into the system a child and came out the very monster they were trying to lock up in the first place."

Silence filled the space and Hannah tried to regain her composure. She saw the faint outline of the makeup girl who helped her as she brushed away a tear.

"I am responsible, Marcus, for any pain that I've caused families who have been in the place I am now, for not stepping up all those years ago to stop a sideshow that was getting out of control. And if I'm not guilty of that, then in the very least I'm guilty of not stopping it when I was an adult and I knew better. I told myself it was okay, I was bringing people comfort. I told myself that if people walked away feeling better, then my fee wasn't blood money. But when I grew up, I knew that if I had to keep telling myself those things over and over again it meant they were lies."

Hannah was aware that they were zooming in on her face. "That's the thing about the truth, I guess, you only have to tell that to yourself once. It's the lies we have to convince ourselves of."

A group had quietly gathered behind the cameras to watch Hannah let everything spill out, the cascade of sadness and ugliness. "We were both failed by the adults that day. Your penalty was prison, mine was losing my daughter. I'm begging you, if she is still alive, please let's both do better for Grace than was done for us. The thing I'm begging you for is Grace's safety. I have nothing to offer in return, except that I see you, Marcus. I see the truth and I see the lies, both mine and others, that destroyed your life. If Grace is still alive, I hope you can stop the lies from destroying her too. If she isn't, please tell me where I can find her. She didn't do anything wrong, and if all I can give her is a dignified resting place she deserves at least that." Hannah nodded towards Jack that she was finished, and stood up.

"Okay. Thank you, Hannah." The camera went back to Jack as Hannah was disconnecting her microphone, preparing to leave. "I'm sure that people have many questions, and hopefully there will be answers forthcoming. If you're just tuning in, we have just heard from Hannah Smoke herself, who has publicly named the man who took her child, Marcus Keegan. If you have any information, please contact the FBI using the number at the bottom of your screen."

But Hannah wasn't quite done. She balled her fists, making a beeline to where Rick stood. "She's gone, isn't she? It's too late." She didn't look at his face, staring straight ahead into his chest instead.

He put his hands in his pockets and looked at his feet. "Yeah."

She tilted her head up to look him in the eye. "I'm sorry for everything I did that made this happen."

"Hannah..." He looked everywhere but at her.

"And I know I shut you out of decisions but it wasn't because I didn't trust you or value your opinion..."

He ran his hands through his hair, brushing over her with a passing glance. "It's not your fault, I just didn't want Grace to get hurt."

"Rick, I need to say this, please."

He lowered his eyes to hers.

"Because I can't stand here and say to you that I wouldn't do the same things again." A new batch of tears overflowed and she swiped at them. "I mean, there's a bunch of things I know I wouldn't do again but when it comes to desperate things to save our daughter..."

"I know." Rick grabbed at her hands as she reached for him, stopping her from bringing him closer. "I know you were only trying to save her, Hannah. I never doubted it."

"But you doubted *me*. And you left. You *left*..." She struck his chest.

"Because I had to..."

"And the fucked-up thing is..."

"I can't do this Hannah..."

"...is I still love you. You left me with our daughter missing, but I still fucking love you." She sobbed as she struck him with each syllable. "Not in some stupid romantic way because that's over, but as fact."

"I know..."

"I mean," Hannah shrugged and wiped her face with the back of her hands, "she's gone and what now except I still love you."

"I just can't Hannah. I'm sorry," he stammered. "Take care of yourself." He kissed her on top of her head, and walked out.

Chapter Fifty-Three

"Do you two ever speak?" Asha asked, surprised by the sadness of a simple breakup considering the larger tragedy that enveloped it. *A family destroyed*, she thought.

"Not for a very long time, but I'll have to tell him soon." When Asha tilted her head, Hannah explained. "This article, people are bound to start calling him and I should warn him. I owe him that much."

"Of course. And Marcus..."

"There are people who think that a juvenile facility is not that bad, that what happened to him is not a big deal since Marcus would have just been in 'juvie'." Hannah made quotation marks with her hands. "But juvenile doesn't mean everyone is under eighteen and it doesn't mean the people you're locked up with are any less dangerous."

She remembered how Marcus looked that day, a skinny kid wearing a cartoon t-shirt and shorts, scanning the room with confused fear. He was older than Hannah, but equally powerless in stopping the freight train the adults had set in motion.

"From what I've learned, the Marcus that went in was not the same Marcus that came out. He spent two years in a maximum-security facility for dangerous juvenile offenders before a technology developed that showed Kylie had not been attacked by her brother."

"DNA?" Asha asked.

"No." Hannah shook her head. "This was still in the 80s." She sighed. "I can't tell you how many times I go over in my head how DNA technology, literally just a speck of time away at that point, could have saved so much grief. Whoever had killed Kylie had also urinated on her body."

Asha shivered and Hannah nodded.

"Exactly. Shortly before DNA, you could sometimes determine blood type from a urine sample. Whoever urinated on her had type A blood, Marcus is type O. Later in the early nineties when DNA became more available, the semen was tested. It matched a drifter with a history of violent crime." Hannah swallowed. "He spotted Kylie outside alone—I don't remember if she was walking home from school or to a friend's house, but she never got there."

Hannah bit the inside of her cheek. "The ripple effect of something like that is breathtaking. Everyone sees the first tragedy, but after all the years of working with families that have had a similar tragedy, I can tell you murder is the gift that keeps on giving. The pile of bodies that followed in this case alone—first Kylie, then Mrs. Keegan, Teddy Shieves, Katherine... When a person dies violently, it's a curse that grows like a spider's web."

She looked at Asha, her eyes haunted by grief. "We're sitting here right now and it's still cascading and I don't know what to do."

Hannah gathered her ashtray and dumped the remains of the burned yet mostly unsmoked cigarettes in the garbage. "Once the blood type results that eventually cleared Marcus came to light he had nowhere to go."

"What happened to Mrs. Keegan?" Asha asked.

"She died of an accidental sleeping pill overdose a few months after Marcus was incarcerated. I suspect they called it accidental for politeness more than accuracy."

Asha felt something twist in her chest. "He had no one."

Hannah swiped her hands on her jeans then gripped the countertop. "And when you have no one—no one pestering law enforcement to get things tested, no one looking into every possible petition you could bring before the court, a slow system comes to a standstill. So, there was Marcus, exonerated. He had survived it all, only to be acquitted with no one particularly interested in looking out for him."

Asha frowned. "What does happen in that case? Foster care?"

Hannah scoffed. "For foster care people have to agree to take you. Imagine this kid, now sixteen and topping six feet tall, who has recently been acquitted of murder but known to suffer from mental illness and recovering from the baggage that comes with the fresh hell of juvenile prison, as well as an untimely murder and suicide in his immediate family. The prospective homes weren't exactly rushing to take him. He was put into a public mental institution that housed other juveniles who were eligible for foster care. If you're wondering what the other kids there were like, well, that's where he met Teddy Shieves, so it's not hard to imagine. That was the connection we missed."

Asha's head snapped up. "The man with..." she trailed off and went pale.

"Yes. Let's just call him the man with the blanket. He knew Marcus. People who were there at the time reported that Teddy was enamored by Marcus, but Marcus wasn't the social type. Apparently though, he let Theodore trail him, had some sort of sympathy for him, which made him an undying hero in Theodore's eyes. Marcus didn't so much engage him as talk at him—that's how it was explained. No one was ever able to confirm contact between them after Marcus was released to his own care, but they did say Theodore was devastated. There's no evidence he in any way aided in the kidnapping, but if there's anyone who would have recognized it as Marcus's work, it would have been Teddy."

Asha sat back and looked Hannah over. "The way you speak about them... It seems you feel sorry for them. Theodore and Marcus. Especially Marcus. You feel some sympathy for him."

"No." Hannah shook her head, then shrugged. "Maybe it depends on how you define sympathy, but I'd say that's too strong a word. I'd say I have an understanding of him, but not sympathy for his choices. Taking Katherine and Grace was planned out for a long time. He knew what he was doing was wrong and went to great lengths to hide it. He didn't consider what his revenge on me meant for them, he didn't take his revenge out directly on the adults or the system that ruined his life or even me, because my girls were the easier target. Underneath all of the self-justification going on in his mind, ultimately, he chose Grace and Katherine because they were easy, not because it was righteous. That part makes him a monster. But I do realize that Marcus Keegan was not a monster that appeared out of thin air. He was dropped into a perfect storm of shit. If the adults in charge had done right by him, he could have been just another person dealing with some mental illness, not the danger he is. And it's important to remember that, Asha." Hannah shook her finger. "It's very important because, in your line of work, people will try to use that to manipulate the truth. They'll try to paint a story to say that because someone's circumstances led them to do something horrendous, justice should be lenient. That he himself was the victim first and I wasn't a very good person. That ignores one very important fact. That some things cannot be fixed. Some people, even after you've unpacked all the background that made them what they are, they can't be changed back. Some people *need* to stay in prison forever."

"But there's been no trace of him since?" Asha asked.

"For his final trick, both he and Grace disappeared into thin air."

"How long has it been?"

"25 years, 5 months, and 13 days."

Asha tried to imagine all of those years of not knowing, an impact crater that obliterates the rest of your life.

Her own mother, thousands of miles away right now, was probably scrubbing something hard enough to take off the finish because she was so mad at Asha, while at the same time looking out the window, hoping to see her coming up the walkway. There was one time, when Asha was little, that her mother had lost track of her for fifteen minutes at the beach. Asha thought about how her mother still went pale as she told that story twenty years later and her heart skipped a beat. She made a mental note to call Mum as soon as this was over.

"How did you manage all that time?" she asked.

Hannah straightened in her seat. "I held on for dear life, waiting for the day I'd get some news."

Chapter Fifty-Four

Hannah read the address again, pausing before she knocked to confirm she was in the right place. The woman who had helped her at the previous location spoke enough English that she could explain why Mr. Mateescu wasn't where she had expected him to be and where she could find him.

She had worked with people in missing-children circles for decades now and they were, for the most part, decent salt-of-the-earth types that meant well. She rubbed her hands together fighting both the cold and her nerves as she waited for her knock to be answered.

Romanian orphan cases were often made sticky by a web of cultural complexities that didn't bear many good intentions out. Reunions were complicated here, even when an adoptee had no misgivings about their upbringing. Then there was the issue of the birthmother's shame, a shame that was powerful despite a government that had begged women to produce as many children as possible and hand them over to the state in the first place. But the cryptic message about the sick adoptee needing help to locate their family due to a medical condition gnawed at Hannah, which was why she stood at the door of the stucco cottage a few days earlier than expected.

The door swung open and the similarity between this woman and the woman who had helped her at the previous stop was striking, the exception being the scowl of disapproval this woman had framed by her babushka. "Buna zuia." Hannah stumbled over the words, hoping the attempt would be appreciated. "Numele meu este Hannah."

"I know you," the woman grunted with a thick accent and turned her back on the doorway, walking further into the house. "I no agree."

She didn't slam the door in her face, so Hannah assumed she was to follow despite *she no agree*.

Maybe good English was preferred to bad Romanian. "Stefan Mateescu asked me to come. He sent a message about finding a birth family."

Hannah worked with an international group that helped reunite children that had been separated from their families for various reasons. They ranged from sinister non-custodial kidnappings to accidental family separations during times of war or poverty. Sometimes the family was seeking the child they lost, sometimes the child was aware that the family they grew up with wasn't the one they were born into and they wanted to find them. She closed the door behind her, keeping out the brisk air.

"Feh." Babushka woman dismissed Hannah with a wave, but when Hannah didn't move, she pointed to an interior door.

"I should go in here?" Hannah asked.

"I no agree you be here." She nodded in affirmation.

"I understand."

"You go." The woman waved. "I no agree, you go."

She was like an angry cat, giving Hannah a hard time for existing, but Hannah couldn't help liking her a little bit. She turned the knob and walked into the wood-walled room. A fire blazed in the corner and Hannah knew that "I no agree" must have been maintaining it, since the man in the bed was in no condition to get up and deal with it himself. He didn't even flinch when Hannah walked in the room, just lay there in bed as the light from the fire danced across his face.

"Mr. Mateescu?"

His eyes opened and blinked a few times, as if he was having a hard time distinguishing between reality and dream. He gave Hannah a blank stare for a few moments, and then his face brightened while he broke out in a dry grin that showed a shrinking collection of yellow teeth.

"You made it," he cried out in a faint, raspy voice. "I was hoping, I don't know how much longer I have. I can speak, but the writing, she is a struggle." His voice was so faint Hannah wished there was a way to turn down the crackling of the fire. "I hear you have done some good work for our children. Thank you."

"Your message said you wanted assistance for someone from your orphanage? How can I help?" Hannah pulled up a chair alongside his bed. "We have worked out a roadmap that we have used for Romanian adoptees raised all over Europe who are interested in meeting their birth families."

"You are from the U.S. You know about our country? About all the children raised by the state?" He stared at her.

"Yes, and we've had some great success in helping people find each other. I can put you in touch with some organizations to help with the process. Do you have contact information for the adoptee, the one seeking her birth parents? We prioritize cases where there's a medical issue involved."

He stared at Hannah openly. "This is what my message said?"

"Yes. Is that not correct?" Hannah's face screwed up tight. "Is it the birth family seeking the adoptee?" This was not unusual. Language barriers often caused details to be confused.

He pointed to the dresser. "Can you bring me that water?" After he took a weak sip from the cup Hannah held to his lips he said, "Mary keeps the fire going to keep me warm. Nice woman. I don't have the heart to tell her it's drying me out so badly I'll turn into a mummy before I'm even dead." He barked out a raspy laugh. "You will have to forgive her—she sent the message to you and I'm sure she said what she thought was best. You are here now, that's what matters."

"I don't understand."

He didn't seem to hear her. "She always wants to put a nice side on things, so she's not very direct when news is distressing." He shrugged. "But maybe it's not, I don't know."

He took another sip of water, then lay back on the pillow. "I'm getting weak, so please no questions until I'm done. Over twenty years ago, a young girl was dropped at our door. This was not unusual."

Hannah nodded.

"But she was dropped, like when people do this in US, leave a baby on church steps? We didn't know who she was. Ok. We still take care, must be Romanian. We never find out who she belonged to, but still."

"All right. That's a bit more complicated. What about the medical condition?"

"No."

"No?"

"I know what people say about our orphanages, how they were mistreated. It is a national shame. But not everyone involved didn't care for the children, Ms. Smoke. Months went by and there was no one claiming to be her parents, no connection to a family we could find. When a couple came in and fell in love with that child... They had money. Money we sorely needed for the other children. We rushed her paperwork."

Hannah nodded, not knowing where this was going.

"I put it out of my mind. That I had accepted money to rush the adoption was justified, I told myself, because other children needed the large donation the parents were willing to give. Of course, I'm reminded of it every time I see the heat system we have for the main children's house now. That's what was done with the money, along with other repairs. Then about two years ago, I was talking with an advocate from England and she was telling me about this American woman who had brought them a child that had been saved from prostitution. This woman did this sort of thing a lot, she did it after her own child was taken."

Hannah gave him a sad smile. "Because I don't know what else to do with myself."

"I would think God would agree you've chosen wisely. She pulled a news story up from the machine and I looked into the eyes of the child who paid for our repairs."

Hannah stopped breathing. She had heard that a lot over the years, of course. Countless Grace sightings everywhere. But it still knocked the air out of her, especially coming from such a sweet old man. She found a breath and shook her head. "I wish it were true."

"I am not lying, Ms. Smoke."

She shook her head again. "I didn't say you were lying. I know you believe what you say. But over the years, many people have believed the same thing. The truth is my Grace probably..." A small sob escaped her chest, before she could collect herself. "She likely passed shortly after being kidnapped," Hannah said in a whisper.

"She didn't talk much," the man continued, oblivious to the turmoil in Hannah. "She said only one word: purse."

Hannah froze. "Excuse me?"

"It took us a long time to figure it out, until one of our ladies who spoke a good deal of English told us. She kept trying to pull the bags off the shoulder of any woman who came by. Purse. What a funny word, isn't it?"

Hannah swallowed. It wasn't that she *believed*, but that detail startled her in the way a lightbulb popping would. Her memory flooded with images of Grace pulling purses around, trying to sashay on chubby little legs and pushing her curls out of her face while repeating that same word.

"Go in that drawer," he pointed. "There's some pink papers."

Hannah pulled the papers sitting in the drawer out, hands shaking, and stared at the faded writing on them.

"Maybe I'm wrong." He started a fit of coughing.

Mary came in and shooed Hannah towards the door. "Enough."

"If I am right," Mateescu said through her, "I beg for your forgiveness. I didn't know."

"You, I no agree," Mary growled, waving Hannah out. "You will go!" But Hannah couldn't move.

"I thought I was doing some good." He leaned and almost tumbled out of bed. "I didn't know I kept her from you." More coughing, blood coming up now. Mary got up. "Leave!" And she slammed the door in Hannah's face.

Chapter Fifty-Five

"Oh!" Asha got so excited she knocked over the recorder with a clumsy hand.

"Bollocks." She couldn't hide her grin as her trembling hands confirmed it was still working while Hannah watched her, a hint of an amused smile playing on her lips.

This is it! Mystery solved and a happy ending? Brilliant! Asha let the flood of adrenaline and relief overtake her. The big story that would save her career had landed, and she could have it all. Not some shitty salacious exposé on Hannah's failings, lies, or criminal responsibility. It was breaking news of hope. It was a screaming headline *and* happy news. How often did a journalist get to see that?

She felt some moisture around her eyes and blinked a few times. *Get a grip, Asha.* She cleared her throat. "So that was about a month ago, you say."

Hannah nodded.

"That's recent, but also a lot of time to keep that inside. What did you do? What happened next?"

Hannah groaned. "Actually, the first thing I did was to shove the file in my bag, then get on the next flight back to Heathrow and try to forget about it."

"But that story..." Asha exhaled.

"Is one of many I've heard over the years. It wasn't even the most convincing. I mean, *Romania*?"

"I don't understand?" Asha's face fell to the floor.

"Grace has been spotted everywhere. It's part of the horror, following up on leads that you want to believe in, but that never actually lead anywhere. In the two decades since she was taken, Grace had been spotted," Hannah started counting on her fingers, "attending preschool in Canada, on a train headed into Oregon, living as a vagrant on skid row, attending medical school in New York City, and yes, even countless overseas sightings."

Hannah sighed. "I would love to say that these give you some sort of hope, and I guess at first they do, but every time it turns out to be nothing, it steals a piece of you. And one day, you get a sighting and you realize that it's just another cross to bear. That you no longer truly believe that a striking resemblance or an unusual circumstance means something, because you've been punched in the gut time and time again when they don't. And then there's every time the remains of a child are found, and you get stabbed with that horror over and over again. I hope I don't sound bitter. Everyone that tells me these things is only trying to help, I recognize that."

Asha deflated, the screaming headline in her head — *Baby Grace Found!* — disappearing in a puff of smoke. "No, not at all."

"Good. Because every person who has ever reported something, I am grateful for. It doesn't matter that they are wrong." Hannah scoffed.

"Although I guess to say that belies the fact that I prayed for years that someone would be right. They never were. So, I put his information aside, like all the other reports through the years." She shrugged. "It's not that I don't follow up on any of them, but it serves me well to at least attempt sanity."

Hannah gazed out towards the one unlit spot in the backyard, the spot where the crumbling slab of the former pool house stood, its tragedy hidden in the darkness. She cleared her throat. "I know it might sound cold, but I find a lot of parents have to compartmentalize this information. Set aside specific times to deal with it." She pointed out the glass door. "I had them tear it down about four years after it happened. The few people still speaking to me directly at that point wanted me to move. My mother wanted me to move in with her," Hannah made a pained face, "and while I give her credit for trying, that wouldn't go well under even the best circumstances. Anyway, I couldn't leave this place."

"Is it because you could sense her here? Like when people stay around after they die?" Asha's voice cracked as if the question was difficult to get out.

Hannah didn't answer but picked her head up to look at her, the earliest hint of alarm apparent on her face.

"I've been wanting to ask this for hours." Asha swallowed, barely able to get the rest out. "Do you see her here? Is she here now?"

Hannah's face relaxed. "It's not an unreasonable question. Why did you wait to ask?"

Asha turned off the recorder.

Chapter Fifty-Six

2015

Asha put the kettle on for tea, relieved to finally have a minute to herself. Even though it had been a decade since Rory had stepped through their door, the news that he had been struck by a car hit their family hard. Asha had barely a moment to herself to process as her parents hovered, so when they finally needed to step out to check in on Gran, she claimed a headache and stayed behind.

The whole thing was weird in a horrible way, how inseparable they had been as children, but passed each other without a word since that day at the lake.

She couldn't look around her house without reliving some memory of him. She looked at her table and saw all the lunches they had together, usually playing with their food and driving Asha's mum bonkers. She looked at Mr. Whiskerpants dozing on his favorite chair, now older and slower, and remembered how much affection Rory gave him as he wasn't allowed a pet. She looked out the window and saw the stone wall at the back of the garden, which Rory would climb and walk atop of to get to Asha's house. For the past two days since the accident every time she looked out the back window she half-expected to see ten-year-old Rory standing there, waving Asha to come out for some adventure or another.

But he wouldn't. His garden wall days, along with the rest of his days, were tragically over, along with any chance of them reconnecting.

It felt complicated, possibly, in a twisted way, Asha pondered, more complicated than if she had still been close with him when he died.

Unresolved came to mind as she stood by the kettle and inhaled the steam as water boiled, taking in the silence that embraced her heavy heart. He had been at a pub with some friends, she thought of them as *new* friends, and tripped off the sidewalk into the path of an oncoming car. He had lasted about twenty-four hours before he succumbed to internal bleeding. Whatever tried to get him in the lake took him for good this time. Asha shivered at the thought.

The doorbell rang as a bolt of lightning flashed, threatening a downpour to come. Asha frowned and considered not answering, but thought better of it.

And when she opened the door, there stood Rory.

Chapter Fifty-Seven

2019

"He was standing there, as much as you are here now."

Hannah transfixed on Asha. "And then?"

"Um, nothing." Asha shook her head. "He, looked at me, and then started to fade away until he wasn't there anymore, and I was freezing on the porch staring at nothing." Asha gave a sad laugh. "Just, feeling heartbroken and scared, and crazy."

"Did it happen again?" Hannah asked.

"Twice. Not exactly in that way but I spotted him."

Hannah reached out and grabbed Asha's hand. "Did it ever happen with anyone else?"

"No." Asha shook her head.

"How did you feel? Seeing him?"

"Confused." Asha waved off her answer. "Actually, it felt like *he* was confused. He didn't say anything this is all coming from what I felt." Hannah nodded as Asha let this experience that she had locked away spill out of her. "I felt like he was confused and looking for where he was supposed to be." Asha rubbed her eyes. "I don't know why I'm telling you this."

"Because you assume I understand Asha, and you're right, I do." She squeezed her hand tighter. "Were the incidents after Rory passed the only times something like this happened to you?"

Asha gave a vigorous nod. "Yes. Thank God. Those made me feel crazy enough."

Hannah gave Asha's hand a final pat before she let it go.

"You don't need to tell anyone if you don't want to. And yes, what you describe is part of the reason I couldn't imagine moving." Hannah smiled. "Rory showed up because whatever came after the lake accident, he had been close to you. It's not unusual for such things to happen with those that die before their time. It's as if they don't know what to do so they hang around the people they cared about, people who they trust. If Rory was on your doorstep, it's because your childhood friendship lingered with him. He was going to someone who felt safe."

"This happens?"

"People don't talk about it much," Hannah chuckled and shrugged, "except maybe to people like me. But when they do the stories are strikingly similar, down to the bolt of lightning."

"Is that why you stayed? You thought Grace would show up here if she had passed?" Asha turned the recorder back on, then reached into her bag for something.

"Maybe." She shook her head. "But what I was thinking changed minute to minute since I wasn't all that mentally stable. You were when you saw Rory, so it's hard to compare. I wanted her home, the only one she knew, to still be here if she came back. But that fucking pool house, it drew me in like a magnet, drew me in and gave me ideas of how I could finally get peace, finally just, let go and drift off with some lovely pills."

"Oh Hannah..." Asha started.

Hannah gazed into the blackness outside. "I would sit in there for hours and hold the bottle in my hand, slowly turning it to listen to them clack together with their promise of how they would take away all my pain and bring me back together with Grace." She looked up. "I had convinced myself that even in the afterlife she needed her mother."

Asha shook antacid tablets into her palm.

"I got close too," Hannah said. "I was right there, those pearls nestled in one hand and a glass of cheap wine in the other, when I said the weirdest thing out loud. I said, *I'm sorry, Mrs. Keegan*. I'm not even sure what I meant by that. Maybe I was taking her way out because I felt her tragedy too, that her tragedy had become mine. I don't know." Hannah looked up. "I saw her sitting in her kitchen decades before and me sitting out there, both the same broken woman. And then something snapped, because I thought of Marcus." She exhaled. "It hit me that she hadn't been there. That woman's family was destroyed and I don't know if she prayed for a miracle or not, but she did get something. She did have a chance to get her son back, to be there for him."

Hannah reached her arm out across the table and grabbed Asha's wrist. "What if Grace was found? How would someone explain to her that *I* couldn't take it? What if she had been through fucking hell and survived, only to be told *your mother didn't stick around just in case, because she was too sad*."

Hannah looked at Asha gritting her teeth and loosened her grip.

"The hell with that. Maybe Marcus would have been okay if she had hung on. Up until then, I was so focused on my failings that it hadn't occurred to me that, despite how much I had fucked up, I might still be needed. It was about three AM when I called Randall and told him he needed to get someone out here to demolish that thing." She gestured out the window. "I was playing a dangerous game of self-pity in there and it wasn't the way I should have been honoring Grace or Katherine. I needed a place where I could be with her by myself and feel it, even the sadness, but also feel her brightness inside of me. Grace couldn't just be my tragedy. I had to remember she was my joy. I had to fight so I could be ready when she needed me again, be it in this life or the next. So, I made a room for her that I can go to when I'm in a good place to take in the memory of her full on. Does that make sense?"

Asha wasn't sure any of this made sense but nodded anyway.

"It was the first time I really saw it, the cascade of people dying and how it could keep going if I didn't get my shit together." Hannah nodded. "And I did. I held on. And now," tears glittered in Hannah's eyes as her voice grew thick, "that time has come. She needs me again, and I made it."

A dark spark lit inside of Asha, the realization that whatever Hannah had left to reveal, it would not be a happy ending. That the best-case scenario, one where Grace was found— and she now had no doubt that Hannah had something— centered around a grave. Whether it was a story of devastation confirmed or something Hannah had known all along remained to be seen. But that's where Hannah was headed, Asha could feel it in her bones.

"Would you like to see it?" Hannah asked, her hand over her heart. "My setup to honor Grace?"

Asha swallowed. "Yes. Of course." She tried to push visions of Norman Bate's taxidermized mother in a rocking chair, out of her mind.

Hannah nodded. "Randall hasn't even seen it."

Asha pretended to gather some belongings, but surreptitiously opened her phone in her pocket and pulled up Charing's number, so she could call her with the touch of a button if necessary. She suspected Charing was nearby, and would probably get to her faster than any 911 service.

Hannah didn't notice, she was staring past Asha into the fire. "I think you should see it, Asha. You should see Grace *as she was,* not just the victim she is to everyone else. That's what I hope will come out when you write this. Up until that day, she was very happy. I want you to see it," her voice lowered, "to know it."

"Ok." Asha inhaled through the butterflies in her stomach and made sure she had her phone at the ready, wanting to be prepared for whatever Hannah was about to show her. "All right." She hoped her fear was hidden. "Show me."

Chapter Fifty-Eight

Grace's room was left exactly as it had been when she was taken. But it was the sacred relics that waited for her to come toddling through the door again that served as a punch-in-the-gut reminder of what was lost while the world feasted on scandalous news reports.

A fuzzy blanket folded on the dresser waited patiently for someone to keep warm. A teething ring complete with impressions sat beside it, waiting for someone to soothe. Something broke inside Asha when she saw the worn and faded tiny shoes placed neatly on the floor in front of the dresser.

There were no remains here, and she chided herself for letting her overactive journalist imagination get the best of her. *Yes, but, it would have made one hell of a story.*

Hannah's eyes followed hers. "Those were her favorite." The tiny sneakers had a Sesame Street character's beaming face on the side. "It didn't matter what she was wearing, she had to have those shoes on. She was going to outgrow them soon and I remember being worried that... Are you alright?" Hannah examined Asha, who had grabbed a dresser to steady herself. *Those shoes,* something prickled at the base of Asha's neck. *Something's wrong.*

"I'm fine," Asha huffed.

Hannah's mouth popped open into an "O." "I didn't feed you enough." She put her hands on her hips. "I was so wrapped up in the past that I forgot."

"I'm fine." She forced herself upright and sniffed to change the subject. "It even smells like a baby in here." *Not remains but something is not right.*

"I know. And being in here is a lot, even for me, but at least I can smile from it sometimes." Hannah's eyes followed Asha's around the room. "It always ends in tears, but I can smile still, you know?"

When Asha didn't answer, Hannah filled in the silence for them both. "I left everything the same, which in many cases would make sense, but," she put her hand on the carriage bed, "she only had this a few weeks when..." Her voice lowered. "Obviously this wouldn't do if she had been found even all those years ago. I guess I'm just too weak to change it."

"Weak?" Asha fought through the anxiety. *It's from talking about Rory*, she told herself. *Stop freaking out, you're almost there.* She could feel that Hannah wanted to spill something. "No. I know you don't like the word strong, but it's appropriate."

Hannah studied her. "Do you think so?"

Asha grabbed a tissue to wipe her forehead, then had a moment of panic when she thought it might have been an old box she shouldn't touch, part of what was waiting.

"It's all right," Hannah gestured, observing Asha's every move. "Those are mine, for exactly that."

Asha crumpled the tissue and tossed it in the wastebasket. "Listen to me Hannah, I have a mother. And I'm old enough now to see all of the things I didn't see as a child. The fretting, the hope." She shrugged. "The hurt you cause when you up and decide to build a life overseas even when there's nothing wrong with the place you've come from. I know that has hurt her. It hurts her and she knows where I am, she knows that I am happy and doing exactly what I want."

Hannah flinched and stopped breathing, and Asha worried she might have offended her by comparing a child living abroad to, this. But she continued, unable to stop.

"I didn't mean any disrespect. Seeing all of this and how much you lost, I think about how that would have broken her. How Katherine was lost and how so many people were hurt and then how the media was so cruel." Asha squared her shoulders and looked at Hannah. "I know you're scared. But I want to let you know that I'm here to help. You can trust me with whatever has not been told, I'm going to make sure this story gets people's attention. If there is any chance you could get new information from this, it would be—"

"It would be a miracle," Hannah interrupted.

"Yes." Suddenly, this was personal for Asha and her anxiety dissipated. If *she* could move the needle on finding out what happened to Grace she could save Hannah. She could somehow make her own mother feel better about why her daughter had left home, prove it had purpose, that she wasn't thousands of miles away just to write stories about cats in trees and tarted-up starlets.

She wouldn't just save her job, she could be the kind of journalist who made a difference in the world, the ones she'd always admired. She could help people instead of just chasing headlines.

Asha smiled at Hannah and saw hope for the first time that day. "People are found years later. Those girls in Ohio? They were missing for years. And the other girl. Oh goodness, I can't recall her name but she helps others now too."

Hannah nodded. "Elizabeth Smart? I've met her." Hannah clasped her hands together. "A remarkable young woman on her own and that's before you consider what she experienced."

"Yes." Asha paused to blow her nose. She told herself it was because of allergies and not because she was getting emotional about how kids lived in their own world, but they were their mother's entire world. "It would be my honor to try," she said, and she meant it. "To bring this all back so everyone remembers and maybe we find something. But you need to give me the piece that's missing."

"Sure." Hannah turned her back, and a shiver went up Asha's spine.

"But," Asha took soft steps approaching her, as a nameless fear crept through her gumption, "maybe we do find her, and it's not a miracle."

"The not knowing was the worst. I lived with that for years." Hannah was barely audible.

"Of course."

Hannah spoke to the corner she was facing, like a child in time out. "I never gave up."

"You found something." Asha reached her hand out, then thought better and withdrew it.

"I did track down the name and address that was on that paperwork." Hannah's shoulders sagged.

"The papers from Romania?"

"They led to a record regarding a change of citizenship due to adoption."

"It's her?" Asha held her breath.

Hannah turned around but wouldn't look at Asha. "She's a grown woman now and this will turn everything upside down. What would I say? How do I tell someone this without ruining their life? It's not what I want. I've asked myself a million times if it isn't better to just walk away knowing that she's okay, walk away and let her have the peaceful life she's settled into. I don't know what to do here, I really don't. I feel like maybe telling her is putting my own needs before hers."

"Oh my God." Asha felt a jolt go through her. "Okay. Hannah, like you said, what if she finds out elsewhere? What if she digs and finds the answers to these questions herself? What if, in doing so, she ends up in danger again?"

Hannah shook her head, but Asha knew she had to convince her to tell the truth. This was not something she could go rogue on, Hannah needed to agree.

"Ms. Smoke, Hannah, the important thing is you make sure she knows of your concerns. That she knows your intentions and even your reservations. But you have to do it. With all of the DNA tests out there, scary as it might be, it must be done. There's too much chance that if it is Grace, she will find out who she is by accident. One minute, she's sending a sample out to one of those ancestry companies, next thing she knows, the FBI is breaking down her door. It wouldn't even be the first time such a thing has happened."

"I know." Hannah's breath hitched. "I don't want that."

"She can't read about herself on the internet somewhere before she knows your suspicion. And then if she agrees, you've got the whole process of DNA testing to confirm."

Hannah's hands covered her mouth. She turned away again, head hanging down, and Asha could see a tear drop on the floor.

"What?" She took a step closer. "Hannah, what is it?"

"I've already done it."

Asha startled. "What? Wait, how in the world...?"

"When I found out she lived not too far away and then where she worked, I drove there. I sat in my car outside of the building she worked at. And then I saw her walk out." Hannah shook her head. "It blew me away. It took every ounce of fight in me to not run up to her and take her in my arms. But I needed to know. I needed to know for sure. I followed her as she walked to a coffee shop. I know, this all sounds wrong, but I didn't know what else to do. Before she went in, she spit something into a tissue and threw it in the garbage. It was gum."

Asha's face snapped up.

"I took it."

"When, um," Asha swallowed. "when did this happen?"

"I had it tested. I didn't want to alert anyone, so I had one of my contacts run the DNA on them for me."

Asha staggered back. The peaceful farmhouse that surrounded her suddenly felt like a prison. She became keenly aware of the thick stone walls around her. "Where—where was the place you got this from?"

"The results came back a week later along with mine..."

"Answer the question. What coffee shop..."

"... linking us as a parent and child relationship. It was Grace. And since then I have struggled with how to tell the woman who was raised as Asha Bennett that she was born Grace Smoke."

Asha didn't dare look directly at Hannah, for fear that what she would see in her eyes screamed the truth. "No," she whispered. "That's a mistake." But it was her habit, to spit her gum in a tissue before she got her afternoon cup of coffee. And she knew. She could see now why the baby in that photograph in the bathroom looked so familiar. She was a younger version of the child in the photographs her parents had back home.

"I'm sorry," Hannah whispered. "I didn't know how to tell you."

Asha stumbled over a large toy that started to play a song as she staggered backwards and bile rose in her throat, because damn if the tune it played wasn't *familiar*. "No. You're mistaken. I have parents. They wouldn't do that. I have a mother." Even as she said it, Asha knew how flimsy that was. She was adopted at two years old, she'd always known that. "No, that's not possible." Romania was thousands of miles from here. And her birth certificate was British.

"I'm sorry. I didn't want to scare you." Hannah reached a hand to her.

"You're crazy," Asha recoiled as she backed her way out of the room. *Her* room.

"I'm so sorry. The DNA and—"

"Shut up! Shut up about the bloody fucking DNA!"

"We can test it again, if you like. Maybe I am wrong," Hannah pleaded.

"Stay away from me!"

Asha flew out of the house, leaving the recorder and her notebook behind.

She fumbled for her phone as she ran, putting as much distance between herself and Hannah as she could.

Randall must have stayed, because as she ran down the driveway he came after her, calling out her name. She didn't stop until she reached the gate and called Charing. As the phone rang, she turned to the lawyer. "Open this fucking gate right now!" she screamed. She must have been a frightening sight, because he didn't argue.

She ran past the first gate and all the way to the second, onto the road and away from a story she wanted no part of. She didn't stop until Charing pulled up by her side.

Chapter Fifty-Nine

AFTER

Asha was learning what it meant to be a victim of kidnapping. Awareness of the events she couldn't remember brought trauma, not healing. And that trauma cascaded its way down to her parents. Hannah had been right about that—tragedy is the curse that keeps giving.

"I'm sure you have a lot of questions."

Asha glared at the man speaking to her from across the table. She had to remind herself that this wasn't his fault and she forcibly relaxed her shoulders.

"I have many things going on right now, 'some questions' doesn't even begin to describe it," she said. "You'd be surprised how many of them have nothing to do with what happened and piecing it all together. For starters, do *I* need a lawyer? How do I protect my parents? And what about me? What about my life and what I want? Because when this comes out, all of that is going to be over." She crossed her arms and looked out the window. "It was over the moment I understood."

Tom Wolinsky, a man central to Hannah's story, had come to life as she told it. The only change Asha detected was he now sported a full head of white hair to go with his formidable but fatherly presence. Tom gave Asha what she assumed was supposed to be a reassuring nod.

"Those are all reasonable questions and concerns. I won't deny that I'm coming from a different perspective, the one where you even being alive and having had a good life is a relief to all of us who worked on your disappearance."

"But to me..." Emotional exhaustion overwhelmed Asha.

"To you, that good life has just been pulled up by the roots and there is no good news to be found. That perspective isn't wrong either."

Asha looked back at him and sat down, relieved to at least be understood that much.

"I do have some answers for you today, but I can count all of those on one hand. The questions we don't have answers for could probably fill the Grand Canyon and I'm afraid that if we fail to locate Marcus, we may never get any of those."

Asha stifled a shiver at the mention of her unknown enemy. A person whom she had to fear for her very life and someone she didn't even know existed two weeks ago. "That may be the worst part, this idea that there's someone out there. I look around on the street and wonder about everyone now."

Tom opened a file and rifled through some papers. "We have been able to piece a few things together that we are following up on. Once you were found," he paused when Asha winced at the word "found," as she hadn't felt lost to begin with, "we knew something important that we hadn't known before—that he was able to leave the country. Now, smuggling you away was always a possibility, it happens still today with cargo, but more likely he was able to obtain passports for both of you. Counterfeit documents would not have been difficult to come by in the 90s. The only question was how deep he wanted them to go. Something simple just to allow you to cross a border, something attached to an existing person, or something that came with a complete travel history. All that would have been necessary was money and a connection. We know he had money from the estate, the connection, that's what we're looking into now. Who he may have associated with, either in detention or otherwise, who was known to make forged documents or was known to associate with someone who did."

"But that's just, it's an awful lot of trouble just to drop a kid at an orphanage. It just seems a lot simpler to..."

"Be done?" Tom nodded. "This was never a standard kidnapping from the start. He could destroy Hannah's life without destroying yours, thereby staying superior. He likely enjoyed slipping out of the country right under our noses."

"You think she was destroyed?"

He looked at Asha. "You spent a day with her. Would you say Hannah is whole?"

Asha looked away.

"There's a self-righteousness to Marcus, one that would take satisfaction in not killing an innocent child, especially considering that's what he himself was accused of to start all this. The goal was to hurt Hannah. Taking you away, letting her believe you were dead but not knowing, would accomplish that goal. Letting you live and leaving you to fate would satisfy his ego. If he kills you, he's everything they said he was when they put him in jail in the first place." He shook his head. "He loses what he has manufactured in his mind as the moral high ground."

"But Katherine Willard?"

He looked at Asha carefully, probably wondering if she knew Katherine appeared to have been holding her tight when she was killed. "All those details point to a desperate escape attempt. The fact that she was killed possibly made him more determined for you to get out of this alive even if it was for his own selfish reasons."

Asha rose out of her chair and leaned into the window looking over the Manhattan skyline, arms crossed above her head. Somewhere, a few blocks over, her parents, the ones that didn't see dead people, waited at their hotel. Asha had told them everything, but had waited until they arrived in New York.

Everything, save for the part about Rory, what it meant, and how she feared it might make her more like Hannah than she ever wanted to be.

That's what kept her up at night now. Every creak in the darkness made her heart beat a little faster.

But in their eyes, nothing had changed about who Asha was to them. Outside of a few select investigators, the small circle involved in the story at the Metropolitan, and Hannah, nobody knew who Asha really was. But the clock was ticking on her secret and she sighed. "I don't know what I should do."

Tom didn't require explanation. "You need to take care of you. So yes, you should probably have a lawyer. I wish I could say everyone will act in your best interest as this proceeds, but experience has told me better. I know Randall has been—" Asha shot him a look and he cut himself off.

"For your parents, I would imagine they would also require some help, but less so. The fact that you're an adult now and they did nothing illegal when they adopted you at least takes away any issues in that regard. Any legal steps taken on their behalf would be more in the interest of safety and privacy."

"And me? What about my life?"

Tom stared into her with sad eyes. "There is no going back, is there? When this breaks, and we have to assume it will, millions of people will think of you not as Asha, but Baby Grace."

"I am not Grace. I mean," she flailed her arms, "I understand that is true but I have no feeling or connection to that at all." She pretended not to remember how it felt to be in that room, to hear the jingle played by the toy when she tripped on it.

"Of course, you don't. And to the people who know Asha, that's who you'll remain. But for those that don't know you and see only Grace, the cure for that will be time."

Asha scoffed.

"I'm serious." He pointed outside to the city where millions of people went on about their day, oblivious to the drama on the 43rd floor of the government building. "We could go out there right now and announce to the world that you are Grace and it would be pandemonium." He nodded. "It would. But the thing about pandemonium, Asha, is it cannot be maintained. It's a supernova that burns out. People will come to accept and you will be allowed to move on with your life." He got up from the table to join her in gazing out the window. "It happened that way with Hannah. The story never went away but the day-to-day chaos did."

Asha gave Tom a warning look at the mention of Hannah.

He shrugged. "Whatever you decide, it's up to you. She has agreed to keep this quiet permanently if that is your desire."

"As if I trust her!" Asha leaned into the glass, not entirely sure if it wouldn't be easier if the window just disappeared and she tumbled into oblivion. "After what she did?"

"Hannah is," Tom paused, "not well. Not a lock-her-up level of not well, but not well nonetheless. What happened has made her impulsive and reckless at times. I guess what I'm saying is Hannah doesn't always make good decisions, but she's had a lifetime of bad influences that helped her get there." He looked at her. "When she says she will keep this quiet, I believe her. But I'm also going to ask you to consider the opposite."

"Well, I lived quite happily with no one knowing I was," she swallowed, "that baby."

"And if you keep it quiet, you will live under the weight of someone finding out." He turned back to pick up a file and held it out to her. "And they will. There's too much here. Someone is going to spill it. I wish that weren't true but there's a time limit to the courtesy of people keeping their mouth shut. And it won't be in a way you can see coming. Think it over, long and hard, but if you're seeking advice—whatever it's worth from the man who couldn't find you in the first place but is damn well invested in your welfare—I say pick a time to rip off the band-aid. Then you'll live freely. Under a microscope for a time, but then freely."

"And what about him? What happens when Marcus finds out I'm alive and have been located?" They locked eyes and the world went still. "What happens then?" Asha could only manage a whisper.

"I think..." He sighed and his gaze drifted out the window, looking on the people moving like ants below them. "I pray that's when we catch the bastard."

Chapter Sixty

The announcement from the morning news made Hannah stop in her tracks, causing her coffee to slosh over the rim of her cup. She'd known this was coming, but had understood the story wasn't being published for another month yet. She broke out of her surprised stupor and grabbed a paper towel, wiping up the mess as the newscaster went on. Hannah didn't need to look at the screen to know she was salivating, she could hear it in her voice.

"*Grace in Plain Sight*," she announced with glee at Hannah and the rest of the world. *"That's the headline of this morning's explosive article. And it brings the welcome news that not only is Grace Smoke, the victim of a kidnapping more than two decades ago, alive, but that she discovered her true identity as a reporter working on this very story."*

Hannah pushed away her hurt feelings. She created this mess, and her hurt feelings were childish given the circumstances. Besides, the hurt she felt today of not having any direct contact with, she acknowledged, *Asha*, was nothing compared to the hurt that she felt when Grace's whereabouts were unknown and she seemed likely dead.

She sat at the table and let her head fall in her hands, repeating the mantra that got her through the past year. *Grace didn't die. You got what you wanted. You got your miracle that she was alive and grew up happy. Time brought you this miracle, maybe time will bring you another.*

But if this would be it, Hannah willed herself to believe that her being alive was enough. If Hannah being in her life caused Asha more pain, she would stay away.

Hannah threw the soiled towel in the garbage, and eyed her iPad on the kitchen table. She knew she should get on reading the article. It would be painful, Asha would have some less than glowing things to say about how Hannah had handled the situation which would all be as accurate as it was devastating, but Hannah had gotten her say: she had to let Asha have hers. There was also the urgency of getting through it before the press started clamoring for comment, Hannah didn't want to give anyone the opportunity to regurgitate their interpretation of Asha's words without having seen them with her own eyes.

The doorbell rang and Hannah sighed. *Too late.*

Her spine tingled as the voices that lived inside her head hummed, the same voices that she denied existed in a desperate attempt to save Grace decades ago. They whispered at Hannah about what could be, and she grunted at the intrusion. They had made their presence known when she spotted Asha in that coffee shop after all those years, they had chittered in anger when Hannah told Asha that everything she had done to Barbara Silver, that everything she had done in her profession, was a lie. In the last year Hannah had spent countless hours wondering *what if*, but in the end the voices didn't bring Grace home the first time and she wasn't ready to trust them again.

Only three people knew the code to get through the gate, Randall, Tom, and Joanne, so Hannah wasn't surprised to see Randall standing there. She didn't even give him a chance to say hello.

"Good news travels fas—" Randall cut her off by reaching out to push Hannah's door open further, so she would see Asha was standing next to him. Hannah's breath caught.

And the voices in her head went silent.

"Hi." Asha gave an awkward wave. The two women stared at each other with full understanding of what this meant, that this was their beginning, maybe not mother and daughter as it once was but at least as *Asha and Hannah*. There were going to be countless minefields and hurts to be worked out but this was *a* beginning and it was *theirs*. Hannah almost drowned in new hope that there was going to be something left for them after all that was lost.

And behind them, Hannah saw Katherine for just a moment as she sat on the edge of the driveway fountain, her elbows perched on her knees and her head resting in her hands, a smile playing on her lips.

Thank you, Hannah thought.

Randall looked between them. "Asha said it was her turn to show up without warning."

Hannah was still frozen in place, and Asha shot Randall a worried look.

"Can I come in?" She gestured towards the door.

Hannah stepped aside. "You never have to ask to come in here."

***

"*Grace in Plain Sight.*" The headline caught his attention and stopped him in his tracks. He reached down for the paper, the slight tremble to his hand conflicting with the assurances he gave himself that this didn't matter, it didn't matter because it was done and he no longer cared, precisely why he stopped keeping track of her all those years ago, granting the innocent whatever fate determined.

It only took the first sentence of the article to confirm that, yes, this headline meant what he thought it did. He paid for his purchase, tucked the paper under his arm and walked on, blending into the crowd around him.

A Thank You From Jennifer

Thank you for following Hannah and Asha's story to the end. Or if my suspicion is correct, the end of their beginning. (Yes the next book is in progress – and it's a doozy!)

I am an independent author and your opinion matters not just to me, but to other potential readers. Your stamp of approval through a review or rating tells other readers that this book is worth a try, or at the very least is not some AI generated hot mess. Reviews are what will allow me to keep plugging away at this crazy writing thing. If you take a moment to write a few words, I promise I will read and consider your feedback with gratitude.

Acknowledgments

After countless hours, multiple books, files stuffed full of false starts, a more than one existential crisis, the idea that it's time to think about writing acknowledgements seems surreal. As I write this I'm 99% certain the only person who will ever lay eyes on this will be me.

But just in case:

To my husband, who didn't bat an eye when out of nowhere I said *hey I'm going to write a book,* who never said a word when I spent significant money hiring editors or attending conferences, who didn't laugh at me for having the audacity to think I might be able to pull this off: I am so lucky to be married to someone who thought my chasing this ridiculous dream was worthwhile. You shall forever be my Stewie Griffin asking *how's that novel going hmm?*

To my babies Andrew, Angelina, and AJ, (cut me a break the three As seemed like a good idea until I had to say it out loud), thank you for being the kind of kids who thought it was completely normal for your mom to one day just decide *I write novels now.* At minimum you're all good at pretending it was normal. I love you to the moon and back, and if anything I hope you've seen that chasing a big goal makes you a better person, regardless of the result. And yes of course I want people to read this, I want them to enjoy it, but just the fact that I did this and had the grit and patience to stick through the process is something that I know has made me a better person. Chase your ridiculous dream. Please clean your room first.

To my father, who made those trips to the bookstore a regular routine of my visits, and bought me all the Sweet Valley High books even though they, and I quote, *cost an arm and a leg and are the size of a pamphlet.* I was ten, Dad. I wasn't exactly ready for your WWII tomes. But you bought me every book I asked for when you weren't rolling in dough, and I know that mattered.

To James, our cat, who while I was working on this book showed up in our yard and declared *I live with you guys now.* Your contribution was countless interruptions and hair on the furniture. You were not any help, but you have a certain charm so you can stay.

And finally, to my mother, who started all of this. For my first novel ever, she handed over her personal story and let me do whatever I wanted with it, even if it meant it really wasn't hers anymore. Watching the events of your own life being pulled and twisted into something new is traumatic, but she let it happen because it was for me. For that first book and every one since you've proven to be the best beta reader, the one person willing to tell me what you didn't like because you understood I took this seriously, so you did too. To anyone who didn't enjoy this book, I don't know what to tell you, my mom liked it.

The mistakes in this book are entirely my own, whether they be of the typo or factual variety. Every time I was "done" some little sparkle revealed itself to me that demanded an update and yes, much of this was after the last round of professional edits. So my apologies for anything that left you screaming *but this is not right!*

I want to acknowledge professional help from people who were happy to tear me to shreds in exchange for money. I highly recommend this to my fellow writers. Stick to the ones who expose all the parts of your story that are wrong wrong wrong. You can find people to tell you about how good it is for free, usually people who haven't actually read your work.

At the top of this list is Gabriela Lessa. I found her in the best way, in the acknowledgements from another novel where the author stated of Gabi "even though we've never met and your feedback made me cry, I know this book is better for it." You weren't just an editor, but an educator and both that first book and this one are better for all of your criticisms and the tears they caused.

I need to take a moment to acknowledge my people, the unrepped writers. Because writing is hard, and then you get to query which is somehow worse.

But do it. Even if you don't plan to pursue traditional publishing, please put yourself through the fresh hell that is querying anyway. Because while the odds are against you landing an agent, even agents that don't take you on as a client may help make your book better - *for free.*

I did have close calls with some well-known agents who took an interest in this book and gave real feedback. Not the form letter kind, but specific to my story: what was working, what was not, what they thought could make it better. And while sometimes that stings because it's like someone pointing out the parts of your baby that are ugly, the sting wears off and you start to see it. And if you're lucky, one day while you're randomly folding laundry, the way to make that ugly part turn pretty occurs to you. So every agent that requested a full, read it, and bothered to give real detailed feedback is someone I owe a debt of gratitude. We didn't ultimately end up working together, but I recognize the lucky spot

I was in to have that feedback when you're getting thousands of queries and can't respond to them all.

Writing books is long lonely work. It's peaks of *this is awesome* followed by valleys of *I suck*, usually spaced about 5 minutes apart. It's sacrifice after sacrifice both of time and resources, where all of the work and sacrifice makes no guarantee of any success. It's doing this thing over and over again and asking yourself *why* you are doing it while being unable to give it up. It's the career path that begs the question *but what are you going to do for money?*

Writing is weird.

But I see you, my fellow writers, doing this weird thing with me. And if I can get here, to that place where I finally felt ready to throw this baby out into the world with all its pretty and ugly parts to let fate decide what happens - I promise you can too.

Jennifer Crown

June 2025

About the author

Jennifer Crown is a writer based in New Jersey surrounded by a bossy cat, a patient husband, and three kids who are growing up too fast. When she is not writing, she can be found trying to keep her sense of humor while holding the fraying ends of her chaotic life together. She can be reached at jennifercrown.com

Printed in Dunstable, United Kingdom